Tallowood Bound

Karly Lane lives on the mid north coast of New South Wales. Proud mum to four children and wife of one very patient mechanic, she is lucky enough to spend her day doing the two things she loves most—being a mum and writing stories set in beautiful rural Australia.

ALSO BY KARLY LANE

North Star
Morgan's Law
Bridie's Choice
Poppy's Dilemma
Gemma's Bluff

Karly

LANE

Tallowood Bound

ARENA
ALLEN&UNWIN

First published in 2015

Copyright © Karly Lane 2015

Arena Books, an imprint of
Allen & Unwin
83 Alexander Street
Crows Nest NSW 2065
Australia
Phone: (61 2) 8425 0100
Email: info@allenandunwin.com
Web: www.allenandunwin.com

Cataloguing-in-Publication details are available
from the National Library of Australia
www.trove.nla.gov.au

ISBN 978 1 74331 727 3

Set in 12.4/17.6 pt Sabon LT Pro by Bookhouse, Sydney
Printed and bound in Australia by Griffin Press

10 9 8 7 6 5 4 3 2 1

The paper in this book is FSC® certified. FSC® promotes environmentally responsible, socially beneficial and economically viable management of the world's forests.

To the Townsville years, 1997–2004

One

Erin dropped her head onto the steering wheel and closed her eyes as she summoned the energy to get out of the car.

She hated this place.

Gran hated this place.

It wasn't that the nursing home was terrible. In fact, as far as nursing homes went, it was rather nice: the grounds were immaculate, the staff were friendly, and the rooms were clean and modern. She didn't hate *it*, just what it represented.

She'd been coming here for the last week and each day was worse than the one before. Her grandmother, Evelyn Macalister, had always been such a proud, independent woman. It was hard to watch her now, trapped inside a withering body, slowly losing her memory. Up until recently her gran at ninety-two had still been doing her own housework, until Erin finally convinced her to get some help and arranged for a local lady to come and clean her house once a week. However, a nasty fall had sent Gran into hospital and then to the nursing home for medical treatment.

If that hadn't been enough to deal with, the doctors had diagnosed Gran's occasional bout of forgetfulness as rapidly progressive dementia. Now she was confined to a bed and forgetting everyone and everything around her a little more each day.

A week ago the nursing home had called to inform Erin that Gran had suffered a fall and that they hadn't been able to reach Erin's mother. Erin had dropped everything in Sydney and headed up to Tuendoc, relieved she'd arranged to be listed as an emergency contact given her mother's habit of disappearing without letting anyone know. Erin's mother, Irene, or Serenity as she now preferred to be called, owned a private health retreat in far northern New South Wales. She was also the benefactor of a foundation to protect orangutans in Borneo and Sumatra, and she went off overseas at the drop of a hat, rarely informing Erin when she was leaving. Erin often only found out her mother was away if she happened to ring her from some remote corner of the world. And this time, despite having tried all week, Erin had so far failed to locate her.

Erin gathered the photo album from the passenger seat and locked the car. Visits were getting harder. While her grandmother had seemed her same old self when Erin had first arrived, she'd been rapidly deteriorating ever since, sinking into a deep depression. She wanted to go home to her beloved farm and the house she'd lived in for the last sixty-five years.

Erin could understand Gran's love of the old house at Tallowood. The lowset, sprawling weatherboard, surrounded by verandahs on all sides, was in need of a new coat of paint, but it still looked as neat and tidy as the day her grandfather had built it. Gran always took great pride in the gardens, and the yard was chock-full of old-fashioned plants not often found in modern gardens—tall brightly coloured sweet peas and snapdragons, hydrangeas with their bright blue and purple clusters of flowers, and Gran's favourite: roses, every colour and scent under the sun. Tallowood was where Gran needed to be.

Erin had spoken to the doctor about getting her released, happy to take care of her for as long as she needed to, but the doctor explained that her grandmother's hip was too badly broken and she would require high-level care for quite some time, so going home wasn't an option for now.

So Erin had to find different ways to occupy Gran and take her mind off her surroundings. Yesterday Gran had been talking about Pop, as well as a few people Erin didn't know, and she'd seemed happy all of a sudden. It had been good to see her looking more positive and to hear her talk about the old days.

Over the years Erin had heard bits and pieces of what life had been like for Gran as a young girl, but she hadn't truly appreciated these stories. It had always seemed as though Gran would be around forever—her father had lived to be ninety-nine and her two older brothers had both made it into their late eighties—but over the last few days Erin had come to realise that her grandmother might not have much time left. She wanted to find out everything she could about Gran's life before the opportunity was lost forever.

It was hard to take in, though. Gran had always been there for her. All through Erin's childhood, while her mother had been busy building up her business, she had spent school holidays in Tuendoc. Gran had always given Erin her full and undivided attention, something she'd rarely experienced with her mother, and Erin had always treasured that.

Her mother had been a strong role model, as had Gran in her own way. Erin's grandfather had died before she was born. There were no cousins, no brothers and sisters. Now, with the thought of Gran leaving her, Erin realised she was running out of family.

She'd always thought she'd marry and have lots of children because she hadn't wanted any child of hers having the lonely time she'd had. But those dreams had come crashing down in her mid-twenties when doctors had discovered the ovarian cysts. She'd had multiple operations and then contracted an infection that had caused such damage she'd had to have one of her ovaries removed. She'd been told that the degree of scarring meant she was unlikely ever to conceive. No longer able to dream of a house full of children, she'd thrown herself into her career instead.

That was when Phillip had come along.

She met him one evening at a friend's dinner party. He was a university professor twenty years older than her, attractive, charming and intelligent, and he made her feel special. When things started to look as though they might become serious, Erin was surprised when he refused to take her usual brush-off. And when she eventually came clean about her infertility, he didn't blink an eyelid.

They were happy together; their life was full and they had everything they needed. Well, almost everything, but Erin was too afraid to continue wishing for the one thing she wanted more than anything: a baby of her own. Instead they had holidays overseas, lazy weekend sleep-ins, two incomes and careers they both loved. However, after the death of Phillip's older brother a few years into their marriage, Phillip tentatively broached the subject of IVF. Erin tried not to get her hopes up with each attempt, but time after time it failed and each time a little piece of her heart died. Eventually, when she couldn't take any more cycles of hope and then despair, Erin refused further treatment.

Then everything started going pear-shaped. Phillip became distant and their relationship began to change. It was all so pathetically clichéd, really; the professor and his attractive assistant having an affair. The affair was bad, but it was nothing compared to the soul-crushing sense of betrayal that followed Phillip's confession on the night he walked out of their apartment.

'She's having your *child?*'

Phillip ran a hand through his usually impeccable head of hair and began to pace. 'I didn't mean it to happen like this, Erin. But I'm fifty years old, and now that Charles has gone I'm the last of my line. Don't you understand?' he said, his eyes imploring. 'My branch of the tree ends with me. This is my only chance to have a child. Dakota has given me that opportunity.'

She *could* see. She *did* understand, but it still hurt like hell to have the man she loved, the man she'd made a life with, suddenly decide he needed to trade her in for a younger *working* model, named after a state that had four dead presidents carved in a rock.

She wished she could say she'd walked away with her head held high, that she'd stayed composed and dignified. But she hadn't. She still cringed when she recalled how terrified and pathetic she'd been. 'I don't care about the affair. I forgive you. I'll do anything,' she'd pleaded. 'We still have our name on the list for adoption, it could still happen for us.'

'No, Erin, I don't want to adopt,' Philip said. 'You're missing the point. I don't want my family name to *die* with me. I want my own child. My *own* blood.'

It wasn't fair! *She* wanted her own child too.

Erin stood staring on in shocked silence as her husband packed a bag and walked away with a woman half his age who was having his baby.

Two

As she headed towards her grandmother's room at the end of the corridor, Erin shared a smile with a nurse bustling past. Inside, she found Gran staring out the window from her bed. Gran had been such a lively woman, no one ever believed she was in her nineties. She was always baking a sponge or putting on the kettle after a long morning in the garden. She wasn't this small hunched woman staring out the window with a blank expression.

'Gran?'

Her grandmother slowly turned her head and looked at her. Erin waited for Gran's familiar welcoming smile, but for a long moment there was no smile, no recognition, not so much as a blink of the eye.

'It's Erin,' she said hesitantly, unable to believe she was introducing herself to the woman she'd loved her entire life.

Slowly a smile of recognition tugged at Gran's dry lips before she gave a small sigh and lifted a hand towards her.

Erin stepped closer and took her hand, noticing how cool it felt. 'Do you want me to get you another blanket, Gran?'

'No, dear. I'm all right. Just tired,' she said, looking out the window again.

Erin pulled a chair closer to the bedside and looked down at the hand she still held. Her grandmother's hands, which had spent a lifetime working in the garden and on the farm, were thinner than Erin remembered. The network of blue veins and tiny bones stood out beneath the pale, paper-thin skin.

'I brought your photo album in. I thought you might like to look through it with me,' said Erin, placing the album on the bed.

Her grandmother remained staring out of the window, seemingly disinterested in anything else.

Erin opened the album and turned to the first page. 'You were such a beautiful bride, Gran. And look at Pop, he was so handsome.' The photo of her grandparents standing beside an old car made her smile. She looked up in surprise when Gran reached over to turn the album slightly so she could get a better look.

'So young,' Gran said softly. Her eyes searched the image that had gone brown around the edges. 'I always imagined that when I married I would wear a white wedding gown.'

Erin looked back at the photo. In it her gran was wearing a demure dress that hung just below her knees, with a fitted jacket over the top. It was hard to tell what colour the dress was in the black and white photo, possibly a grey or brown. Her hazel eyes, so much like Erin's, were indistinguishable in the old photo, but she knew they could sometimes appear green or, in certain lights, blue-grey. Her dark hair was pulled back in an elegant chignon and she looked every inch the 1940s Hollywood starlet.

'Why didn't you?'

'Roy wouldn't let me,' her voice drifted off.

Erin frowned slightly at the strange comment but didn't ask her to elaborate. It was hard to accept this new vagueness, when her gran had always been so alert. 'You still looked beautiful, Gran.'

'Such a long time ago,' she whispered, shaking her head, her eyes watering. 'How did it all go so fast?'

Erin swallowed past a hard lump in her throat and reached across to turn the page, hoping to distract her grandmother. She smiled at the next photo of her grandfather dressed in his uniform. 'And this is Pop?'

'Yes,' Gran said eventually, studying the photo with a sombre expression.

'Where was this taken? In North Queensland?' Erin asked, remembering her gran had grown up there.

'Yes. That's where your grandfather and I were raised. We were next-door neighbours. Childhood sweethearts.' Erin's grandfather had died before she was born but, from the little her mother had said about him, she'd gathered he'd been a stern, rather cold man. He didn't look that way in these old photos, but fighting in World War Two had changed a whole generation of men.

She flipped through some pages of photos of a tropical-looking town with lots of military vehicles lining the main street. The photos were filled with men in all kinds of uniforms—Australian, American and others she didn't recognise.

'What was it like in Townsville back then? It must have been a culture shock, all those Americans suddenly moving into town,' said Erin.

'Yes. It was,' said Gran. 'It changed everything.'

Erin considered her gran's answer. She seemed to be almost looking *through* the photo, but it wasn't the lost, blank expression she'd been wearing when Erin had arrived. 'Tell me what it was like, Gran,' she said, easing back in the chair.

She watched Gran's face soften and her eyes take on a faraway look.

Three

Townsville, 1943

Evelyn pushed open the gate, hearing the familiar creak as the hinges protested, and headed into town to start her shift for the Red Cross. She'd wanted to join the Women's Auxiliary Australian Air Force, better known as the WAAAFs, but her father wouldn't allow it. He considered it unladylike and was determined that no daughter of his was going to be in the armed forces. Evelyn couldn't think of anything more exciting. She looked longingly at the recruitment posters hanging around town. Compared to the WAAAFs, with their neatly pressed uniforms and air of comradeship whenever she spotted them out and about, her work with the Red Cross seemed rather dull. Evelyn shook off the sulky thoughts and straightened her shoulders. What she did was nothing to be sneezed at. The Red Cross provided a vital service and she should be proud to be part of it.

She approached the makeshift hospital in Chapman Street, which consisted of a row of modified houses. An American nurse hurried across the timber walkway that had been constructed to join the houses together, and smiled at her absently before disappearing into the building.

It was strange, but most of the time she barely batted an eyelid at what was happening around town. It was only now and again when she stopped to think that it made her shake her head in amazement. The construction of a row of concrete slit trenches, dug into the middle of Flinders Street for air-raid shelters was amongst the first of the radical changes to their town. It seemed unlikely they'd ever be used, and a tad overcautious to many north Queenslanders, but they were now part of the landscape as was the barbed-wire fencing along parts of The Strand. The enormity of the changes was hard to digest. Townsville had lost something of its laidback innocence over the last few years. It had gone from a sleepy country town to a bustling, sprawling city within a few months, leaving the local population still scratching their heads at the speed with which their lives had been turned upside down

Americans had only ever been seen on the silver screen or in fancy magazines, then suddenly here they were, walking the streets of Townsville. It had been exciting, at first. The soldiers with their loud voices and strange accents flooding the streets, splashing their money—and attention—freely around town.

The novelty had dimmed a little over the last few months, though. Shortages of milk and fuel added to the exorbitant prices being charged for fruit and vegetables and caused a lot of strain on the local population. Blocks of ice were almost impossible to get hold of since the Americans had contracted the iceworks for the majority of the local supply, leaving the locals to line up from three in the morning in order to buy the precious commodity.

Yet for the younger generations the war had brought unexpected opportunities and it was sometimes hard not to get caught up in it all. While she wasn't as Yank crazy as some girls she knew, she loved the air of excitement the war had brought to town. She loved talking to the nurses and staff who frequented the Red Cross dances, listening to their descriptions of their lives back home, which sounded so different to life in Australia. She loved the new ideas and latest innovations being adapted in town, milk bars popping up and new cuisine being introduced in an attempt to lure American clientele into restaurants and cafes.

Evelyn looked up when she heard her name being called. Her best friend, Dolly, was waving madly from the back of a US Army jeep. She was helped down by a soldier who, having jumped out of the back of the vehicle, lifted her out and set her down on the footpath. Dolly kissed his cheek and laughed at the chorus of catcalls and cheers that followed from the other men in the jeep before it roared away.

'Who was that?' Evelyn asked as she stopped in front of her beaming friend.

'That was Larry.'

'What happened to Reuben?'

'He shipped out,' Dolly said with an offhand shrug.

'I thought you really liked him?'

'I did. But, you know, what's a girl to do? There's a war going on and these Yanks come and go. There's plenty of fish in the sea,' she said with a wink.

'You're terrible,' Evelyn said with a smile and shake of her head. Over the last year or so Dolly had transformed into a blue-eyed, blonde-haired sex kitten, her outgoing personality completely suited to this new era. Evelyn's parents had never really approved of Dolly, she'd always been a rather rebellious, outspoken child, but Evelyn liked her. Dolly said and did the things she could only dream of doing. Her friendship with Dolly had been the only thing she'd ever stood up to her parents over. She knew that underneath all that bravado there was a kind and gentle soul. However, Dolly's reputation was becoming the subject of gossip and Evelyn's parents had once again begun to voice their displeasure at the girls' friendship. But really, there was little they could say when they both volunteered at the Red Cross, doing their bit for the cause.

'There's a group of us going to the movies on Saturday night. Why don't you come along?' Dolly said.

'And watch you and Larry devour each other all night? No, thanks,' Evelyn laughed.

'Oh, come on, you *never* come out with me. Just once. Please?'

'I'm engaged, Dolly.' Not to mention her father's reaction to her going out with Dolly. She knew well his views about the types of young women who went out on the town. In his mind, they were all asking for trouble. No daughter of his was safe going out on the streets with *all those bloody Yanks hangin' around*.

'Which is why you need to get out and see what you're missing,' said Dolly. 'It can't hurt to compare what's out there. How else are you going to be sure Roy is really the one for you?'

'I don't need to compare anything.'

Dolly had not been overjoyed when Evelyn had told her she'd decided to get engaged to Roy before he left to serve in New Guinea. 'Why on earth would you want to stay at home and mope when you could be out having fun?' she said.

Dolly was loving the fact she could get all the silk stockings she ever wanted, not to mention chocolates and sweet treats from these charming foreigners. How they managed to get hold of half the things they did was hard to imagine, but they showered the locals girls with gifts. Add that to the sweet-talking and courting, and what hope of resistance did the average girl from Townsville have?

It was something that had not gone unnoticed by the rest of the community. There was an undercurrent of unease rippling throughout town. Hostility towards the Americans seemed to be simmering just below the surface, waiting for something to set it off. Food was ridiculously expensive as the district's resources, which had previously catered for a population of thirty-odd thousand, suddenly had to accommodate an extra fifty thousand people. The logistics of feeding that many personnel were a nightmare. Shop owners were making a killing, to the detriment of their own community in many cases, and for the average local family it was becoming increasingly difficult to buy the essentials like milk, butter and fruit.

Like most families, Evelyn's grew their own vegetables, kept chooks and had a variety of fruit trees in the backyard, so they were somewhat self-sufficient, but they didn't have a cow to milk and they still needed staples like meat, providing they could find any ice for the icebox to keep it in. Rations were something they had all grudgingly grown used to, but it was galling that there was a very lucrative black market for those with enough entrepreneurial skills to buy and sell these sought-after items.

'You'll just have to cope without me on Saturday,' said Evelyn.

'Mark my words, you'll look back on your life and wish you'd done something crazy while you had the chance.'

Evelyn ignored the small twinge of regret that followed Dolly's warning. She was looking forward to married life. No longer under her parents' roof, living by their rules, she'd finally have some autonomy. Besides, it wasn't as though she was ever going to be able to do what she really wanted, which was to go away and study. Women didn't need a university degree, at least that's what her father had always said when she'd timidly brought up the subject. Sometimes she wished she was more like Dolly, who would have done whatever she pleased and not worried about who she hurt in the process. But Evelyn couldn't do that. Her family was strict, but she knew her parents loved her and her sister very much. She'd never be able to do anything to hurt them, it just wasn't in her.

'Just think then,' Evelyn said, forcing a smile and dismissing her troubled thoughts as she linked arms with Dolly, 'you'll be living it up for both of us. God knows you've been going through enough men for two women.'

The girls were still laughing when they rounded the corner and came face to face with Mrs Huxley, who ran the Red Cross volunteers with an iron fist.

'Late again, I see, girls,' she snapped.

Evelyn tried not to flinch under the weight of the woman's disapproving glare. Beside her Dolly rolled her eyes and Evelyn groaned silently. Dolly seemed to enjoy needling the woman as often as possible, but Evelyn found everything about Mrs Huxley disconcerting. From the enormous bun tightly pulled back on top of her head, to the sharply angled nose that had given her the nickname of Bandicoot by those brave enough to whisper it behind her back.

'You might try and remember that you are representing the Red Cross when you come here and conduct yourselves in an appropriate manner.'

'Oh, come on, Mrs Huxley. There's no law against having a bit of fun, is there?'

'I'm well aware of what you call a bit of fun, Miss Rowland,' she said in a distasteful tone. 'However, I would have expected better from you, Evelyn. I'm sure your mother wouldn't approve of you dillydallying and carrying on.'

'Sorry, Mrs Huxley,' Evelyn murmured, tugging on Dolly's arm before her friend could say anything else to annoy the woman further.

'You know, if Bandicoot would just go out and get a good—'

'Dolly!' Evelyn interrupted, staring at her friend with equal parts of dismay and mirth.

'Well it's true. You don't see me getting all hot and bothered about someone laughing, do you?' she said with a wink, as they entered the building and prepared for another long day.

Their work with the Red Cross was important, Evelyn knew that, but it really wasn't very glamorous. They packed comfort parcels for the men overseas, sold cakes to raise money and rolled bandages and collected medical supplies headed for the front lines, but she wished she could do something . . . more.

She could be a driver, work in transportation. She'd even written to Roy and asked him to write to her father and convince him, but Roy hadn't been overly supportive either. *Why would you want to drive around a bunch of hobnobbing officers? Or worse, drive trucks?* he'd replied. The fact was she didn't quite know the answer to that, why it was she wanted more from her life. All she knew was that the WAAAFs would have opened up a whole new world for her. She might have ended up anywhere, and that possibility would have been thrilling had there been even the remotest chance her father would allow it.

Swallowing back a frustrated sigh, she ducked her head and hurried around the ever-disapproving Mrs Huxley to get to work.

Four

The next morning a knock at the front door surprised Evelyn: visitors to the Ward house rarely knocked. She opened the door to find a tall stranger in uniform standing on the front step.

'Hello, miss. I'm wondering if you can tell me whether I have the right address. I'm looking for Miss Evelyn Ward.'

She pushed the screen door open cautiously. 'I'm Evelyn.'

The stranger's serious face broke into a sudden grin and Evelyn found herself distracted by his good looks.

'Hi, my name's Jimmy Crenshaw,' he said, swapping his cap to his other hand before extending his arm.

Surprised, Evelyn hesitated before reaching out to shake hands. 'Hello.'

Reading the confusion in her face, he said, 'Sorry to drop in unannounced, but Roy asked me to stop by when I got to Townsville and let you know that he was doing fine.'

'Roy?' Evelyn was even more confused. How on earth did an American airman, by the look of his uniform, know Roy?

'My squadron just got in from New Guinea. I met Roy up there.'

'Oh,' Evelyn said. 'Well, that was very kind of you. His family live next door. I'm sure they'd love to see you while you're here. Any friend of Roy's and all that.' She felt unexpectedly nervous as she looked into his eyes. They really were very attractive: framed with thick, dark lashes, they were a lovely deep chocolate brown, like the colour of those fancy dark chocolates she and Dolly had drooled over last Valentine's Day in the shop window downtown.

'I was just over there, but no one was home. I'll try them again later.'

'Oh. Would you like to come in for a cuppa then?'

'A cuppa?' he said, a little unsure.

'A cup of tea? Or a cool drink? I know most Yanks prefer coffee, but I'm afraid we don't have any.'

'A cold drink would hit the spot just fine, thank you kindly, ma'am,' he said, before offering her a lopsided grin. 'And I'm not a Yank, I'm from the south.'

Evelyn smiled. 'Well, to an Australian you're all Yanks.' She led the way down the hallway to the rear of the house and into the kitchen. She poured some freshly squeezed lemon juice into a tall glass and topped it up with water. 'How are you handling the heat?' she asked as she handed him the drink and showed him to a chair at the small kitchen table.

'Better than some, I guess,' he grinned. 'I'm from Louisiana, I'm used to the heat. Besides, New Guinea's much worse.'

'So I've heard. Roy said in his letters that it rains all the time. It comes out of nowhere the same time every day and then, as if someone turns a tap off, it just stops.'

'Yep. Just like that.'

It was odd having a stranger sitting in the kitchen, and an American one at that, but what else could she do? It would have been rude not to invite the man in when Roy had asked him to call on her.

'So, you're in the air force?'

'Yes, ma'am. I'm a pilot.'

'It must be a wonderful feeling, being able to fly.'

He smiled again and tilted his head slightly. 'There's nothing quite like it. The world looks different from up there. You suddenly realise just how small we all really are in the grand scheme of things. Have you ever been in a plane before?'

Evelyn shook her head regretfully. 'No. Never.'

'Well, if it's any consolation, now is not exactly the best time to be up there. It kind of spoils the enjoyment when you have a Jap on your tail trying to shoot you down.'

He was making light of it, but Evelyn thought it must play constantly on his mind. Almost daily there were reports of aircraft either being shot down or crashing. It was not a career for the faint of heart.

'You're here for some R&R?' she asked, changing the subject.

'Partly. Our aircraft are undergoing some modifications, so we have some work to do, but then we get some time off.'

21

The front screen door creaked and then banged shut, announcing the arrival of her parents and sister who had been in town. A flutter of unease started in her stomach as she heard their footsteps approaching the kitchen, but she pushed them away. Why should she feel uneasy being found with a visitor?

'Evelyn.' Her father said her name more as a statement than a greeting.

'Dad, Mum, this is Jimmy Crenshaw. He's a friend of Roy's.'

'*Our* Roy?' her mother asked, surprised.

'Sir. Ma'am,' Jimmy said, standing to shake her father's hand and nodding to her mother. 'And who's this?' he asked, turning his smile towards Evelyn's younger sister.

'I'm Betty.' The younger girl said quickly and batted her eyelids at him. Evelyn inwardly rolled her eyes.

'I hope this isn't too much of an intrusion, but Roy wanted me to come and check on Evelyn and remember him to you all while I was in town.'

'How do you know Roy then?' her father asked. Mick Ward had returned home from the Great War with shrapnel in his leg which had left him with a permanent limp, but it was his years working on the railway that had toughened him up. It was hard work and bred even harder men. He ruled his house with the same iron fist he used with his men.

'We often work with the Aussies on certain missions. And Roy plays a mean hand of cards. When he heard I was headed to Townsville he asked if I'd stop by.'

'Well, you boys seem to be doing a fine job up north.'

'We're certainly doing our best, sir. Plan on turning those Japs right back around.'

Over a cup of tea Mick and Jimmy talked at length about the war, and Mick tried to explain the finer points of cricket to their American guest. Eventually, as the afternoon grew later, Evelyn's mother asked Jimmy to stay for dinner. Evelyn alternated between listening to the men's conversation and helping her mother as she bustled around the kitchen. She found Jimmy's accent fascinating, with the slow drawl of the south but a hint of something else, which Jimmy told her was Cajun, the French-Canadian influence that remained strong in some parts of Louisiana. There was a quiet watchfulness about him. He wasn't like some of the other Americans she'd come across. He seemed content to sit and listen most of the time.

Evelyn's father was one of the many of his generation who weren't excited about the Yank presence in Townsville. For Jimmy to have won over the usually reserved man spoke a lot about his polite charm.

Evelyn caught Jimmy's eye and they shared a smile. She was worried about her father boring him, but he seemed genuinely interested in their conversation. At dinner he complimented her mother profusely and made the older woman blush. 'Oh, it's nothing special. Just a baked chook.'

'Chicken,' Evelyn added when he looked up from his plate, puzzled.

'Well, it's the best meal I've eaten in months.'

'It's always nice to cook for an appreciative audience,' her mother said, patting her hair demurely.

'I always appreciate your cooking,' her father said, scowling.

'You're not a guest, dear.'

Evelyn bit back a smile as she listened to her father muttering about smooth-talking Yanks and saw that Jimmy was also doing his best not to smile or make eye contact with anyone.

'You mentioned earlier that you missed your family gatherings. What kind of meals do you have back home?' her mother enquired.

'Well, ma'am, the thing I miss the most is a good ol' crawfish boil. We boil up a whole heap of crawfish, corn on the cob and potatoes in big pots and then we cover a table in newspaper and just dump it all out in the middle and eat it hot.'

'You eat everything straight off the table?' her mother gasped.

'Yes, ma'am. Ain't nothing tastes better,' he said with a shake of his head, before suddenly remembering his manners and adding hastily, 'Except for the meal we just ate, of course.'

Her mother took a moment to digest this news before curiosity got the better of her. 'What other types of food do you eat?'

'The south is renowned for its food. We eat lots of gumbo, with shrimp, oysters, crabmeat, and sometimes with chicken. Crawfish étouffée and jambalaya. That's like a big stew with rice,' he explained when he caught her mother's confused expression. 'You can make it with sausage, chicken, turkey and even alligator.'

'Alligator!' her sister squeaked.

'Yep, alligator. We've hunted and eaten gator for generations where I come from.'

'Is it really like chicken?' Betty asked.

'I guess, if chickens had a whole bunch of sharp teeth and a surly attitude,' he grinned.

Evelyn laughed and Betty scowled at her.

After the men had been shooed from the kitchen, the two sisters began clearing the table while their mother prepared a pot of tea.

'Isn't he a *dreamboat*,' Betty said wistfully as she wiped the plate Evelyn handed her.

'He's far too old for you, young lady, and I wouldn't let your father hear you talking like that,' their mother scolded.

'He's not *that* old,' Betty pouted. 'Besides, I think an older man is romantic.'

'I think you should spend more time watching what you're doing with the good china and less time with your head in the clouds.'

'Oh, Mum, I'm almost fourteen. I'm not a child, you know.'

Evelyn and her mother shared an amused smile.

'Here you go, take this out to the men.' Evelyn's mother handed her a tray with the tea and cake carefully set out on it.

'I'll take it,' Betty said quickly.

'No, you'll finish those dishes, young lady.'

Evelyn smiled to herself as she headed down the hallway towards the sunroom at the front of the house. Her sister was becoming a pain lately, trying to imitate the older girls she knew around town. Evelyn didn't understand her younger sister's need to act so grown up. When she'd been fourteen she'd still been climbing trees in the backyard. They were as different as two siblings could be. Betty was interested in fashion, gossip and movie starlets, and would sit in front of her mirror for hours, recreating the latest hairstyles of her favourite idols. Evelyn was more at home pottering in the garden. Nothing quite beat the feel of dirt between her fingers, the satisfaction she got from picking vegetables which she'd tended and nurtured from seeds.

Evelyn put the tray down and poured two cups of tea, handing one to her father and the other across to Jimmy. Their fingers touched briefly as he accepted the dainty cup from her. Evelyn gave a start and Jimmy quickly gathered the cup in his big hands, saving it from spilling. Flustered, Evelyn felt her cheeks heat up and she dropped her gaze to the cake she hurriedly dished up.

By the time her mother joined them, she'd gotten herself under control and the evening continued without any more awkward incidents.

'Well, I guess I should be going,' Jimmy said eventually, sounding more than a little reluctant. 'Thank you once again, ma'am, I truly did appreciate your kind invitation to dinner,' he smiled and took her mother's hand, kissing it before shaking her father's hand heartily and thanking him for the conversation. Evelyn couldn't believe how easily the man seemed to have charmed her parents within the space of one afternoon.

'I'll walk you to the door,' Evelyn said, leading him from the sunroom and out onto the front verandah.

'You have lovely parents.'

'Yes, and I'm wondering who they are,' she grinned. 'You've certainly managed to win them over.'

'I wasn't trying to win anyone over,' he protested with a small frown that instantly made Evelyn feel bad.

'I didn't mean that you . . .' she faltered. 'What I meant was that it usually takes a lot to impress my father, and you've somehow managed to do that in one visit.'

'You have no idea how much of a relief it is to be able to sit at a real dinner table and be part of a family again. It was nice, and it meant more to me than any of you could possibly realise.'

'We'd like to think someone would do the same for Roy,' she said, feeling a stab of guilt that she hadn't thought of him all evening.

'Roy's a lucky guy,' he said quietly, holding her gaze. The roar of a jeep down the street broke the silence and they both fidgeted self-consciously for a moment until he took a step back, shuffling his hat in his hands awkwardly. 'Well, I better go,' he said. 'You have yourself a good evening.'

'Goodnight, Jimmy.'

'Goodnight, Evelyn,' he said softly, hesitating briefly before turning away.

She watched as he walked down the street, eventually melting into the darkness, and tried to work out why she felt as though she'd just been hit by a train.

Five

Evelyn smiled as she placed the warm eggs into the basket and filled the water and feed dishes. She loved her girls, listening to them cluck as they scratched around in the yard. There was something about chooks that soothed her. They didn't judge or make any unreasonable demands. They were simple, uncomplicated animals. On the outside she supposed that's how everyone thought of her too. She didn't like confrontation and was happy to go along with things. Even though part of her dreamed of travel and seeing exotic places, deep down she really was content with the simple things.

Roy had often talked about owing a property someday. His father had been working on a cattle property down south when he'd met Roy's mother and moved to Townsville to be with her. Roy had always found it hard to understand why his father had given up life on the land for love. He couldn't understand a man allowing emotion to rule his head in that way, but Evelyn secretly thought his parents' story was romantic.

Roy was more like her father. He was a man who rarely showed his emotions and preferred to let his actions show his love. 'A real man works hard and makes sure his family is provided for,' she'd once heard her dad say to Roy. Still, Roy's dream of living on the land and raising cattle appealed to her, and maybe they were right—all the romance and sweet words in the world wouldn't put food on the table or a roof over your head.

Betty called for her from the sunroom and Evelyn put the basket of eggs she'd just collected on the kitchen bench. She heard her sister giggle as she walked down the hallway. At the doorway she froze, her eyes widening as she spotted the familiar figure seated across from her sister.

Jimmy stood and smiled, although he looked a little less self-assured than last time.

'Miss Evelyn,' he greeted her politely, his large hands holding his cap tightly in front of him.

'Just Evelyn,' she murmured, swallowing nervously.

'Isn't this a nice surprise, Evie?' Betty said, seemingly oblivious to the tension in the air around her.

'It is,' she agreed quickly.

'What's in your bag?' Betty asked Jimmy curiously.

'Betty,' Evelyn chided, but Jimmy chuckled and bent down to retrieve the paper bag at his feet, handing it across to her little sister. 'Just a thank you for having me to dinner the other evening.'

'Butter! And sugar! Oh, Evie, look,' Betty gushed in excitement. 'Tea and . . . What's in here?' she asked, holding up a small wrapped package.

'Sweets.'

'Sweets? Oh, you mean lollies? Evie, lollies! I'm going to show Mum.'

Evelyn stared after her sister as she ran from the room and realised she was now alone with the handsome pilot. 'Thank you. But you didn't have to do that.'

'I wanted to.'

'It really wasn't necessary, it must have cost a fortune.'

Jimmy shrugged but didn't comment, changing the subject instead. 'I was wondering if you and your sister would like to go get an ice-cream with me.'

'Ice-cream?'

'You haven't had ice-cream before?'

'Of course I've had it before . . . just not lately.' It was hard to buy luxuries like ice-cream when you couldn't even get hold of fresh milk on a regular basis.

'Then I'd like to remedy that situation immediately,' he said with a grin.

'Can we, Mum? Please?' Betty's squeal interrupted them and Evelyn looked over to see her sister standing in the doorway with her beaming mother who'd come in from the garden.

The three of them walked down Clarendon Street, along Charters Towers Road and onto Flinders Street with Betty talking almost the entire time. Usually this would annoy Evelyn no end, but today she was almost thankful for her sister's presence. Jimmy confused her. He was so handsome, and unlike any man she'd ever met before, and she suspected she was a little infatuated with him. This was not good. In fact, this was very bad. She was not usually more than vaguely interested in the Americans who had flooded their town. She often found them a little obnoxious, despite their smooth charm and rather dashing uniforms.

She was glad she was engaged to Roy. Sensible, down-to-earth, no-frills Roy. Actually, she was surprised that Roy had even bothered giving the time of day to a Yank, let alone become friends with one. But in all fairness, Jimmy did seem different. He genuinely wanted to know about Australia and Australians. She liked that about him.

They had to line up to be served at the milk bar, one of many local businesses that had brought in American-style foods like hamburgers, milkshakes and ice-cream.

Walking from the cafe, Evelyn and Jimmy followed Betty, who had run ahead to catch up with some girls she knew from school in order to fill them in on the dashing Yank who had bought her ice-cream.

'You realise you'll never get rid of her now, right?' Evelyn said dryly as she watched her sister giggling with her friends.

Jimmy's soft chuckle made her insides quiver a little. 'That's okay. I don't mind. She's a good kid.'

Evelyn eyed him sideways. 'She's a brat.'

'She reminds me of my cousins.'

'Do you have a big family?'

'Big and loud.'

'So are you the black sheep then?'

He looked at her a little oddly.

'You seem more content to watch and listen.'

31

'Yeah, well, sometimes you learn more about people by watching. But I guess back home I'm louder.'

'What's it like in Louisiana?'

'Hot. Humid like here, but different.' He smiled at her raised eyebrow. 'We have lots of bayous and we love our food.'

'Is a bayou a river?' Evelyn asked hesitantly.

'Kind of, but they're covered in marsh and don't flow real fast.'

'Like a swamp?'

'Yeah, but the bayou is so much more than just a swamp. It's—' he paused and looked around as though searching for the right words—'it's a forest in water, full of ancient cypress and tupelo trees, covered in Spanish moss and so quiet in places it almost feels haunted. And we have green water hyacinths that smell just like watermelon when you dip the pink flower in the water.'

'A flower that smells like watermelon?' Evelyn laughed, caught up in his vivid description of his homeland.

'I swear,' he grinned, and Evelyn found herself mesmerised by his smile before realising she'd been staring and averted her gaze quickly.

They walked down to The Strand and sat on a bench overlooking the bay. Across from them Magnetic Island rose from the turquoise water.

'We don't have views like this though,' he said as they sat quietly looking at the sparkle of the sun playing across the water.

Trucks, buses and planes drowned out the usual sounds of the gentle waves lapping against the shore. The port was full of naval vessels, and landing craft ferried personnel and an endless parade of vehicles and equipment to and from the big ships anchored in the bay.

'You don't like us much, do you?'

Evelyn looked up at his quiet words and found him studying her.

'Us?'

'Americans.'

'I like Americans just fine.'

'You don't like the US military being here then.'

Evelyn dropped his inquiring gaze and looked out over the congested bay. 'This isn't our town any more.'

'There's a war on.'

'Really?' she asked, feigning surprise.

'We're trying to help.'

'I know. It's just hard to sit back while someone else turns your home into a place you no longer recognise.'

'Things will go back to normal once we win this war.'

'Will they?' Evelyn had her doubts about that. Nothing would go back to the way it had been before the war. Once the war was over, she'd be a married woman, expected to settle down and raise a family. It was what she wanted, she reminded herself firmly. She wasn't sure why she was having such conflicting thoughts lately. Maybe it was Dolly, always trying to change her mind about her hasty engagement. What else could she have done, though? Roy had surprised her with the proposal in front of both their families at his farewell dinner. Everyone had been so happy. Her father had beamed at her . . . beamed!

For the briefest of moments she'd felt cornered, but she'd quickly hidden it beneath a smile. How could she have said anything but yes? It was the next logical step for them. But since that night she'd found herself occasionally feeling like an animal trapped in a set of headlights. Then she would feel guilty and ungrateful. She shied away from examining the tightening of her chest the thought provoked.

'You don't wear a ring?'

Jimmy's words surprised her and she looked down at her hands. 'No. I . . . there wasn't time to get a ring. It was a bit of a spur-of-the-moment thing.' To say the least.

'You don't really talk about him.'

Evelyn glanced up at him sharply. 'What do you mean?'

'You haven't asked much about him. Don't you worry?'

'Of course I do. Why wouldn't I be worried about him? He's my fiancé,' she pointed out, partly to remind herself. 'Besides, I gathered from your visit the other day that he was doing well . . . otherwise you would have said something.'

When Jimmy chuckled softly, Evelyn frowned a little. 'What's so funny?'

'Aussies,' he said with a shake of his head. 'You know, I asked Roy if there was any special message he wanted me to pass on to you, or a letter, but he just said, Tell her I'm all right. What kind of thing is that to tell the woman you love?'

'Well, Roy doesn't like to make a fuss.'

'Seems to me it's not just Roy. Your menfolk don't seem to know much about courting.'

'Is that what you call what you Yanks do when you come here?'

'I know that Aussie women appreciate men with manners.'

'And money, let's not forget that,' she added dryly. 'They appreciate what American servicemen can get them, the stockings and chocolate and all the fancy dances. Australian servicemen can't compete with that.'

'So Australian women are shallow?' he asked with a twitch of his lips.

'No more than American men are willing to overlook it to have some fun.'

'So money, charm and manners don't work with you?'

'Apparently not,' she said, realising she'd dug herself into a hole. 'There's more to life than sweet words and money.'

'Like?'

'Loyalty. An honest, hard-working man is a very important thing to have.'

'This is true, and Roy is definitely that.'

The ground was dry beneath their feet, ants busily scurried about their work and the hum of insects could just be heard between rumbling trucks driving past and the drone of aircraft overhead.

'I think it's time we headed home.' Evelyn wasn't sure where this conversation was headed but she didn't feel comfortable having it, partly because she felt like a fraud for defending Roy when earlier she'd been having doubts about her feelings towards him. Maybe it was a timely reminder that she needed to stop wasting time thinking about things that just weren't possible. She'd made her choice, she'd accepted Roy's proposal, and she would just have to forget about flowers and chocolates. That wasn't who Roy was. It hadn't bothered her before, so why did it suddenly feel as though she were somehow settling for less than she deserved?

Six

Over the next few weeks Jimmy became a regular visitor to the Ward household. He always brought gifts, sometimes staples, often more exotic things like lollies, which always pleased Betty. Jimmy didn't disappoint her parents either; he somehow managed to find material for her mother who had been complaining about the lack of any decent fabric to sew up some new dresses. Then there was the occasional drum of fuel that her father found out the back near the shed. That in itself was worth a small fortune, fuel rations being what they were. When her parents protested that what he had brought them was too much, he just smiled and shook his head, saying that just to be part of a family for a little while and have some small comfort of home was worth far more than a few sweets and lengths of material.

Often Jimmy would be waiting outside the Red Cross building when Evelyn finished her shift and they would stop for a milkshake or something to eat on the way home. A few times Dolly accompanied them, and the outings were great fun. For all her flirting and brashness, Dolly was good company. Evelyn always felt better if Dolly, or even her sister, was with them during their outings. That way she could push away the niggle of doubt she always felt whenever she was with him. *He's just a close friend of the family, our adopted Yank,* she'd tell herself firmly. But she never was much of a liar and it was growing harder to keep up the charade with each passing day.

Over Sunday lunch, after the whole family had returned from church, Jimmy casually asked her father if it would be all right if Evelyn accompanied him to an upcoming dance. 'If I had an escort I would be less likely to be harassed by some of the more determined local women,' he said as a way of pleading his case. Evelyn held back a snort at that. Very few servicemen complained about the attention local women paid them, but in his defence, Jimmy did manage to look extremely pained about the situation.

'Well, I suppose that would be acceptable,' said her father eventually.

'Can I go?' Betty chimed in hopefully.

One look from their father soon silenced her and she lowered her head and went back to her meal.

The afternoon of the dance Evelyn took her best Sunday dress from the wardrobe and laid it out on her bed. When Betty walked in she studied her choice critically. 'Is that what you're wearing?'

'Yes. Why?'

'It's a little bit . . . well, maybe you could ask Dolly for a lend of something?'

'A little bit what?'

'It's . . . boring.'

Boring? 'It's a perfectly good dress. I wear it to church all the time.'

'Exactly. To *church*,' Betty emphasised pointedly. 'This is a *date*.'

'It's *not* a date. It's a *dance*.' Evelyn looked at the dress apprehensively. Did she really want to look boring? She had only been to a handful of dances, working alongside ladies from the Red Cross or occasionally with her mother's church ladies.

'I guess maybe I could borrow something from Dolly,' she relented.

Dolly was more than happy to lend her something, although Evelyn declined most of the outfits, knowing there was no way her father would allow her to leave the house dressed in them. In the end Dolly handed her a gauzy grey and pink floral dress. The fitted sweetheart bodice had gathered short sleeves and a lightweight A-line skirt that floated to her knees and swirled when she turned.

'It's beautiful,' Evelyn whispered in awe as she smoothed the skirt down gently.

'But it's so . . . dreary. Are you sure you wouldn't rather the blue one? It would be stunning with your dark hair.'

Evelyn sent the discarded frock on the bed a nervous glance. Her parents would have a fit if she wore that. It hugged every curve of her body and left nothing to the imagination . . . at all. 'No, this one's perfect,' she beamed. 'I'll get it back to you tomorrow.'

Dolly waved a hand briskly, 'Keep it. I only bought it to wear for a job interview once.'

Betty seemed mildly satisfied by her dress choice when she arrived home, and asked, 'How are you doing your hair?'

'My hair? I don't know, down I suppose,' Evelyn said as she wiggled into the frock.

'Sit down.'

Her younger sister's tone surprised her, and Evelyn found herself doing as she was told. Armed with a magazine, hair-brush and bobby pins, Betty went to work. When Evelyn looked at the end result, she was flabbergasted. Who was this woman staring back at her? Her dark hair had been parted and twisted and pinned into an elegant chignon at the base of her skull.

'You look beautiful,' Betty whispered as she stood behind her and admired her handiwork in the mirror.

'Are you sure it's not too much?'

'It's perfect,' her sister said with a frown, ready to protect her creation if Evelyn tried to touch it.

A wave of nervous anticipation fluttered to life, and she placed a hand over her stomach. *This was just a dance, it was not a date,* she repeated firmly and tried to ignore the lingering doubt which continued to hover in the background, quick to pounce if she allowed it an opportunity.

⁓

When Jimmy arrived to pick her up, Evelyn's breath caught at the sight of him in his dress uniform. He looked like a movie star with his dark hair slicked back and his medals gleaming.

'Wow,' Betty breathed beside her, and Evelyn couldn't have agreed with her little sister's assessment more.

'All right, off you go then,' her father's gruff voice broke the appreciative silence. 'Stay away from any trouble out there.'

'I'll take care of her, sir. You have my word,' Jimmy promised, shaking her father's hand firmly.

It wasn't a frivolous warning on her father's part. Fights were commonplace at night in this disturbing new culture of loose morals and outrageous behaviour.

Evelyn tried hard to contain her nervous excitement. The warm night air was heavy with the sweet smell of hibiscus and bougainvillea, and she could smell something else—the tantalising scent of soap and aftershave on Jimmy's skin. He was walking closely beside her and suddenly her stomach was aquiver with butterflies. As they neared the main street and approached a group of GIs gathered around a parked vehicle, Jimmy pulled her closer against him, keeping his arm around her securely.

They entered the Red Cross recreation hall and Jimmy led the way across to a long table that had been set up wtih drinks, offering her a glass of fruit punch. They weaved their way through the crowd and finally spotted Dolly, who was waving them over to a saved table. She looked stunning in her tight red and black polka-dotted dress. It clung to her voluptuous curves and drew admiring glances from the uniformed men. Her date for the evening, Teddy, was yet another in her long list of acquaintances, and he looked as though he could hardly believe his luck.

It was nice to forget the war for a little while, and the rest of the problems that went along with it. For the next few songs, Jimmy and Evelyn were content to sit and watch the others dancing as they sipped their drinks. However, when she'd finished her drink, Evelyn slid a sideways glance across at Jimmy and was surprised to see he looked strangely nervous. 'Is everything all right, Jimmy?'

'Sure. Everything's just dandy. Are you having a good time?'

Evelyn nodded enthusiastically. She was. This was so much better than a quiet evening at home in front of the radio. She watched the couples on the dance floor as they twirled and spun around; part of her longed to be able to dance like that, but she was too terrified of making a fool of herself to ever attempt it.

'Would you like to give it a go?'

'Oh, no,' she shook her head. 'I couldn't dance like that.' The men were throwing their dance partners in the air and sliding them between their legs on the floor. It all looked a little daunting.

'We wouldn't have to jitterbug,' he chuckled. 'Come on, I'll teach you something simple. I'm no Fred Astaire but I can get by.'

Evelyn briefly resisted his tug on her hand as he got to his feet, before reluctantly allowing him to lead her onto the dance floor.

'Just follow my lead,' he said, pulling her close and beginning to move to the fast tempo of the music. 'There ya go, you're a natural,' he beamed down at her as she slowly lost her initial anxiety and began to enjoy herself.

She wasn't sure what dance they were doing exactly, but at least they were having fun. When dances were announced that she was more familiar with, like the good old Pride of Erin, she felt far more confident, but then a slow song came on and she felt the butterflies flood back as Jimmy stepped closer, wrapping her tightly in his arms as the singer crooned something soft and gentle into the microphone.

Evelyn felt a little self-conscious with her arms trapped against his chest, until Jimmy reached down and placed her arms around his neck. The sudden contact with his chest sent an unfamiliar quiver through her. Nothing more than a thin layer of clothing separated their bodies, and through the fabric Evelyn could feel the warmth of his skin imprinting against her own.

She'd never felt this way before; her body's reaction was both exciting and alarming. They were only dancing, yet somehow it felt as though they were doing something far more intimate.

When the song finally ended, Evelyn found she couldn't immediately step away from him. They stood there, oblivious to the crowd, still trapped in their own bubble as the band launched into another upbeat rendition and couples danced on around them.

Eventually Evelyn dropped her arms from his neck and took a small step back, trying her best to avoid his gaze as she returned to her seat. She was grateful that Jimmy didn't try to talk about what had happened, she wasn't sure she even knew herself. They sat out the rest of the dances, content to chat to other people they knew, and after a while Evelyn managed to relax again.

'I don't want to go home yet,' Dolly protested after the announcement of the final dance for the night.

'Then don't. Let's go for a coffee. The cafe across the street's still open,' Teddy said, his Brooklyn accent making Evelyn smile.

Stepping outside the hall the air was cooler but still warm, and the moon hung in the black sky, bright and beautiful.

The sirens cut through their chatter as they stepped off the kerb to cross the street and for a moment the four of them stared at each other.

'Air raid!' Teddy said, grabbing Dolly's hand and hurrying towards the closest of the slit trenches, dodging the crowd of people who'd evacuated the hall at the sound of the siren. People were milling around in the street, some blatantly unfazed, looking skyward curiously, while others were taking the shouted advice of the air-raid wardens to head for shelter. Jimmy and Evelyn followed the wardens' instructions and climbed down into the cement, pit-like fortress. The steps were narrow and steep, and Evelyn tried not to focus on how claustrophobic it felt all squashed together in the dark trench. There had been two previous, uneventful attempts at bombing over the last week with no real damage resulting, unless you count the coconut tree south of town that was hit. Locals were becoming a little blasé about the Japs being a threat in the bombing department, but her father had remained wary, despite the unconcerned attitude most people were displaying. 'Lucky the Japs couldn't hit the side of a barn, because the clowns running the show in town wouldn't have a clue what to do if they managed to hit a target.'

Looking up, Evelyn saw that the night sky was clearly visible through the slits in the box at street level. Eventually a low droning sound became audible and Evelyn held Jimmy's hand tightly. It didn't feel real. Townsville couldn't be bombed, surely? This had to be some kind of drill. Despite the war being so visible in Townsville, it still somehow didn't seem real. And yet here they were, huddled together in a bunker, with a Japanese bomber circling overhead. Evelyn shivered slightly, despite the humidity.

Jimmy slid an arm around her shoulders and pulled her close to his side. Her trembling stopped, but her heart rate continued to pound, for different reasons now.

'What is it doing?' Evelyn asked. The plane sounded as though it was circling the city without dropping any bombs. Bright searchlights held the aircraft in their beams, following its every move.

'They're taking their time and getting their bearings,' said Jimmy quietly.

Machine-gun fire rattled in the distance but it was obvious the plane was too high and it was doing nothing to deter the enemy.

The sound of another aircraft approaching soon had everyone searching the night sky to locate it. 'There,' Jimmy said, pointing slightly to the left as the American plane got close enough to identify. 'It's a Bell P-39.'

The machine-gun fire continued, despite the fact it seemed to be having no impact on the big plane. Then bright red tracer bullets erupted from the smaller P-39 and a burst of light exploded as it made contact with the tail of the Jap plane. A loud cheer went up inside the bunker.

Jimmy slid his arm back around Evelyn's shoulder and pulled her close to his side. She found herself studying his strong jawline, no longer interested in the drama in the sky above them. She felt safe and protected; the heavy weight of his arm across her shoulders and the warmth of his big body beside her chased away any fear. There was no other place she wanted to be.

He looked down at her, but his expression seemed to change as he read something in her eyes she hadn't even been aware was visible. Everything around them ceased to exist. The other people, still watching the spectacular light show provided by the bomber moving out to sea, were oblivious to the exchange happening between them.

Slowly Jimmy lowered his head towards her. There was nothing and no one, only Jimmy's warm coaxing lips and the heady sensation of freefalling into the darkness.

There was another cheer and the spell was broken. Evelyn looked up to see everyone was still looking out to sea, apparently excited by the hit the Jap plane had taken and the fiery trail of destruction that followed.

She didn't care about the Japanese and their bombs. If the whole Imperial Army landed on The Strand right now she truly wouldn't care because at that very moment she knew beyond a shadow of a doubt that she had fallen head over heels in love with Jimmy Crenshaw.

Seven

The damage from the bombing raid the night before was minimal, with the only fatality being a coconut tree that had been cut in half. The rest of the bombs had fallen into Cleveland Bay, but the whole town was talking about the narrow escape.

At the dinner table her parents were discussing the events.

'This is the third raid. I really think we should consider going down to Iris's house in Sydney,' her mother was saying.

'If this is the best the Japs can do, we don't have much to worry about.'

'Maybe the girls—'

'I'm not going to Sydney,' Evelyn cut in. She'd have to leave her friends behind . . . and Jimmy.

'No one's going anywhere,' said her father. 'Besides, if we left, the Yanks would probably move into the house and we'd never get the bloody thing back.'

And that, it seemed, was the end of that. Evelyn took her plate to the sink and rinsed it, distracted by the panic the thought of leaving Jimmy had caused her. Her thoughts returned to the kiss they'd shared and she jumped when the cutlery slipped from her fingers and clattered into the sink.

'Careful, love,' her mother chided from the table.

'Sorry,' Evelyn mumbled.

'Your mother tells me you're going out again tomorrow night,' said her father gruffly.

Evelyn froze momentarily, before forcing a calmness to her expression and turning to look at her father. 'That's right. Jimmy will be there.'

'What would Roy think about that?'

'Seeing as Roy sent him here to visit us, I'd say he wouldn't have a problem with it.' A mixture of anger and guilt flooded her. Anger because she resented having to think about Roy when she was feeling so happy; guilt because she was forced to remember she *shouldn't* be happy, she had no right to be having these feelings while she was engaged to another man.

'I don't know. It doesn't seem right to me.'

A swell of irritation made her answer more tersely than normal. 'After everything he's done for us, you expect me to turn down an invitation?'

Her father frowned at that but said, 'Make sure you're home early. I don't want any rumours starting up. You don't want word getting back to Roy that you've turned into some floozy like that Rowland girl.'

Even though she wanted to defend her friend, there was no way she could when everything her father had heard about Dolly was true, and more. The Rowlands had always been no-hopers, according to her dad. Dolly's father had worked on the railways until his back had given out on him and he'd turned to drink. It fell to Dolly's mother, a skinny woman with a long face, to take in people's washing and ironing in order to feed the family. The older sons were always in trouble, and rumour was they were in cahoots with some Yanks who were making a lot of money on the black market. Evelyn had always had to fight hard their entire childhood in defence of that friendship, and it seemed things hadn't changed all that much now they were older.

There had been no further air raids, and the party-like nightlife continued on unabated for both civilians and military personnel alike. She'd tried to talk herself out of going to the dance tonight, but the truth was she *wanted* to be with Jimmy again. Everything about this situation was wrong, and yet she didn't want to resist the pull he had on her.

The band was playing a slow, soft jazz number and Jimmy gathered Evelyn close. She circled her arms around his neck and rested her cheek against his chest.

'Are you having a good time?' Jimmy asked, bending his head towards her ear. She felt a small shiver run through her at the intimate gesture.

'I am. Thank you.'

Jimmy stopped moving and Evelyn looked up at him in surprise. 'What is it?' she asked warily.

'I've been struggling, Evie, ever since the day I met you,' he said. 'I've tried to stay away from you, but the thought of not seeing you makes me break out in a cold sweat.'

'Jimmy,' she said, then faltered as she saw his pained look.

'I know you're Roy's girl,' he said, 'but I can't get you out of my head.'

Evelyn opened her mouth to reply but no sound came out. This was crazy. It was worse than crazy, it was wrong . . . So why was her heart doing backflips inside her chest?

'Say something, Evie,' he said, sounding anguished by her silence.

'I . . . Jimmy . . .'

'Mind if I cut in, mate?'

Evelyn's gaze flew to the soldier in Australian uniform who stood behind Jimmy, tapping him on the shoulder.

'As a matter of fact I do,' Jimmy said, his hold tightening fractionally on her waist. 'We're in the middle of something.'

'Let me rephrase it for you, *Yank*. I'm cutting in.'

Jimmy shook off the soldier's hand and turned to face him. 'Take a hike, pal.'

'Bloody Yanks, you think you can just come in here and take our women?' He looked Evelyn up and down before spitting on the ground at her feet. 'Fine, I don't want any Yank's whore anyway.'

The hit came hard and fast and Evelyn found herself pushed backwards into the couple behind. Within seconds a crowd had circled the two men exchanging punches. The Australian soldiers cheered their man on, and the Americans, far outnumbering the Australians, did likewise. Jimmy was more agile than the stockier Australian and managed to duck and weave, avoiding the majority of the hits, landing a few solid blows to the Australian's stomach. The Aussie doubled over briefly, then rallied and hit Jimmy a smashing blow to the side of his head. Evelyn could only stare on, hands across her mouth to contain her horrified gasps. Already Jimmy's eye was beginning to swell, and a cut to his lip was dripping blood across his face. The Australian wasn't faring much better; despite their differences in build they seemed fairly evenly matched. It wasn't long before smaller fights broke out around the hall and the dance floor became a battlefield. The band had stopped playing and were hurriedly dragging their instruments off the stage. Evelyn searched the room for Dolly and found her laughing and cheering on Teddy, who was weaving and ducking to avoid another man's wild swings.

Evelyn felt her wrist being grabbed and began to struggle wildly until she realised it was Jimmy, and she allowed him to drag her out of the melee, dodging and weaving. He shielded her from the fighting as they made their way towards a back door, down a narrow laneway and out into the street. Military police had converged upon the hall, dragging away uniformed men and doing their best to stop the chaos.

She couldn't look at him. Now that the shock had worn off, her face flooded with shame as the Australian's words came back to haunt her. *Whore*, he'd called her. Evelyn turned away and began walking. What had she done? How could she have allowed her emotions to get so out of control? The soldier was right, she *was* no better than a common whore. Roy was off fighting a war, putting his life in danger every day, and here she was out dancing and falling in love with an American! What on earth could she have been thinking?

For a little while they walked in silence, and from the corner of her eye she saw Jimmy gingerly touching his jaw.

'Evelyn, hold up a minute,' he said.

'How badly are you hurt?' she asked, stopping. He'd wiped most of the blood off, but his eye still looked red and no doubt he'd eventually have a black eye.

'It's nothing serious,' he dismissed, looking closely at her. 'What about you? Are you okay?'

'I'm fine,' she said. But she was angry . . . at herself more than anyone.

'Look, I'm sorry about the fight.'

'It doesn't matter,' she said and turned to walk away, but he stopped her, taking hold of her arm.

'It *does* matter. I would never have put you in a position like that if I could have helped it, but there was no way that guy was getting away with what he said.'

'I said it doesn't matter,' she said, jerking her arm out of his grip.

'Damn it, Evelyn. Stop,' he snapped. 'Is this because of what I said before?' His voice had lost its softness and there was an urgency to it now. 'Tell me you don't feel the same way about me. Tell me you haven't thought of me almost every second of the day since you first met me,' he demanded roughly.

She had never been able to lie very well. 'This . . . can't happen.'

'It's too late, Evie, it's *already* happened. You can no sooner stop having feelings for someone than hold back the tide.'

'You don't have feelings for me . . . you've just been away from girls for a very long time, and you're just missing . . . *that*.'

Evelyn frowned. She couldn't bring herself to imagine Jimmy having sex with some other woman, couldn't say it out loud.

'I haven't been away from girls all that long, and I'm pretty sure I know the difference between *that* and what I'm feeling for you.'

For a moment she imagined herself and Jimmy locked in a passionate embrace, like the romances Dolly sighed over in movies. She wasn't sure where all these lustful thoughts and feelings were coming from, she sure hadn't experienced them with Roy. In fact the closest she and Roy had ever come to . . . *that* . . . had been a night of ardent kissing when they'd found out he was leaving the next day for basic training.

'You need to find a girl who can show you a good time,' she snapped, angry that the thought of him with someone else stung so terribly.

'I don't want any other girl.'

'Jimmy, I'm engaged . . .' Her words faltered as he moved in closer and the scent of his aftershave filled her senses.

He kissed her with the lightest of touches, but gradually his lips became more urgent, sending liquid fire through her veins.

Roy had never kissed her like this. The thought was enough to shock her to her senses and she pushed at his chest until she could squirm free of his embrace. Angry tears filled her eyes as self-loathing swelled up inside her. 'Leave me alone, Jimmy. Go back and find some other woman willing to show you a good time.'

'What the hell are you saying?' he said, his expression furious.

'I'm saying this is wrong and I don't want to see you any more.'

'Evie,' he pleaded.

Evelyn shook her head but held strong. 'You're *not* falling in love with me,' she said firmly, 'and I'm *not* in love with you.'

She caught the flash of pain that crossed his face and quickly turned away. This was insane. There was no future for them, she had to end it before it got completely out of control. Being called a whore tonight had been a slap across the face. It was a wake-up call, a warning that if she didn't stand up to this now it would be too late and the damage to everyone would be irreparable. She quickly crossed the street and ran along the footpath, not stopping until she reached her front gate. As she climbed the stairs, she paused, her gaze drawn to the forlorn figure watching her from the shadows at the end of the street and fought the urge not to run back.

Eight

Evelyn took on more volunteer work over the next few days—anything to keep herself occupied and, more importantly, out of the house should Jimmy drop by to visit.

Her plan seemed to be working; she hadn't seen him and apparently neither had anyone else in the family.

'Where's young Jimmy today?' her father asked as they sat down to eat their Sunday meal.

Evelyn kept her head down and concentrated on cutting her chicken.

'I haven't seen him for a few days, Evelyn? Have you?' he continued.

'No. Maybe he's working a lot.'

'What did you do?' Betty demanded.

Evelyn glared at her sister before her mother said, 'Just eat your dinner.'

'Well, he was just dandy last time he was here,' her sister complained. 'Then nothing. I miss him.'

'You mean you miss the sweets,' Evelyn snapped.

'Girls,' said their mother with a frown. 'You're giving your father indigestion.'

Thankfully there was no further discussion of Jimmy's whereabouts, and each day she didn't hear from him, Evelyn told herself it was exactly what she wanted. Then, waiting for Dolly one afternoon down at Pallarenda Beach, she was forced to face the realisation of just how poor her attempt at denial had really been.

'Hello, Evie.'

She turned at the familiar voice, her heart in her throat and an unmistakable rush of joy flooding her body.

'Jimmy. What are you doing here?' she asked breathlessly. There were a lot of military personnel relaxing on the beach and in the shade of the trees, but the chances of him being here at the same time as she was seemed a little too coincidental.

'Don't blame Dolly. I asked her to help me out. I wasn't sure that you'd agree to meet me if I asked.'

The truth was she wasn't altogether sure she would have been able to keep away. So much for her attempt to stay on the path of virtue.

'I love you, Evie. It's as simple as that.'

'Jimmy, please,' Evelyn said, her voice cracking slightly. Inside, her emotions were waging a battle between joy and pain.

'Just hear me out,' he cut in, quickly closing the distance between them. 'I know how hard this is on you.'

'No, you *don't*. You're not the one cheating on someone who trusts you. You have nothing to lose, Jimmy. I have everything: a best friend, my family . . . neighbours.'

'Roy's my friend too. You think I don't feel bad about what's happening?'

'Have you even thought about the fact that you'll be gone soon and I'll be left to face the consequences? I'll still be here and I'll have to live with the shame of cheating on Roy. His family will know! *Everyone* will know! Why can't you understand? You need to walk away before this goes any further.'

Jimmy closed the gap between them and claimed her mouth in a fierce kiss that ignited a matching response, full of urgent and desperate need. His arms slipped around her tightly, strong and secure, anchoring her to him and keeping her from melting into a pool of wanton lust at his feet. Where was this coming from? This was not her. She was quiet, sensible, sane Evelyn, and yet there was an inexplicable feeling of completion. She felt as though she belonged right here in his arms.

They were both breathing heavily by the time they pulled apart and Evelyn wondered if her expression was mirroring the astonishment she was feeling inside.

'I don't want to walk away. Can't you see I'm head over heels in love with you, Evie?'

'We've only known each other a few weeks, Jimmy, this can't be love. It's just this stupid war.'

'You're right. The war has *everything* to do with it. I've seen life end in a split second. I've watched my buddies die in front of me, Evie. It makes me realise you can't take life for granted. None of us knows how long we have, or what the future may hold. You have to take happiness whenever you find it.'

'So we live for the moment, and then when you get your orders it's *Thanks for memories, see ya around?* I can't do that, Jimmy. It's not who I am.'

'Evie, I've had the chance to be with more women than I could even count since this war started, and you know what? Not one of them ever made me feel the things I feel just by thinking about you. And that's the God's honest truth. I've never wanted to be with anyone the way I want to be with you. That's how I know this is real. It hasn't happened at the best time for either of us, but it's happened nonetheless. I'm not talking about this ending once I leave. I'm saying I want to spend the rest of my life with you, Evie. After this crazy war ends, I want you by my side . . . forever.'

Evelyn stared at Jimmy, stunned. Part of her was still stuck back on whether he'd meant he'd actually *been* with more women than he could count or just had the *opportunity*. Then his words sunk in.

She felt it too. She knew she was head over heels in love with Jimmy Crenshaw and the knowledge terrified her.

'Evie, baby, please. Not seeing you these last few days has been eating me up inside.'

Truth be told it had been the worst few days of her life too. It was a telling realisation. Roy had been away for over six months, and while she was worried about his safety, it was not the same gut-clenching fear she experienced when she thought of Jimmy leaving her to head back into battle. She didn't love Roy in the way she knew she should love the man she was supposed to be marrying. What she had with Jimmy went far deeper. It scared her to compare the two feelings now that she knew what love felt like.

'I don't know what to do,' she all but whispered.

'Yes, you do. Listen to what you *really* want, not what everyone else wants.'

'I made a promise.'

'To get engaged,' he agreed, pulling back slightly so he could look down into her face. 'You're not married, you haven't broken any promises said before God. Don't throw away this chance we've been given.'

Those words cut through her uncertainty. What if this *was* a gift? It was almost like a miracle. Had the war not happened, had Jimmy not been sent here, their paths would never have crossed. This was a once-in-a-lifetime opportunity. Was she brave enough to take it? Or would she turn her back for the sake of a promise she'd made to a man she *loved* but had never been *in love* with?

In her head it sounded ridiculous, no one fell in love after just a few days . . . but then again she'd known Roy for eighteen years without actually falling in love with him, so what did she know?

'Give me the rest of my time here to prove it to you. I promise, if you're still unsure, I won't cause any trouble between you and Roy. No one will ever know.'

He obviously hadn't lived in a small place like this before. Everyone *always* knew what was going on.

Could she live with the regret of letting her chance at true love walk away? If she let Jimmy go, she would never see him again. His life was on the other side of the world, not just the other side of Australia. He would be lost to her forever.

Evelyn searched those dark eyes above her and felt her own brim with unshed tears. If love was supposed to be so wonderful, then why did they have to go through so much pain to get it?

'Yes?' Jimmy prompted as he watched her intently.

'All right,' she finally agreed softly.

The relief in his face brought a smile to her lips. Yes, she was going to cause pain and anger and feelings of betrayal, but right now, wrapped in Jimmy's arms and seeing the tenderness of his smile, she knew she had to take the chance.

Nine

Over the next few days Evelyn and Jimmy spent as much time together as they could. Evelyn told her parents she was working extra volunteer hours and she and Jimmy snuck away to explore the countryside. Jimmy managed to acquire a vehicle, never the same one twice, and they took daytrips up into the surrounding rainforest, swimming and picnicking, enjoying their brief escapes from reality. Evelyn glowed from the inside out, and even the knowledge of what would happen when her family found out couldn't detract from her happiness.

The day was warm, and the water cool against her skin. When Jimmy reached out and drew her close to him, her body responded immediately. She'd never been this close to a man before, never run her hands across the fuzzy softness of a man's naked chest before. She liked the feel of his rougher skin as it rubbed against her softness. As Jimmy slowly slid down the straps of her swimming costume, she felt her blood scorch inside her veins, and not even the icy coolness of the mountain-fed creek could ease the sensation. Evelyn arched her back as he cupped her breasts in his warm, strong hands and slowly rubbed his thumb across the nipple, drawing a broken groan from her.

Against her stomach she felt the steely length of him, pushing urgently at his trunks, and the knowledge that she had brought him to this state filled her with a mix of confidence and power.

Slowly she ran a hand down his chest and felt him freeze. His hands momentarily stopped their gentle kneading and she felt his breath catch as she moved closer to the hardness demanding her attention. Her hand closed around him through the material of his trunks, and she felt him shudder against her as his breath hissed from between his lips. His fingers moved to cover her own and for a moment he guided her hand to move along the length of him, then he stopped her, dropping to rest his forehead against hers. In a strangled voice, he said, 'Enough.'

'Did I hurt you?' she asked, confused by the sudden halt.

'No,' he chuckled almost painfully. 'But if you don't stop now, you'll be getting a bit more than you were bargaining on.'

Realisation dawned and suddenly she wasn't confused any more. Slowly she eased away, the cold water seeping into the warmth their bodies had created and making them both gasp slightly. Slowly she slid her bathing costume down over her hips and stepped out of it, throwing it up onto the rocks beside the waterhole. His dark gaze followed her every movement silently.

'Are you sure you know what you're doing?'

'No. But I'm a fast learner so I expect I'll pick it up as we go,' she said, smiling.

'Evie, I'm not—'

She leaned forward and kissed his lips gently. 'I want you to,' she said, wanting him to make love to her, to stop this ache that was becoming unbearable. She was fairly sure the only cure for it was Jimmy. When he looked as though he was going to protest some more, she slipped her hand inside the band of his swimming trunks and he was left with no doubt that she knew what she wanted from him.

'Sweet Jesus, Evie, you have no idea what you do to me,' he groaned against the side of her neck as she ran her hand along the length of him.

'I have some idea,' she breathed back. The sensation of feeling him so hard and smooth against her sent her pulse into a frenzy.

In one swift movement he whisked off his shorts and gathered her against him, moving them closer to the edge of the pool so her back was against a rock worn smooth by the water over thousands of years.

He kissed her, his mouth taking her lips greedily before breaking away and lowering to her breast. Evelyn gave a surprised gasp as he took the nipple into his mouth, pulling against the sensitive skin and sending her spiralling over some invisible edge she had no idea she'd been standing near. But still it didn't ease the ache. Lifting his face he nipped and sucked his way up her neck, smoothing away her hair and burying himself into its flowing softness.

'I want you so bad, Evie, but I don't want to hurt you,' he whispered hoarsely.

'I'll be fine. Please, Jimmy,' she begged, unsure of how to put into words the need she had for him.

Slowly, carefully, he moved against her and she felt him nudge between her thighs. The pressure was excruciating, but at the same time her body welcomed him, drawing him deeper inside with each gentle thrust, in and out, until finally she gave a whimper and shortly after felt him shudder. A long helpless moan followed before he collapsed against her, his breathing harsh and laboured.

She still ached inside, but this time it had a different quality; she felt sore but somehow satisfied.

'Are you okay?' he asked, cupping her face in his hands and looking into her face carefully.

'I'm fine,' she said, unable to meet his gaze, feeling suddenly shy, which seemed ridiculous after what they'd just shared.

'Baby, look at me,' he coaxed gently.

Evelyn lifted her gaze reluctantly.

'Do you regret it?' he asked with a frown of concern.

'No,' she said. 'Never.' As his face slowly relaxed she managed a shy smile. 'Was it . . . all right? For you, I mean.'

'Oh, baby,' he breathed out a shaky breath and then chuckled, pulling her head forward to rest on his chest as he kissed her temple. 'Thank you.'

'For what?' she asked, lifting her face.

'For trusting me enough to be your first.'

'First and only,' she clarified, bringing his palm to her mouth to plant a kiss on it gently.

His eyes darkened at her words and his hold tightened on her possessively. 'I promise after this is over I'll be back to find you. You know that, right?'

'I know,' she said, blinking away the sting of tears his words evoked. She didn't want to think about life without him, even for a short time. She couldn't bear to think about what would happen if this war raged on for too many more years.

As they dried off on the rocks, Evelyn laced her fingers through his and held them up to inspect them. Jimmy smiled tolerantly as he watched her turn their hands this way and that. The sun caught the big ruby in the ring Jimmy wore on his left hand and it flashed a deep blood red.

Around the edges were engraved the words *US Air Force*. 'Does everyone get one of these?' she asked.

'My parents gave me this when I got my orders.'

'They must be very proud of you.'

'Yeah, I guess.'

'What are they like, your family?' she asked, curious to know everything about this man who'd become such an important part of her universe so quickly.

'Loud, crazy,' he told her with a grin. 'There's always lots of eating and music. Lots of laughing. *Laissez les bon temps rouler*,' he said cheerfully. 'It means, let the good times roll. Not that there's much to be laughing about at the moment. Ma's got two of her three boys away at war. My ma's a real worrier. My dad is always saying, *Ain't no point in worrying, cher*, but she always does,' his Cajun accent pronouncing the term of endearment as *sha*.

Evelyn caught the wistful look on his face and gave his hand a reassuring squeeze. How hard it must be for these men sent so far away from their families and everything they held dear. This was how it would be for the thousands of young Australians spread across the globe as well, longing for home.

'What are your brothers like?'

'Patrick was always the daredevil. He'd be the first to jump off something or take up a dare. He's over in Europe in the army. Thomas is younger and the brains of the family. He's studying to be a lawyer.'

'And what about you, where do you fit in?' she asked with a smile.

'Somewhere in the middle. Not as brave as Patrick and not as smart as Thomas.'

'I think you're pretty brave, and not everyone can fly a fighter plane, so you can't be too dumb.'

'And I got you to fall in love with me, so maybe there's some truth in that. Must've taken some smarts to get a gal like you to fall for a guy like me,' he winked.

'Where do you think we'll be a year from now?' she asked after a while.

'Sitting on a porch swing, looking out over the bayou and planning the rest of our lives together,' he said without hesitation. 'Do you think you can do that, Evie? Do you think you could be happy with me in Louisiana?'

Evelyn had thought about it a lot since the day Jimmy had declared his intentions, and the simple truth was that she could. She'd miss her family terribly, and living in a new country, despite the fact they spoke English—well, mostly—would take some getting used to, but she was prepared to deal with all that. 'I don't care where I live as long as it's with you,' she said solemnly. And it was the truth. Nothing else mattered. She wanted to make a life with this man, and as long as he was there beside her she knew she'd be fine.

Ten

Erin walked into the house and sat down at the kitchen table, utterly exhausted. She wasn't sure how she felt: numb, empty, emotionally wrung out were a few descriptions that sprang to mind as she folded her arms on the table and laid down her head.

It was hard seeing Gran fade away before her eyes. She hadn't been prepared for that when she'd come to Tuendoc. She'd thought Gran would be fine after a little TLC. Erin realised now that she'd probably been a tad naive. Although, in her defence, she had been a little distracted by her marriage having just fallen apart.

The knock on the back door came unexpectedly, ending her brief moment of solitude. She ran her fingers quickly through her long wavy brown hair in an attempt to restore some order. She caught a brief glimpse of herself in the hall mirror as she walked past, and frowned. She'd spent a good forty-five minutes straightening her unruly hair this morning, but it had stubbornly returned to its long loose curls already. As she approached the screen door, she found herself looking at a broad-shouldered man in a hat.

She watched as he took off his sunglasses, hooking them into the neck of his T-shirt. He tipped his hat back on his head a little and looked at her, as if waiting for some kind of reaction.

Erin's eyes widened. Jamie McBride.

Despite her shock, she did notice that for his part Jamie didn't seem as surprised to see her. A grin broke out across his face and she felt her heart give an odd little kick which momentarily distracted her. She wasn't seventeen years old any more, she shouldn't be having that same giddy reaction.

'Erin,' he greeted her with a slight nod of his head. 'You're looking good.'

'Jamie,' she stammered, caught off guard by his blue eyes crinkling a little in the corners in a way they hadn't at nineteen, but which she found more than a little attractive just the same. Erin cleared her throat and mentally shook off her shock.

'I would have been around sooner, but I've been up at Binawhile.'

Erin remembered the property the McBrides owned further out west where they rotated their cattle prior to bringing them back to their place in Tuendoc to fatten for market. She'd been there once, and she squashed the memory quickly when the majority of images associated with that visit involved Jamie and her teenage self making out at every given opportunity.

'I heard about your gran's fall,' he said quietly. 'She was complaining about those curtains before I went away.' Erin saw genuine concern in his expression. The McBride family had always been close to her grandparents, the two families having been neighbours for two generations.

'She's so damn stubborn,' Erin said, shaking her head. 'She should have waited, not tried to climb the stepladder herself.'

'I should have taken them down before I left.'

'Gran wouldn't have wanted to bother you.' She was like that, independent to a fault, and determined not to become a burden on anyone, which was what made it so hard to watch now as she lay in a nursing-home bed, completely dependent on others. 'How did you know I was here?'

'I saw the car. Besides, who else would it be? Not like anyone expects your mother to make an appearance.'

It should have stung to hear her mother criticised, but she couldn't really argue against it. Her mother hadn't been back here in years. Some people became born-again Christians, but her mother had become a born-again hippie. Despite her mother's sometimes embarrassing lack of regard for social trends, Erin was incredibly proud that, even with the added burden of being a single parent, she'd bravely ventured into a small business with a long-time friend, Carol. They'd turned their modest health food shop, the Health Hut, into a multimillion-dollar chain of stores.

Then, after Erin had left home, her mother had decided it was time to make some lifestyle changes. She'd sold the house, turned the business over to Carol and her son, and moved to Nimbin to become a spiritual guide and aura cleanser. Somehow her mother and Gran had drifted apart over the years, and as far as Erin knew, her mother hadn't been back to the farm in a very long time.

'Mum sent over a casserole. It's out in the car, I'll go bring it in.'

'Oh. Thanks,' she said, but he'd already turned and walked away. She'd been meaning to drop over and visit his parents, but it was always getting late when she got back from the home, and maybe she was also a little scared of running into Jamie again. 'Oh, don't be ridiculous,' she muttered under her breath. She was a grown woman, not the giggly seventeen-year-old who'd fallen head over heels in love with the boy next door while she was on summer holidays. It wasn't even as though it was the first time she'd seen him after all those years. Every time she'd seen him she'd had the same stupid reaction. It was beyond pathetic.

If she was lucky he was away when she visited Gran, but whenever their paths crossed it was always awkward, at least on her part. It never seemed to bother Jamie, in fact he seemed to enjoy making her uncomfortable. The times she'd come home with Phillip, he'd been even worse than when she visited alone.

'So where's the old man?' he asked as he walked inside carrying a tea-towel-covered dish.

Erin gritted her teeth and concentrated on not reacting. She was pretty sure the 'old man' comment was not a term of endearment. Jamie had never made a secret of the fact he thought her marrying a man twenty years older was insane.

'Phillip,' she said, stressing his name pointedly, 'didn't come with me.'

'He doesn't come along for moral support?' His thoughts on that were more than a little obvious.

'I don't need moral support.'

'What kind of dick leaves his wife to deal with all this alone? He should be here.'

'It's no longer his concern, and this is really none of your business, so I'd appreciate if you'd just drop it.'

'What do you mean it's no longer his concern?'

'What part of *It's none of your business* don't you get?' she asked.

'The part where you say something like it's no longer his concern and then don't explain.'

God this man was infuriating. He didn't even have to speak and he could annoy her, but when he did speak it was usually to say something he knew would rattle her cage. Did he seriously have nothing better to do with his time?

'We're getting a divorce. Okay? Happy?'

'At the risk of making *me* sound like a dick, yes, actually. That makes me incredibly happy.' He grinned.

He had the audacity to stand there and grin after she'd told him she was getting a divorce? Who grinned when someone told them they were getting divorced? It was rude. Not to mention insensitive. There was nothing happy about divorce.

'Oh, come on, Erin. You know I can't stand hypocrites. You seriously expect me to stand here and pretend I'm not glad you finally got rid of that jerk?'

'I've given up expecting anything remotely civilised about you, Jamie McBride. So no, please, don't go and change now.'

'Ouch. That wasn't nice.'

'Bite me,' she snapped.

His laugh followed her into the kitchen. He put the casserole dish down on the bench and unhooked a coffee mug from the timber stand near the jug.

'Make yourself at home, why don't you?' she said, folding her arms across her chest as she watched him.

'Don't mind if I do,' he said, holding up a second cup in silent query.

She would have just said no if it would mean getting rid of him, but he wouldn't go until he was ready, so she gave an impatient sigh. 'Fine. Yes . . . please.' She wasn't going to sleep tonight anyway, not with a list a mile long of things that would need to be taken care of.

Jamie spooned the coffee granules and sugar into the two cups, then lightly touched the wonky old mug stand. 'I don't know why she kept this thing. I made it in woodwork one year for a Christmas present.'

It had sat on Gran's bench for as long as she could remember. 'She kept it because you made it for her,' Erin said quietly.

Jamie cleared his throat and turned his back on her as he fiddled with the teaspoon. His reaction shouldn't have surprised her. Gran had practically been his grandmother as well. But he was the quintessential Aussie farmer— stoic, resilient, hardworking and tough. She hadn't seen the sensitive side of Jamie for a long time. Images of another place and time rushed to mind.

Jamie, tall and lean, his dark hair a bit too long at the back, wearing a stock hat, faded jeans and a cocky smile.

She'd been so lovesick over him back then or, as Gran would say, smitten. They'd spend afternoons swimming in the creek and going for long drives down narrow dirt roads and finding secluded places to . . . She immediately squashed the memories. The effect of raging hormones and crazy dreams had always been a recipe for disaster.

Erin took a biscuit tin down from the cupboard. 'Let's have coffee out on the verandah,' she suggested, leading the way outside.

The side verandah was where afternoon tea was always taken, while morning tea was usually on the back section. In winter they followed the sun.

Erin chose the side verandah; it had always been her favourite. The view from here took in the gentle slope down to the bottom flat and, just a little further over, the tall row of trees that lined the creek bank.

They sipped their coffee in silence for a while, listening to the gentle sounds of farm life going on around them. Gran's chooks scratched around beneath the orchard and chased insects. As a child Erin had loved feeding the chooks corn from the cob and collecting their eggs. She'd been reliving the experience over the last few days, taking care of Gran's girls for her. The sound of mooing drew Erin's gaze to the herd of cattle grazing along the bottom flat.

'Are those yours?' she asked, looking over at him.

'Yep.'

'They look . . . happy.'

'Happy?' he said with a sideways glance. 'Yeah, well, they should. They're being fattened on some of the best grazing pasture money can buy.'

There had always been cattle on Tallowood. After Pop died, Gran had continued to run the property for quite a few years, although Erin had been a little young to remember a lot about that time. After a while it had become too much for Gran to handle and she had sold off the stock and agisted the land to the McBrides, keeping only a few house cows and her beloved chooks. Then about ten years ago Jamie had taken over his father's agistment to graze his own cattle on Tallowood.

'So what are your plans?' Jamie asked.

'For?'

He shrugged and reached for another jam drop. 'How long are you staying here? Or are you heading back to the big smoke soon?'

'For now I'll stay here. The doctors aren't very optimistic that Gran will get back here any time soon, but I don't feel right just leaving her there. I can work from anywhere, so I guess there's no hurry to go back.' Go back? The last place she wanted to be was back at the apartment.

She cringed at the memory of bumping into the occasional person who knew Phillip had moved out. The pity and sheer awkwardness of their expressions had made her feel *so* uncomfortable. *Thank goodness for Roxy*, she thought. They'd become friends two years ago when Roxanne had started work as her personal assistant. Roxy had never liked Phillip, and the feeling had been somewhat mutual, which had often made it tiresome as she was constantly having to defend one against the other. Looking back, however, maybe Roxy had seen Phillip's true colours a lot clearer than Erin had. Nope, she definitely wasn't in any hurry to return to the city just yet.

'So what happened?' asked Jamie, looking at her.

There was no need to ask what he was talking about; that little gleam clearly told her they were talking about Phillip again. The last person Erin felt like talking to about Phillip and their upcoming divorce was Jamie McBride. 'I don't want to talk about it.'

'It must have been bad.'

'It's really none of your business, Jamie. Would you just leave it alone?'

'Okay, fair enough,' he said. 'Sorry, I won't ask any more.'

She highly doubted it. 'So what about you? Any plans to settle down yet?'

'Why? You makin' me some kind of offer?'

'Dream on. I just thought you might be getting a bit too old for this Casanova routine.'

'Jeez, you're not holding back today, are you? You make me sound like some geriatric sleazebag.'

'You're not getting any younger,' she told him, raising her eyebrow before draining the mug quickly and standing up. She gathered the cups without bothering to ask if he was finished. She couldn't cope with any more Jamie McBride this afternoon.

'I take it that's my cue to leave?'

'You always were quick off the mark,' she muttered, heading inside.

'That's me. Is this the same album Gran had with her yesterday?'

After placing their cups on the bench, Erin saw he was idly flipping through the photo album she'd left on the kitchen table. 'Yes.'

Her expression must have given away her curiosity.

'I dropped by to check on her,' he said.

'I've been taking up old photos for her to look through. She doesn't talk much unless you ask about the pictures,' Erin said sadly, recalling those blank stares that were growing longer and more frequent every day. 'It's like she's a different person when she starts remembering those days.' Erin paused, running her fingers over the photos on the open page. 'But every day I think we lose a little bit more of the old Gran.'

She didn't realise she was crying until she felt a rough thumb wiping her chin, moments before she was pulled into a hug. The smell of grass, diesel, leather and jam mixed together on the soft work shirt Jamie wore. For a moment she allowed herself to rest against him, taking comfort from the strong arms holding her and the solid chest against her cheek. Then she realised she was finding it all a little too comfortable.

It wasn't supposed to feel like this.

He was just being neighbourly, comforting an old friend . . . and yet, the strange sensations she was feeling were like the touch of an electric fence. It jolted her back to her senses and reminded her that she was supposed to be a married woman . . . until she remembered that she wasn't any more.

She pushed away from Jamie and straightened her hair, fighting the urge to snap at him. It wasn't Jamie's fault she was angry. It was Phillip's. But he wasn't here, and Jamie was, and if he said one single smart-arse comment she was going to bite his head off.

'Thanks. I'm okay now. But I'm really tired, and I think I need to go and lie down for a bit. I'll see you later.' She didn't look him in the eye, and she didn't stay and wait for his reply, just turned and walked into her bedroom, closing the door and burying her head under her pillow as a cocktail of anger, embarrassment and sorrow battled it out inside her.

Eleven

The next day, Erin made it a point to stop in next door and thank Jamie's mother for the casserole and return her cleaned dish. Patricia and Neville McBride just didn't seem to age. They looked the same as they had when Erin was a child. They were hard-working, salt-of-the-earth people and Gran had thought of them as family.

'It's good to have you back. Jamie said you were thinking of staying for a while,' Pat said, pouring tea into a cup as they sat at the kitchen table.

'I'm lucky that I can do my job from home. I may have to go back for the occasional meeting, but I don't really have to be in the office, so I figured I'd stay until we sort everything out.' Gran's long-term care was a rather uncertain factor at this point in time and something Erin was working closely with the doctor to try to figure out.

'Still enjoying your job then, love?'

'Yeah, I am. I'm still loving my job.'

It had been shortly after Erin was born that her mother had gone into business with Carol. The health craze had been in full swing and the two of them had had no idea what they were about to create. One shop became two, then three, then more, until they had established a chain of stores across the country. The Health Hut, with its trademark Polynesian-hut store front, had become a fixture in most major shopping complexes along the east coast of Australia. Now they were in seven other countries. After finishing her marketing degree at university, Erin had accepted a job with Carol and her son, Steven, who was a few years older than Erin. It made sense, since her mother had taken out shares for her shortly before she'd gone off in search of inner fulfilment. If Erin was going to work for a company, she thought it might as well be one she had a stake in. She'd worked her way up the ladder from the lowly position of marketing clerk, through assistant marketing manager and then state manager, before finally achieving her goal of marketing manager of the whole company.

'Any word from your mother?'

Pat had never been one to hide her feelings about her mother's odd behaviour. The two women had gone to school together, but there seemed to be no great love lost between the pair.

'No. Not yet,' Erin said, and heard the snort of disgust from the other woman.

'How she can leave all this for you to deal with when it's her responsibility as Evelyn's daughter? It's unfair.'

'Now, Pat, love,' Neville put in, calm as ever. 'Don't go butting in when it's none of your business.'

'It's okay, I know it seems strange,' Erin placated with a tired smile, 'but it's easier if I just handle it. Mum's . . .' She hesitated. 'Gran and Mum have a tense relationship.' Which put it mildly. It was something she'd grown up with and something neither of them would ever talk about, so Erin had just gotten used to staying neutral.

'Well, she should be here, not out traipsing all over the world.' Pat sighed and gave an apologetic smile. 'Anyway, enough of that. So tell us what's been happening with you? Evelyn was always filling us in on things, but it's been so long since we've seen you.'

She winced a little at the guilt that comment produced. The visits she'd made recently had usually been quick ones, leaving no time to see anyone else when she wanted to spend as much time with Gran as possible.

'Not much. Work keeps me busy.'

'Jamie mentioned that you and your husband have broken up. I'm sorry to hear that, love,' Pat said gently.

Erin could just imagine how sorry Jamie would have been when he'd told them. He was more like his mother when it came to keeping his opinions to himself—he didn't. 'Oh, well, these things happen,' she said, forcing a smile.

'It sounds like a bit of a rest here is just what you need. You take your time.'

Erin did smile at that. She loved Pat's huge, well-meaning heart. It was a lot like Gran's.

'How's Tanya?' asked Erin, picking up her cup. Tanya McBride was a few years older than Erin, and although they'd spent time together when she visited her gran, they hadn't stayed in regular contact over the years.

'She and Martin live up at Binawhile. Martin works for a big farm supply store up there and he's doing really well. We've got a new grand-baby too.'

'How many children do they have?' asked Erin, vaguely recalling Gran keeping her up to date with Tanya's children.

'The new baby makes four.'

'Wow, four?' Erin breathed.

'You'd think they knew what caused it by now, wouldn't you?' Neville added with a wink, and Erin couldn't help but smile, hiding her heavy heart and feelings of inadequacy.

'Oh, be quiet, you. It's nice having a new little one to fuss around.'

The back door banged shut and interrupted the conversation. 'That'll be Jamie,' Pat said, standing up. 'I better go get another cup. I'll be right back.'

Within moments Jamie made his entrance, his work clothes covered in dust and grime.

'You couldn't get enough of me yesterday, huh?' he asked, raising his eyebrow slightly as he stopped beside the table and snagged a biscuit from the plate.

'I came to visit your parents, actually.'

'You don't have to pretend, we're all friends here, Erin,' he said with a wink, the whole biscuit disappearing into his mouth in one go.

'Stop tormenting the girl, Jamie. Just ignore him, love. He

hasn't changed much,' his mother said with an affectionate shake of her head as she came back out onto the verandah.

'Go and get changed, we have a guest,' Pat told Jamie, slapping his hand as he went in for another biscuit.

'No, that's not necessary, I have to get going anyway,' said Erin, standing.

'Don't let this one scare you off. You know he's all talk.'

'Erin's not scared of me,' Jamie said, standing back to watch her with a small smile. 'Are you?'

There was something about the cocky dare she detected beneath his question that reminded her of another place, many years ago. Jamie had used the same line on her as a seventeen-year-old when he'd dared her to kiss him for the first time. Inwardly rolling her eyes that she'd been so naive back then, she could almost laugh at how blindly she'd been led to the slaughter. Except she couldn't really cry ignorance—she'd known exactly what she was doing. She'd been secretly dreaming about Jamie McBride since she was thirteen.

As kids growing up, they'd sent sparks off each other— Erin had always thought Jamie couldn't stand her. She'd come to Tallowood for holidays four times a year, so it was only natural for her to spend a lot of time playing with the next-door neighbours' kids, especially when the neighbours were like her gran's second family. However, Erin and Jamie usually fought like cats and dogs. More than once, she remembered Gran shaking her head in despair when Erin stormed inside, slamming the door and announcing how much she hated Jamie McBride after they'd had a falling-out while playing. When they hit their teens, the sparks were still there but they were of a different kind. They were sparks of attraction.

'I have some work I need to get to,' Erin said, ignoring Jamie's leading question, dragging her gaze from his mouth and focusing on his parents instead.

'You just yell if you need anything, all right, love?'

'I will. Thanks, Pat.' The two women hugged and she sent Neville a quick smile before heading down the steps that led off the verandah.

'Erin, wait up,' Jamie called and she stopped as he reached the front of her car. He slid his hands into his front pockets, the cocky attitude of a few moments ago gone. 'Look, I'm sorry about the other evening.'

His apology surprised her. 'No, I was rude and you were being unusually kind.'

'Unusually? You know, most people think I'm a good guy,' he said gruffly.

'I'm sure you are.'

'You just can't see it?' he challenged lightly. His gaze seemed overly intense, as though her answer might actually matter to him.

'I didn't say that.'

'You didn't have to. I deserve it after the way I've acted about your ex. I'm sorry. I should have handled that differently. It's just that . . .' He let out a harsh sigh before removing one of his hands from his pocket and rubbing it across his head irritably. 'I really didn't like that guy, you know? From the very first time I met him. Do you have any idea how frustrating it is to watch someone you care about with a person you know is a dickhead?'

His frustration surprised her. This was not the larrikin she was used to. 'Not really,' she said hesitantly.

'It's bloody hard, that's what it is. Every time you brought him home, I just wanted to knock his block off.'

Erin shook her head. 'Why? What could he have possibly done to you?'

'Forget it,' he grunted, shoving his hand back into his pocket and hunching his shoulders a little. 'I just wanted you to know that I was sorry I acted like a jerk.' He turned away and she stared at him, dumbfounded.

'Jamie, wait.'

He stopped but didn't turn around.

'Thank you,' she said.

'No worries. See you around, Erin,' he said, and walked away.

Erin climbed back into her car and drove home. Obnoxious Jamie she was used to, but this other, strangely serious version of Jamie . . . she wasn't sure she knew how to handle him.

Twelve

As soon as Evelyn walked into the house she knew something was wrong. Her parents were seated in the sunroom, waiting for her.

'Where have you been?' her father demanded before she even said hello.

'In town, doing my shift at the Red Cross,' she said cautiously.

'I didn't raise my daughter to be a liar,' he snapped.

Evelyn felt herself turn pale.

'We know you haven't done a single shift in days,' said her mother, furious.

'Your sister saw you get in a vehicle with Jimmy,' said her father. 'She said you and he were . . . very friendly. She watched you drive out of town after you specifically told us you'd be at the Red Cross today. Your mother went down and spoke to Mavis Huxley.'

'Do you have any idea how embarrassed I was when she asked after your health? Apparently you've been too unwell to work for the last week,' said her mother angrily.

Evelyn moistened her dry lips and wondered what her options were. 'It was wrong of me to lie,' she admitted.

'Where have you been all week?' her father demanded.

'Spending time with Jimmy,' she said quietly.

'Doing what?' Betty piped up from the doorway.

'Go to your room!' both parents yelled.

'Why do I have to go to my room, I'm not the one in trouble,' Betty pouted, but she knew better than to argue and quickly disappeared.

'I knew we couldn't trust a bloody Yank,' her father snarled, getting to his feet to stalk to the window.

'This isn't Jimmy's fault,' Evelyn began.

'It's all his fault!' her father spat, glaring over his shoulder at Evelyn. 'Those bastards know exactly what they're doing. Moving in on a town full of women while their men are off fighting.'

'Jimmy's not like that.'

'You will not see that boy again, do you hear me?'

'But, Dad,' Evelyn protested, 'I love him.'

Her father turned around very slowly and Evelyn felt her blood chill. 'Has that filthy Yank touched you?' he asked in a deceptively quiet voice.

'We didn't plan on falling in love, I swear. It just . . . I'm going to tell Roy as soon as I can.'

'Has he touched you?' he repeated.

'Now, dear. Let's not jump to any conclusions,' her mother began nervously, wary of her husband's growing fury.

'We're going to get married after the war,' Evelyn said, straightening her spine and striving for a brave face.

'Over my dead body you are. That bastard's had you, hasn't he?' he yelled, and Evelyn paled.

'Mick, lower your voice, the entire neighbourhood will hear,' said her mother, glancing out the window.

'Maybe they should know exactly what your daughter has become,' he challenged.

'I love him, Dad, and you can't stop us being together.' Panic made her brave, or foolhardy, she wasn't sure which at this moment. Her father's temper was renowned for reducing grown men to tears.

'I can. And I will. You're going down to Sydney to stay with your aunt until this all blows over.'

'No, I won't go!'

'You will,' her father bellowed. 'I won't stand here and allow you to dishonour a fine soldier like Roy for the likes of a dirty Yank,' he said and stormed out of the room.

'Where are you going?' Evelyn's mother called after him.

'I'm going out to look for Jimmy, and he better pray I don't find him,' he snarled as the front door slammed shut behind him.

❧

Evelyn hurried down the street, wiping her eyes as she went. Her father had returned later yesterday evening smelling of beer. Clearly he hadn't had any success locating Jimmy, a fact she was grateful for, but the news that had greeted her early this morning had destroyed any hope she had of convincing her parents to change their minds about Jimmy.

Evelyn knocked loudly on the front door. The paint was peeling and the screen door was ripped and hung uselessly from its frame. The shuffle of feet from inside alerted her to someone approaching, and when the door opened Evelyn found herself staring up at a blurry-eyed man in his early twenties, wearing a stained singlet.

'Well, well, if it isn't little Evie Ward. What are you doing down here in the slums, princess?'

'Is Dolly home, Gus?' she asked politely, ignoring the way Dolly's brother was eyeing her up and down.

'Dunno. Haven't checked.'

'Could you? It's important.'

'Maybe. What's in it for me?'

Evelyn was saved from answering by Dolly's mother coming around the corner. 'You'll get a clip around the ear if you don't go get your sister, that's what.'

Agnes Rowland was not very big, but she obviously put the fear of God into her sons. Gus disappeared back into the house and they heard him call out his sister's name.

'Useless bastard, I could have done that,' Agnes hollered through the door, before shuffling back around the corner to the washing line.

Dolly appeared shortly after, clearly surprised by the visit, and Evelyn immediately burst into tears.

Twenty minutes later, seated on the front step of her friend's house, Evelyn had poured out the whole story. 'I need your help, Doll. Can you get word to Jimmy through one of your fellas? I can't leave without telling him what happened.'

'Of course I'll help. It'll be all right, you'll see. Jimmy's a good sort, he loves you. Everything will be all right. I'm sure of it.'

Evelyn was like a prisoner in her own home for the next two days. If she went out, her mother or her sister accompanied her, and she had to come straight home after any shifts she did at the Red Cross. She had no idea when Jimmy would get word that she needed to see him, or even how it was going to be possible with her mother or sister in tow. Then late one evening there was a tap on her window and Evelyn leaned out to find Dolly waving at her from the shrubbery below.

'Climb down,' Dolly hissed.

Evelyn looked around to make sure no one was around, then cautiously stepped out of her window and clambered down the ladder-like trellis her mother grew the bougainvillea on, biting her lip as she encountered a few thorns on her descent. This was not the first time she'd used the trellis as an escape route: during her childhood she'd preferred this way over the front door, only it was usually Roy enticing her out, holding up a cricket bat or lunch pail to go on an adventure exploring the foreshore.

Dropping to the ground, she hurried across to where Dolly was keeping lookout. She took her outstretched hand and followed her friend down the back laneway and out into the street behind her own.

'Where are we going?' she asked, out of breath from their quick pace.

'Not far. Over there,' Dolly pointed.

Evelyn turned to look, a sob of relief escaping as she saw the shadowy silhouette step out and move towards her. 'Jimmy!' She threw herself into his arms and held him tightly. She didn't want to cry, but the thought of leaving this man, never seeing him again, sent a ripping pain through her heart.

'Evie, calm down. Baby, what's wrong?'

She forced the words through numb lips: 'They're sending me away to my aunt's place in Sydney.'

'What? Who? What are you talking about?'

'My parents. Betty followed me the other day . . . She saw us. She told Mum.' The words came out stilted and abrupt; she barely recognised her own voice. Her mind was moving at a thousand miles an hour while all the time she heard her father's words over and over again: 'This ends now.'

'So they're sending you away, to keep you away from me?'

Evelyn nodded. 'If I don't go to Sydney, my father will make trouble here. He's ready to go to your commander and make a complaint. He can get you into serious trouble. I won't let him.'

'Evelyn, baby, look at me,' Jimmy said quietly, tipping her chin up so he could look into her eyes. 'It's going to be okay. I'll just go over there now and have it out with your father. Tell him straight that you're my girl and we plan on getting hitched.'

'No! You can't.' The thought of Jimmy and her father going head to head terrified her. 'Dad won't understand . . . You can't go over there.'

'He'll have to come around if we're going to get married.'

All of a sudden Evelyn realised just how naive she'd been all this time. Maybe in the back of her mind she hadn't truly expected Jimmy to stick around. Or maybe she'd thought they'd have longer. More time to work on her parents and break it off with Roy properly before she broached the whole marriage thing. There were lots of girls already marrying their Yanks and waiting until the end of the war till they could follow their men to their new homes in America. Maybe by then her parents would see things differently; it might be easier for them to accept. But not yet. Things were such a mess. 'You don't know my father.'

'I won't sneak around any more, Evie. I've only been keeping us a secret this long to keep my word to you. But it isn't who I am, Evie. I won't go behind your father's back any more. We need to sit down and talk to him.'

'No. He won't listen. I've tried. And besides, I need to tell Roy before everyone else finds out. He deserves to hear the truth.'

'Evie, are you serious about marrying me?' Jimmy asked, his face earnest.

'Of course I am.'

'Okay then,' he said, nodding as though he'd made up his mind about something. 'You go to Sydney, keep everyone happy. I'll get down there and find you, then we'll find us a preacher and get married. That way there won't be a damn thing anyone can do about it.'

'Really? You can do that?'

'We're on two weeks' R & R. There's flights going in and out all the time. Somehow I'll find a way.'

'What if you don't? You'll be leaving and I won't get to see you. I don't want to waste what little time we have together.'

'Do you trust me, Evie?'

'Of course I do.'

'Then go to your aunt's and wait for me to call. Until then,' he began tugging at his finger, finally grinning triumphantly and holding up his ruby ring.

'What are you doing?' she asked with a puzzled frown as he took her left hand in his.

'I don't need a bunch of words from a preacher and a bit of paper to tell me when I'm married. Evelyn Louise Ward, right here, right now, under the moon and the good Lord up above, will you do me the honour of becoming my wife?'

'Jimmy,' she gasped, staring at the large ring as it dwarfed her slender finger. Tears welled and spilled over, making it hard to even see straight.

'Say yes,' he said, wrapping his fingers around her hand to hold the ring firmly in place. 'Say you'll be my wife.'

'Yes, Jimmy, I'll be your wife.' There was no other answer she could possibly give. This might be the single most stupid thing she'd ever do in her entire life, but it felt right.

She hadn't ever felt like this with Roy. She'd never have imagined she'd be the kind of woman who'd cheat on her fiancé while he was away at war, it was the worst kind of betrayal, but she hadn't even been aware she was doing it until it was too late. She was head over heels, crazy in love with Jimmy and she knew she couldn't give that up to return to the laidback, easy friendship she had with Roy.

He slid the ring down her finger and she shook her head when she realised he was serious about leaving the ring on her hand. 'Jimmy, no. I can't take this.'

'As soon as I get to Sydney I'll buy you a real one, but until then, will you wear this and keep me with you?'

'But it's your good luck ring,' she said, shaking her head. 'I'm not willing to take a risk like that. Put it back on. I'll wait for a ring when you get to Sydney.'

Jimmy shook his head, his eyes holding hers urgently. 'Please, Evie. Wear my ring? I want you to know that I'm serious. You know what that ring means to me. I wouldn't give it to you unless I already believed you were my wife in every way that mattered. I want you to believe I'm coming for you as soon as I can. I don't need it until I get my orders. Till then, I want you to keep it safe for me.'

'I love you so much, Jimmy. I don't want to leave you.'

'I love you too, Evie. But just think, in a few days' time we're going to be husband and wife, legally.'

Dolly gave a whistle and waved to get their attention. 'Your dad's coming home from the pub. You better hurry up if you don't want trouble.'

'I'll see you in a few days, I promise,' Jimmy said, kissing her one last time, both of them reluctant to break their hold.

Walking away from him just then, knowing that she was leaving for Sydney in the morning, was the hardest thing Evelyn had ever had to do. A thousand things ran through her mind. What if he got his orders and had to leave before she saw him again? What if her father found him before he could meet her? What if, what if, what if . . .

Thirteen

Erin walked into her gran's room, smiling as she looked down at the huge bunch of freshly cut roses she'd picked from the garden this morning. She was hoping the scent of something familiar would do Gran some good, but her smile faded abruptly as she approached the bedside and saw the tubes.

Her gran had looked frail before, but with the tubes coming out of her nose, she looked even worse. Seeing Gran was asleep, Erin put the flowers down carefully by the bedside and tiptoed back to the door, stopping a nurse who was walking past the room.

'Excuse me, but can you tell me why they've put those tubes in my grandmother's nose? Has something happened?'

The nurse shook her head gently. 'Nothing's happened. But because your grandmother hasn't been eating, the doctor wanted to try nasogastric feeding.'

'Oh. Is that normal? Her not eating?'

'It's not unexpected, considering her age and her injury.'

Erin thanked the nurse, then headed back into the room. To Erin, the fact Gran wasn't eating suggested she'd given up, and her heart felt heavy at the thought.

That night, Erin finally managed to track her mother down via her overseas foundation, but she was working in a remote village somewhere in Borneo and the connection dropped in and out, making conversation difficult. She filled her in on Gran's accident and the news that she was now in the nursing home, but her mother's blasé reaction annoyed her.

'It sounds like she's where she needs to be.'

'She is, but, Mum, she's not too good.'

'Darling, she's ninety-two. What do you expect?'

Erin let that go; the static was making it difficult enough without wasting the call on getting upset. 'When do you think you will be back?'

'I wasn't planning on returning for at least another three weeks.'

'I think you should come home now.'

'What do you think I can do for her? She's being well cared for, and you said they won't let her go home. I don't know what you expect me to do.'

'The doctors are worried about her. They've had to start tube-feeding her. She's . . . Mum, she's fading away. I think you should come home,' said Erin, realising she sounded a lot curter than she'd meant to. The image of her grandmother being force-fed through a nasal tube to save her from starving to death had been a confronting sight when she'd visited earlier that day.

'Who gave them permission to do that?'

'They don't need permission. She's not eating.'

Her mother was quiet for a moment. 'Look, I'll try to wrap things up here as fast as I can.'

'Can you give me a time frame?'

'It depends on finding transport out. It could take a while, maybe a week.'

'Just get here as fast as you can,' said Erin, not even sure if Gran *had* till next week. The thought made her feel incredibly sad.

'I know you'll have everything under control,' said her mother. 'You're just like your gran.'

If only, thought Erin. She was almost glad Gran hadn't been well enough for her to tell her about her break-up with Phillip. She was already a failure in her husband's eyes, she didn't want to be a disappointment to Gran as well.

Fourteen

Jimmy sat on the edge of his bed running his hands through his hair in frustration. Time was running out. He'd made a promise to Evie that he'd be in Sydney as soon as he could, but it'd already been a week and he couldn't get a damn flight out, anywhere. It was unbelievable. He was a trained pilot, he lived on an air force base where there were hundreds of aircraft at any given time of the day or night, and he couldn't get a damn flight out of the place.

He'd called the number she'd given him just to hear her voice and his gut had clenched at how miserable she'd sounded. She'd warned him not to call the house, that she'd sneak out and call him when she could, but there was no way he could go that long without hearing her voice and so he'd risked the chance of being caught by her relatives to call her. He hated the whole damned situation. He resented the fact her father had intervened the way he had. Evelyn wasn't a kid, she was a grown woman. Part of him was glad she was no longer under her father's roof. He still felt bad about stealing her from Roy. He was a good bloke, as they said down here.

He smiled at the phrase and not for the first time wondered how his family were going to react to Evie and her strange way of talking. He loved it. In fact he loved everything about her. He was already imagining years from now, happily settled back in Louisiana with two or three little 'uns running around the yard and him and Evie sitting on the back porch swing watching them.

Her call last night changed everything.

'I'm trying my hardest, baby. I promise I'll be there as soon as I can,' he'd said when she'd sounded so wretched he could practically feel her misery over the line. 'Are you okay down there? Are your aunt and uncle treating you right?'

He heard her sniff a little and he could imagine her wiping her eyes and forcing a smile. 'They're treating me fine. But, Jimmy, there's something . . . I need to tell you something important.'

Jimmy felt his gut clench anxiously. For a moment everything in him stilled. He feared she was giving up on him and had decided to stay with Roy instead. He started to break out in a cold sweat at the thought. He was so far away from her, there'd be no way of trying to make her change her mind. He couldn't lose her now . . . not when he'd just found her.

'Jimmy . . . I'm pregnant.'

'What?' Her words had been so unexpected, he'd just sat there dumbfounded. 'You're not breaking up with me?' he asked hesitantly.

'What? Breaking . . . Jimmy, did you hear what I said?' her voice wobbled slightly. 'I'm pregnant.'

Relief rushed through Jimmy's body as her words sunk in. She wasn't leaving him. She was having his baby! He let out a loud whoop of joy that had nearby card players sending him varying looks of amusement and annoyance. 'I'm gonna be a daddy!' he told them loudly.

'Jimmy!' Evelyn sounded horrified on the other end of the phone, but nothing could wipe the grin off his face.

'Baby, that's the best news ever.'

'It is?' she asked after a moment's silence. 'You're not angry?'

'Angry? Why would I be angry? You're havin' my baby, Evie. I'm the happiest man alive.'

'Oh, Jimmy. I was so worried.'

His heart broke when he heard her sobbing on the other end of the line. All he wanted to do was hold her close and tell her everything would be all right, but he couldn't until he got a goddamn flight out of Townsville!

'Evie, baby. I'm coming. I swear to you, if I have to walk to Sydney, I'm going to get there. Just hold on a bit longer. I'll be there as soon as I can. I promise.'

Later, after he'd hung up the phone, he'd sat and tried to calm his jumbled emotions, but nothing could wipe the smile off his face. He was gonna be a daddy!

Early the next morning he was awoken by the loud roar of a jeep pulling up outside and his name being called. Jimmy went to the doorway to find Jacko, the 'go to' guy at the base, looking for him.

'Over here,' he called and watched the redheaded Aussie amble over.

'I hear you're looking for a flight to Sydney? Still interested?'

'You bet. Can you get me one?'

'I got a spare seat, but if you want it you gonna have to run. It's leaving in five minutes.'

Jimmy swore, but sprinted back to his bed, hastily shoving clothes into his duffle bag and making it out the door and into the front seat of the jeep with barely two minutes to spare.

He held on to the side of the windshield as the jeep screeched around a corner and onto the tarmac, pulling up beside the loud whining C-47 Dakota as it prepared to take off.

Jimmy recognised the chief from another squadron who was about to close the door. He saw him running over and held it open for him with a sly grin. 'You must have someone watching out for you, Crenshaw. Ten more seconds and you would have missed it.'

Jimmy grinned. 'I got me an angel waiting in Sydney. She's all the luck I need, pal. I'm on my way to get married.' He sank into his seat by the window and finally breathed a sigh of relief. This time tomorrow he'd be a married man.

∽

Evelyn ran for the phone, as she did each time it rang, and as she did each time she prayed to hear that deep southern accent telling her he was on his way to get her. Once again she bit back the disappointment when it wasn't Jimmy. Her disappointment on this occasion was softened when she recognised Dolly's voice on the end of the line.

'Evie, it's Dolly.'

'Dolly? How are you? Oh, I miss you so much. Tell me what's been happening? What have I missed? How many hearts have you broken this week?' Evelyn paused, waiting for her friend to jump in, but the line was silent. Dolly?'

'I'm here. I . . .' A sob carried down the line and Evelyn held the phone tighter.

'Dolly? What's wrong?'

'It's Jimmy, Evelyn. I'm so sorry . . .'

Her hands went cold as the blood drained from her extremities and her head felt light. She could hear Dolly's voice but nothing was making sense. She wanted to speak, to ask questions, but when she opened her mouth nothing came out. Then a noise started inside her ears, gently at first, before growing louder and louder until it was a deafening roar like the tide crashing against the beach. It drowned out everything, until she felt the tingle in her feet had travelled up her arm and into her fingers, and she dropped the phone to the floor.

Fifteen

Evelyn watched as men in uniform stepped from the train at Central Station. She searched their faces, finding only strangers. There were a few American uniforms here and there around the place but they were growing scarcer with each passing day. Everything was changing once again. The war was winding down.

Everyone said it was only a matter of time until Japan surrendered. Then things would go back to the way they were . . . only Evelyn knew that was impossible. Nothing would ever go back to the way it was. The country had been changed forever. Nothing and nobody had been left unaffected by the last six years of war, and nothing would ever be the way it was before.

It had been six weeks since Jimmy's plane went down. Six of the longest, coldest weeks of her life. Her parents had wanted her to return home, but she couldn't go back to Townsville. She couldn't bear the thought of seeing him everywhere she looked, being haunted by memories of their happiness. There was nothing left for her there. She had no idea what she was going to do. Her parents would disown her, and she knew she couldn't count on her aunt and uncle's hospitality for much longer—especially when it started to become obvious she was pregnant.

She was numb inside and would have still been locked away in her room had it not been for a telegram arriving two days ago to tell her Roy was travelling down on the train to see her. He'd taken shrapnel in his leg, but was able to walk, albeit stiffly, and had arrived back in Brisbane only to be told by her father that she was still in Sydney.

She could have listened to the part of herself that just wanted to curl up and die, to lie in bed until she faded away. She wanted very much to do that, but Roy deserved more. She owed it to him to be there to greet him, and smile. During their time apart, he'd written to her, not regularly, and not long romantic letters, that wasn't Roy's way, but his letters were filled with hope for a future. He wrote of his dreams for the farm they'd buy and his desperate wish for an end to all the mud and death and fighting. She could hear the quiet determination beneath his words.

She hadn't been able to bring herself to tell him about Jimmy. God knows, he didn't deserve to find out through some cold, impersonal letter. She hadn't meant to hurt him; she'd planned on waiting until he got home and at least giving him the courtesy of a break-up face to face. But then it was too late; she was sent to Sydney and everything changed.

After Jimmy's death, her parents had called and advised her not to mention the *Yank,* that it was kinder to Roy that he never know about her indiscretion. If only life were that simple. Maybe she could have gotten away with the lie, never told Roy about Jimmy . . . if she hadn't been pregnant, that was. However, within a few short months her so-called indiscretion would become all too evident. No, it would be kinder to tell Roy what had happened. She would tell him and let him walk away. Then she'd work out what she and her child were going to do.

Only, as Roy stepped down onto the platform and she saw his face light up at the sight of her, guilt threatened to suffocated her. The words stuck in her throat. Babies were born early all the time. Her baby would have a secure future . . . *No,* she thought violently. She couldn't lie to him. She knew she had to at least give him the opportunity to walk away. She'd tell him the truth and let him decide her fate.

Sixteen

The room felt cold when Erin arrived that morning and she crossed to the window and pulled back the curtains, letting in a stream of warm sunshine. Slowly Gran opened her eyes and Erin's heart sank. She hadn't seen a spark of recognition for the last few days, and her gran spent the majority of the day sleeping now. She looked frail and thin, fading away before Erin's eyes.

'Morning, Gran,' Erin said, moving to the chair beside the bed. She waited for any sign that her grandmother knew who she was and tried not to feel disappointed when none came. She prattled on about Tallowood and how pretty the paddocks looked with the dew still clinging to cobwebs on the fences. All the while Gran lay quietly in bed, seeming to listen but saying very little.

Erin finally pulled out the album from her bag and flipped through the pages, bypassing the earlier ones and finding one of her mother, who looked about sixteen, dressed in a white gown, her arm through the arm of a dark-haired boy of about the same age.

'Was this Mum at her debut?' Erin asked, turning the album around and holding it up to show her gran.

She watched as the old woman's eyes slowly came to rest on the photo on her lap, and she reached a hand out to touch the page. 'Me and my Jimmy,' she said softly.

Jimmy? Erin frowned slightly as she peeked to see what photo she was looking at. 'I think that's Mum, Gran. Irene,' she explained gently. She knew it had to be; the deb dress was definitely from her mum's era.

'So in love . . . Jimmy and I . . .' Her voice faded and Erin let out a sad sigh when she saw that now familiar blankness slip across Gran's face and she realised she'd lost her to the memories once again.

Seventeen

Where had the time gone? Evelyn blinked back tears as she watched her daughter dance around the floor, the handsome dark-haired boy at her side. The music was different and so were the fashions, but if she closed her eyes she could almost see Jimmy and herself dancing out there with them.

She'd sensed trouble the moment her daughter had brought Peter home to meet Roy and herself. She knew that look in her daughter's eyes. It was the same smitten look she'd once had when she'd looked at Jimmy. As usual, Roy had shown little interest and she'd had to step in and make the boy feel welcome. She hated the shadow of disappointment that crossed her daughter's face at her father's dismissal. Evelyn had tried so hard to make him love Irene and her heart broke anew each time she saw her husband's rejection of the daughter he'd willingly taken on all those years ago.

I should have told Irene, she thought.

Many times she'd wished she'd been brave enough to raise Irene alone, but it had seemed easier just to let Roy take charge and move them away from North Queensland, away from family and friends to hide her shame.

Only it hadn't been her shame because she'd been too numb to feel anything; besides, she could never feel ashamed of what she'd had with Jimmy. It had been Roy's shame they'd been hiding. He was the one who couldn't bear people gossiping about them. He didn't want to be the 'poor, pathetic fool' he said they would all call him if they knew his fiancée had gone and gotten pregnant to a Yank—and a supposed friend at that—while he'd been away fighting in New Guinea.

Evelyn had tried over the years. She'd tried her best to be a good wife to Roy. She'd cooked and cleaned and dedicated herself to becoming the kind of wife he could be proud of. Only he never was.

She still remembered the day she'd told him about Jimmy and the baby. His face had lost most of its colour and the brightness in his eyes had dimmed. And it seemed from that moment onwards it never returned. She'd expected him to walk away from her, and he had. She hadn't blamed him. She'd returned to her aunt's house and begun packing. She'd had no idea where she was going, only that she had to leave. But then Roy had appeared on her aunt's doorstep, asking to see her.

'We made a deal. I intend to honour it,' he'd said in a stiff, emotionless voice.

'You don't have to do this, Roy. You can return home and go on with your life. I don't expect you to marry me after this.'

'I said,' he told her, 'I intend to keep my end of the deal. We're getting married tomorrow at the registry office down town, and then we're heading to Tuendoc.'

'Tuen *where?*'

'Tuendoc. There's plenty of good land down that way. I told them I was bringing my wife, and that's what I plan on doing.'

'But the . . . baby.'

'I'll take you and the . . . child on, under the condition you never speak the Yank's name out loud again. You understand me? That kid,' he said pointing at her stomach angrily, 'will never know I'm not its father. *No one* will ever know. You got that?'

He'd always been a proud man and the thought of people laughing at him would have been unbearable. And so they had moved away and the past had never been mentioned again.

Over the years, Evelyn had tried to understand her husband. At first she'd put his bitterness and anger down to her betrayal, but as time had gone on, she'd started to realise it went deeper than that. The nightmares had started early on in their marriage. Roy would wake up yelling, covered in sweat and shaking like a leaf. When she asked him about it, he'd simply leave the bed and walk outside, where he'd remain for the rest of the night, staring out at the darkness, reliving things she had no hope of ever comprehending, lost in his private world of pain. His experiences during the war had changed him. Maybe her betrayal had added to the bitterness he carried, but it was more than that. He was not the Roy she'd grown up with. He lost his temper over the smallest things, and she would sometimes find him in their room, the curtains drawn, holding his head and rocking back and forth. She'd stopped asking him to go and see a doctor, it only seemed to enrage him further. Evelyn had done her best to shield Irene from the worst of it.

Until the horrible night when the past reared its ugly head and changed them all forever.

Evelyn had watched her daughter, so carefree and full of life, fall deeper and deeper in love with Peter. Ever since they'd made their debut together, they'd become inseparable. Evelyn had known it was going to end in heartache. If only she'd tried to warn Irene. It wouldn't have done any good, though, she realised later. Young love was blind to anything except what it wanted to see.

The phone call that awoke them late one evening set in motion a terrible set of events. Peter's father called, asking them both to come over and pick up their daughter and saying that there were some rather urgent issues that needed to be discussed.

Upon arriving, Evelyn's heart lurched at the sight of her daughter sitting so dejectedly on the corner of the lounge.

'I'm afraid we have some rather disturbing news,' Dr Brown said gravely. 'Your daughter arrived here earlier demanding to speak with my son. She was quite irate. When I asked her to move along, told her that Peter was not interested in speaking with her, she turned rather abusive. She then declared that she was pregnant to my son and refused to go home until he came down to speak with her. As you can imagine, the last thing we wanted was for the entire neighbourhood to be alerted to this whole sordid mess, so we brought her inside and called you.'

'Pregnant,' Roy all but breathed the word. 'You ungrateful little witch. After everything I've given you, you repay me by getting yourself pregnant by the first boy who comes along.'

'I love Peter.'

'Love,' Roy spat bitterly.

'We're going to get married. He promised,' said Irene, although Evelyn saw the waver of uncertainty behind her eyes. She'd climbed out her window tonight, planning on running away to the city with Peter, only to discover he'd changed his mind and wanted nothing more to do with her.

Prodded roughly by his father, Peter sullenly told Irene that he didn't want the responsibility of a baby and that it would be in everyone's best interests if she got rid of it.

His mother sobbed into a handkerchief, declaring her son's future as a doctor would be destroyed if he was forced to leave school to support a wife and child.

With each accusing glare thrown at her, Evelyn saw her daughter shrink a little more, until all that was left was an empty, dead expression, the same one that had stared back at her in the mirror after Jimmy's death.

'You will not disgrace this family and my name by having some bastard, do you hear me?' Roy growled.

Peter's parents bristled at the implication, but they were clearly not prepared to have their son's promising future stolen away from him either.

111

'Roy,' Evelyn reproached quietly.

He spun on his wife. 'You want everyone knowing what she's done? What kind of parent do you reckon they'll think you are once they find out?'

'Let's just go home and sleep on it for tonight and discuss it tomorrow.'

'I can take care of this with a phone call to one of my colleagues,' Peter's father cut in grimly.

'Can you do it tonight?' Roy asked.

'There's no need to make any rash decisions,' Evelyn said quickly.

'The sooner we put an end to this, the sooner we can all put it behind us,' Roy snapped.

'I agree,' Peter's mother cut in.

'I'll make the call right now,' said Peter's father, leaving the room briskly.

It was all moving so fast. Evelyn saw that Irene was pale and withdrawn. She'd clearly hoped that Peter would stand up to his parents, but he'd refused to even look at her. Evelyn's heart ached for her daughter.

When Peter's father came back into the room, it had been organised for the next day in a private residence in an inner city suburb. They left the Browns and drove home, a heavy silence filling the car.

'I'm not sure we should be rushing into this,' Evelyn said quietly. 'Maybe there's another option.'

'There's no other option. The boy clearly doesn't want anything to do with it.'

'He did, till you and his parents stuck your noses into it,' Irene spat from the back seat.

'He was never going to marry you, and if you think I'm going to help raise another bastard, you got another thing coming.'

'Roy!'

'What are you talking about?' Irene asked, looking between her parents warily.

'Ask your mother,' he snarled.

'Mum?'

Evelyn felt herself go cold as she stared at her husband helplessly.

'The apple doesn't fall far from the tree, does it, *Evelyn*?'

'What's he saying, Mum?'

Evelyn turned her desperate gaze upon her daughter's tear-stained face. How many times had she dreamed of telling her about Jimmy? She used to daydream that one day she would sit down and calmly explain what had happened. She'd tell her daughter all about her daddy and how much he'd have loved her. But she had no right to do that after Roy had sacrificed everything to raise another man's daughter as his own, and she'd given him her promise. Then one day her baby was sixteen and standing before her, heartbroken, in the same position she'd been in all those years ago. Now it was too late to tell her about her father the way it should be told, with love and pride. Instead she'd hear it told as something sinful and wrong.

'I hate you,' Irene said bitterly the next day when Evelyn sat beside the bed after she'd returned from the procedure. 'I hate you both.'

She'd let her daughter down, and there was nothing she could say to defend herself. She'd stood by and allowed Roy to rob her daughter of all the love she should have had from a father. She'd thought that if she loved her enough, she could make up for Roy's lack of interest, but it hadn't worked out that way. She'd just made things worse, and now her baby had also lost her innocence. Evelyn knew that hollow look in the depths of her child's eyes all too well.

She should have stood up to him, she should have made him stop, but it was too late. He'd sapped the life from her. Too many years of hearing what a failure she was, how ungrateful she was, how much of a disappointment she was to him, had robbed her of whatever self-confidence she'd ever possessed.

The worst part was that somewhere along the line she'd started to believe him. Maybe she *didn't* deserve happiness. She should be grateful that he was still willing to take her in and provide for her. The truth was, she just didn't care. When Jimmy was taken from her, she lost the will to care about herself. Not even her child could fix what was broken inside. She'd never stopped loving Jimmy and she could never love Roy in the same way. She had done her best to be the perfect wife, but he knew that her heart would always belong to another man. They were two wounded souls struggling on together, compounding the hurt that had begun years before.

It had been that way until his death. No one could really understand, with his experience, how he'd managed to misjudge such a steep incline and roll the tractor over the edge.

Evelyn still had no idea why he'd chosen that particular moment to end it, but there was never any doubt in her mind that he'd driven over that edge on purpose. Maybe he'd had one of his headaches and hadn't made it home in time to lock himself in the dark and ride it out. Maybe he'd given up trying. Maybe he'd finally just grown weary of fighting his demons day after day. She'd never know. But life after Roy's death was like the calm after a particularly violent storm.

Evelyn was forced to take over running the farm, and found that she quite enjoyed it. She managed most of the tasks alone, having assisted Roy often enough over the years, and for the things she couldn't do, her neighbours were always there to lend a hand. She took back her life, but it was never the life she'd dreamed of. Jimmy was gone, but never forgotten.

It was a cruel joke that she should outlive them both.

Eighteen

Erin stepped out onto the front verandah and breathed in the crisp morning air. *I've missed this smell,* she thought as she closed her eyes and allowed memories, triggered by the fresh, cool scent, filter through her mind. She remembered Gran coming inside on a foggy morning with a pail of fresh milk from her old house cow, Katie. When Katie had passed away, Gran had finally decided to give up milking by hand. Erin smiled faintly as she remembered Gran complaining about store-bought milk: 'It has no taste . . . and where's the cream? Not as good as my Katie's milk,' she'd tsk as she made her tea.

Erin stretched and jogged on the spot for a few moments to warm up before setting off. Jogging was an integral part of her daily routine. It helped her deal with stress. She jogged a lot. At Tallowood it helped her get her emotions under control and give her time to think about things—her gran, her mum and, as much as she hated it, her divorce. She was struggling to come to terms with that, although now the initial shock had worn off she was starting to feel angry. She wasn't sure which stage of grief this was, but it was better than the previous ones of denial and depression. At least anger felt good, and her feet hitting the ground helped pump the fury through her bloodstream.

And she *was* angry. She resented that some other woman had set her sights on her husband and lured him away so easily. After everything they'd been through. She was even angrier at Phillip for giving up on them . . . on *her*. Maybe she'd given up too easily as well. The memory of the night he'd left was still burnt into her brain.

After their last failed attempt, she'd told Phillip she couldn't do any more IVF, purely out of self-preservation. But the night he left, she'd been frantic. 'I'll try again. I'll do IVF as many times as you want.' She'd heard the desperation in her voice, but she hadn't cared, her whole world was crashing down around her. If risking all that grief again would keep him by her side, she'd do it.

'It's no use, Erin. You know what the doctor said last time. I can't ask you to put yourself, or me for that matter, through another round of IVF. I've suffered too, you know,' he said. 'With each loss, I had to swallow back my own disappointment and put on a brave face for you. I can't do that any more, Erin. I'm sorry, but I just can't. I'm done.'

She hated that she'd shown him just how vulnerable she was. It hadn't changed anything, he'd still walked away.

She cursed as she came to a gate. It was annoying having to open and close the damn things, it messed up her rhythm. She fumbled with the keyhole-shaped latch on a chain, jiggling and twisting it to fit over the knob on the post. Why they had to make these things so damn difficult to manoeuvre was beyond her. It wasn't as if the cattle had hands to undo them. She looked around and frowned when she realised there weren't even any cattle in the paddock, then dropped the chain and let the gate swing open. Given her trouble getting it open, it wasn't worth the hassle fastening it again when she'd be back within a few minutes. She picked up her pace as she followed the narrow track generations of cattle had worn in a direct line through the property towards the creek.

She came across two more gates further on and saw the only cattle in the vicinity were all the way on the other side of the paddock, too busy chewing on grass to notice her. As she reached the bottom paddock, she bent over, bracing her hands on her thighs, and concentrated on catching her breath.

The gentle bubble and gurgle of water running nearby drew her attention and she veered off the track to the edge of the bank overlooking a portion of the creek. *It was so beautiful here*, she thought again. It had been too long since she'd taken time out to really look at the place. As a kid she'd lived down here by the creek—knew every inch of it. As an adult, her visits were only a weekend here and there to see Gran, and rarely had she even left the house.

It was a lot more overgrown than she recalled, but if she closed her eyes and listened, it was exactly as she remembered. When they were younger, Erin and the McBride children would entertain themselves down here for hours. She could almost hear the shouts of happy children splashing in the water on a hot summer afternoon. Erin squeezed her eyes tighter and for a brief moment wished that when she opened them she could be back in her childhood once more. She missed Gran, her gentle presence, her greatest supporter in everything she ever did. Telling her stories and always able to give the right advice when it was needed. The woman who was always busy doing something: pottering around the kitchen, cooking, or out in the garden weeding; humming under her breath as she fed the chooks, and seemingly content with her quiet life on the farm. Seeing her fading away to nothing was pure agony. She missed the simple things she'd taken for granted: to sit and have a chat over a cup of tea, to be able to have a conversation without her drifting away behind those blank eyes. She wanted to ask her so many questions. Who was this Jimmy she kept talking about? Why had she never talked about him in any of the stories she told?

Erin had no idea if he was real or just a figment of her grandmother's dementia. Yet the passion in her voice when she spoke suggested to Erin he wasn't someone Gran had made up.

The nurses had warned her that things probably wouldn't get any better. She had to face the fact that she had almost lost what little remained of her gran. A breeze high up in the treetops reminded Erin of a gentle lullaby and she couldn't help but smile as a sensation of utter peace and tranquillity settled on her.

Slowly she opened her eyes and let out a soft sigh. With one last look at the creek below, she turned and headed back the way she'd come.

The sound of a vehicle approaching drew her gaze and she scanned the paddock that stretched out before her until she located the vehicle.

Jamie. She waited for the now familiar spike in her heart rate, and was glad she had a few moments to compose herself before he arrived.

'Hi,' she said as he rolled to a stop beside her.

'Morning. Did you forget something?'

Erin frowned as she tried to work out if she had. 'I don't think so,' she said.

'The gate?'

She eyed him blankly until he gave an impatient sigh and said, 'You left the gate open back there.'

'Oh. Yeah. Well, I was coming back,' she said a tad defensively.

'I spent a long time drafting that mob the other day, I don't have time to waste doing it all over again just because they got out through an open gate.'

'I didn't think I'd be gone long enough for them to notice.'

'Luckily they didn't. This time,' he said.

'Okay, point taken. I won't leave any more gates open.' *Grumpy, much?* she thought, irritated that he was chiding her like some naughty kid.

'This is my livelihood,' he added gruffly.

'Okay. I get it. I'm sorry.' Jeez, she'd said sorry; what more did he want?

'I'm not sure you do.'

'What's your problem today?' she demanded, placing her hands on her hips and glaring at him through his open window.

'I didn't *have* a problem until I came to check on the cattle and found all the gates open.'

'Oh, for the love of God. I won't open another bloody gate. I'll climb the damn things from now on. Happy?'

'No, I'm not happy. I'm bloody frustrated, okay?' he said, rubbing hands roughly across his face and confusing her even more.

'I said I was sorry!' she snapped.

'It's not about the bloody gates!'

They eyed each other with matching scowls before Jamie cursed and threw his car in gear. 'Just forget it. I've gotta go,' he snapped, before revving the engine and pulling away, leaving her staring after him and shaking her head.

'He's doing my head in,' she muttered, turning to go home. She had a busy morning lined up and, thanks to Jamie, all the stress she'd been running off was back.

Fantastic.

Nineteen

A persistent ring woke her the next morning. Erin searched next to her bed for the phone, dragging it to her ear to mumble a groggy, 'Hello.'

'Big night?' came the droll voice on the other end and Erin opened her eyes reluctantly.

'No, Roxy. I just didn't sleep well. What time is it?'

'Six-thirty,' she said far too chirpily for that time of the day. 'Before I leave for work, I wanted to remind you about that conference call at ten o'clock this morning. Carol and Steven are driving me insane, I can't wait until this whole deal is done.'

Securing the contract for placing a Health Hut in the foyer of every resort of a large Pacific hotel chain was a major coup. It was a big step, branching out from shopping centres, but once this deal was finalised the months of planning would be worth it.

Erin threw back her blankets and yawned, giving her wayward mass of curly hair a disapproving scowl in the mirror as she made her way into the kitchen with the phone. 'You can't blame them, this client's huge.'

'A huge pain in the butt more like it,' Roxy grumbled.

'I won't forget,' she promised, tucking the phone between her shoulder and cheek to fill the coffee machine. 'I'm kind of insulted you thought you needed to call me to remind me, though.'

'Hey,' she said defensively, 'I'm covering all the bases. If things go bad, it won't have anything to do with me. Besides, I haven't had a chance to find out what's going on with you lately. How are you doing?'

It was true. Although they usually talked or emailed regularly throughout the day, it was all business. Things had been doubly hectic lately around the office with this new deal unfolding, and without the luxury of tea breaks or lunches, they hadn't been able to talk like they usually did.

'I'm fine. It's just really hard watching her slip away.'

'I wish I could get time off to come out to be with you.'

'No, don't be silly. I'm fine. I'm actually enjoying being out here. I think the break's doing me good.'

'Glad to hear it. You make sure you take care of yourself.'

Erin smiled at her friend's out-of-character motherly advice. Usually Roxy was the one getting her into trouble, not talking her out of it.

In the distance Erin could hear the odd crow sounding forlorn and, in contrast, the cheerful chortle of noisy magpies outside in the yard. It was surprising how she'd come to love listening to the sounds around her, so different to the busy streets and the traffic of her apartment back in the city. Even the loud sound of contented munching sounded relaxing . . . She frowned. *Munching?* Erin pulled the kitchen curtain across and gasped. 'I gotta go. The cattle are out.'

She heard Roxy's confused, 'What?' but she was already putting down the phone. She had to get the cattle out of the house yard and back into the paddock before Jamie found out. 'Crap,' she muttered, rushing out to the verandah and pulling on her fluoro running shoes. Had she remembered to shut the gates after her run yesterday afternoon? She couldn't remember. She thought she had . . . but obviously she'd missed one along the way.

Damn it! Her gaze swept the yard in despair as she saw the damage the cattle had already caused. They'd devoured lots of Gran's plants and most of the roses Erin had been admiring the evening before. The grass was also churned up, with huge divots where cows had stomped their way through, sampling all kinds of new delights the house yard offered them.

'Shoo,' shouted Erin, moving down the steps and heading for the closest of the culprits. Two cows lifted their big heads to stare at her, stopping Erin cold. What the hell was she doing? These things were huge up close. And worse, they didn't seem fazed by her feeble attempt to move them along.

I'll just have to be more forceful, she thought, straightening her spine determinedly. 'Go on! Get!' she shouted, and this time the cattle moved, turning completely around to face her head on.

'This is not good,' she said, anxiously trying to judge how far from the house she was. A low moo drew her attention to the front yard, and she saw with a sinking heart that as well as the cattle in the front yard there were also cattle on the driveway and out on the road!

'Oh, no!' she gasped, as she stared at the scattering of brown and white animals along each side of the road.

Running her hands through her hair, Erin tried frantically to think. How was she going to get them all back in? She edged her way cautiously past the two cows she'd disturbed earlier, who had gone back to munching on rose leaves, and headed along the driveway.

She waved her arms in the air and shouted 'Yah, yah!' at the top of her lungs, startling two young calves and letting out a scream as they turned and ran without warning away from the gate. 'No, not that way, you stupid things. Go back inside.' She tried to cut them off, flailing her arms about in the air and feeling like she was doing a Kermit the Frog impersonation.

Their alarmed mooing triggered the other cattle nearby to call back, and Erin realised that she was in way over her head as an older cow with horns started trotting back down the road towards her. 'Holy sh—'

Grabbing her phone from her pocket, she fumbled with the screen until she brought up the music icon. She needed something to distract them. What the hell kind of music did you play to distract cattle? Something country? She didn't have anything country on her playlist. She kept an eye on the angry one with big horns still edging towards her and hit the first thing her thumb landed on.

A blast of 'Working Class Man' burst from the device, halting the cranky cow in her tracks and causing her to veer away. Encouraged by the cow's reaction to Jimmy Barnes, Erin held the phone out in front of her like a weapon and walked around the nervous-looking cattle until she eventually managed to get behind them. With a combination of waving arms and loud music, Erin shooed the cows back down the driveway. Once they saw the opening into the top paddock, they picked up their pace and scooted as far away from the weird woman with her noisy contraption as they could.

Erin quickly shut them inside then turned the music off, dropping her head on her arm, resting on the cold metal gate, her heart pounding in her chest and her legs feeling weak.

The sound of a car approaching made her lift her head quickly and give an inward grown. Of course he had to turn up now.

'Morning,' a deep voice called.

'Morning,' Erin replied, trying to sound as casual as Jamie, who was sitting in the driver's seat smiling smugly.

'Nice outfit.'

Erin's jaw clenched and she tried to ignore the blush creeping up her neck as she realised she was still wearing her bright polka-dot pyjamas.

'I just got a phone call about some cattle loose on the side of the road,' Jamie continued when she remained silent. 'You haven't seen any, have you?' he asked, titling his head slightly.

'Cattle? On the road?' she repeated nervously. 'Nope,' she said, shaking her head and biting the inside of her lip to stop from saying anything that might give away the fib. She really wasn't very good at lying, but she'd be damned if she'd admit that she'd forgotten to close the stupid gate and let his cattle escape. She tried not to think about what could have happened had someone hit one of them.

She followed his gaze anxiously as he looked past her at Gran's yard and saw the churned-up earth and half-chewed plants.

'So, no trouble here?'

'Nope,' she said casually. 'Everything's fine.'

Erin's gaze slid away from his quickly as she made ready to flee inside. His next words froze her in place.

'Then I guess there'd be a good reason why Mick Patterson's cattle are in your top paddock?'

'What?' she asked faintly.

He nodded his head in the direction of the cattle lazily pulling at grass behind her. 'These cattle belong to Mick up the road.'

'They aren't yours?' Erin asked slowly.

'Nope.'

'But the gate was open . . .'

'I sold a truckload of mine yesterday so there was no reason to keep the top gate shut. The rest of my herd are down in the bottom pasture.'

She'd just risked her life herding *someone else's* cattle off the road?

'Good job, by the way. Interesting technique you had going there.'

'You were watching me this whole time?' she gaped in disbelief.

'Well, you seemed to have the situation under control,' he said, a slow grin beginning to steal across his face.

'I could have been killed!'

'I was ready to jump in if they got away from you,' he assured her.

Erin glared at him, too angry to speak. He'd just sat there and let her make a complete fool of herself. What a jerk! She turned on her heel and headed back towards the house.

'Wait up, Erin. Come on, I was just teasing. You did a good job getting them off the road.'

Erin didn't stop walking. Hearing his low chuckle from behind her, she gritted her teeth and pulled open the screen door, letting it slam shut as she headed inside to try to wash away her humiliation beneath a hot shower.

Twenty

When she came out later, she found a cattle truck backed into the stockyards further across the paddock, and she could make out two men, one on a motorbike with a dog, moving the protesting animals into the yards, while the other stood near the gate ready to close it once the cattle were inside.

The man on the bike must be Mick from up the road, while even from a distance she recognised Jamie standing by the gate. He stood, his forearms resting along the top of the rails of the stockyard, one booted foot propped on the bottom rung as he watched the cattle moving towards him. His hat shaded his face from the morning sun and he looked every inch the rugged country heart-throb.

Erin took her phone from her pocket and ran her thumb across the camera icon and began snapping photos. The dew still clung to the grass and turned spider webs into strands of silver thread. The air was crisp and everything smelled new and clean. The light was spectacular. She zoomed in on the cattle. More clicks sounded as she caught the black and tan kelpie running behind them.

She loved the way the stockyard was a dark shadow in the foreground, as sharp spears of light broke through the clouds, hitting objects with rays of liquid gold. It was a breathtaking display from Mother Nature and it almost made up for the rude awakening she'd received earlier.

Moving the camera across to where Jamie was standing, she zoomed in closer. She loved the camera on her phone; the quality was amazing and the zoom was exceptional. She snapped a few photos of his side profile, admiring the play of shadows across his stubbled chin and the low dip of his hat brim. Then suddenly he turned his head and she was looking deep into two navy blue eyes. Her breath seemed to catch in her lungs, even as she took the photo, but then she quickly lowered the phone and took a step back, feeling more than a little awkward at having been caught photographing him.

Roxy often teased her that she was a frustrated paparazzo. Many times they would be out somewhere and Erin would be snapping photos of everything from their food to their surroundings. When asked why she did it, Erin always said the same thing. 'They're memories.' And they were. There was something special about looking back through her photos and reliving her experiences. They were little mementos of her daily life.

She quickly slipped the phone back into her pocket and turned away. She didn't want him thinking she had nothing better to do than stand around taking photos of him all day. He'd probably enjoy posing for her too, given half the chance. She frowned slightly; maybe she was being a little unfair. Sure Jamie McBride was a pain in the backside and loved nothing better than to annoy the living hell out of her whenever he had the opportunity, but he did have a few redeeming qualities. He'd loved her grandmother and had always been there to lend a hand when she'd needed him. For that alone, Erin could forgive him almost anything.

He was still far too cocky for his own good, though. She could just imagine the laugh he and Mick were having at her expense.

Later, while washing the previous night's dishes, she looked out the window to see the cattle truck heading up the driveway towards the house, and she cursed under her breath. She'd hoped they'd just go off and continue doing whatever farmers did all day, so she wouldn't have to face Jamie again. The truck came to a stop and he swung down out of the cab and headed towards the front steps.

With an irritated sigh, Erin wiped her hands on the tea towel and headed outside to see what he wanted.

'Erin, this is Mick,' Jamie said as she stepped out onto the verandah. A large-bellied man in his late forties climbed down from the driver's side of the cab and headed across. His shaggy beard looked in need of a good trim, and the faded flannelette shirt he wore was dusty and had a rip down one side of the seam.

'G'day. Nice to meet you.'

'Hello, Mick.'

She watched as he scratched the back of his head self-consciously.

'I've only known your gran a few years, we not long bought the place down the road,' he drawled.

Erin was beginning to suspect that maybe the actual name of the property was in fact Down The Road. Why else would everyone keep referring to him as Mick from *down the road?*

'Sorry to hear she's not doing so well,' he continued. 'She's a good woman. Make sure you give us a holler if you need anything.'

The roughly spoken words momentarily clogged her throat. 'Thank you, Mick,' she said, conscious of Jamie watching her closely.

'Jamie said you managed to get this mob off the road all by yourself.' She waited for the punchline about being in her PJs but, surprisingly, nothing came. 'Thanks for that.'

Erin refused to meet Jamie's eyes, but nervously waved off the man's thanks. 'Sure. Not a problem.' *Just don't ever ask me to do it again*, she added silently.

'Well, anyway, better get this mob of troublemakers home. I'm sorry about your yard,' he said, shaking his head as he looked around at the churned-up grass. 'I'll come back this afternoon and fix it.'

'Oh, no, don't bother,' Erin hurried to assure him. 'I've been meaning to prune back the garden anyway, and it's just grass, it'll be fine.'

'I don't feel right about leaving it like this.'

'She'll be right, Mick,' Jamie said. 'I was planning on dropping by this week and taking a load of stuff to the tip anyway. I promised Evelyn a few weeks back that I'd do a clean-up.'

'Well, if you're sure?'

'Yeah, no worries,' Jamie assured him.

They watched as the cattle truck reversed out the drive and turned around. With a final wave Erin went to head back inside the house.

'You really did do a good job this morning,' Jamie said to her back.

Erin turned around and pinned him with a sarcastic look. 'What?'

'Don't stand there and act like you weren't laughing your arse off at me this morning while I chased those stupid cows.'

'Yeah, well, it *was* funny.'

'It was *not* funny,' Erin snapped. 'I was terrified they were going to run right over the top of me.'

'But they didn't,' he said and shrugged. 'You got them off the road.'

'No thanks to you!'

'Hey,' he said, putting his hands up before him in protest, 'who am I to step in and fix something that ain't broke? You had it under control.'

Erin gave a frustrated growl and opened the screen door.

'I'll be back this afternoon,' he called through the door.

'Whatever!' she yelled without bothering to turn around.

She went back to the dishes and finally breathed a sigh of relief when she heard his engine start up and saw his ute heading back down the driveway. She ignored the weird little flutter when she checked the clock to see how long it was till afternoon. It had absolutely nothing to do with the fact

Jamie was supposed to be coming back to fix the garden. Nothing at all.

⌘

The conference call went for over an hour, but thankfully without any hiccups, and Erin worked nonstop through lunch. It wasn't until she heard a noise in the yard that she closed her laptop and went outside to have a look.

She followed the sound around the corner and stopped dead in her tracks. Jamie had just thrown a load of branches into the tray of his four-wheel drive and was pulling his T-shirt over his head, wiping his face with the fabric. With his back to her, he was unaware that she was there, but she knew she couldn't just stand here and stare at him like this. *Move,* a little voice inside her head warned, but still she stood there, transfixed by the smooth muscles of his back—not a body builder's muscles, and not like those in some of the near pornographic images of spray-tanned male models that appeared on her daily Facebook feed, courtesy of Roxy, This was a body muscled by hard work. His thick forearms were tanned, ending in a white T-shirt line which suggested working outside without a top on was not something he did regularly. His waist tapered down into faded denim jeans. They weren't skin-tight, they were obviously made for working, but they gave a nice view of his backside nonetheless.

Oh, yeah, that pesky little voice breathed, *this is why we love country boys.* Erin gave a soft snort; the sound alerted Jamie and he turned quickly, catching her watching him. 'Ah, hi,' she said, clearing her throat. 'I didn't realise how late it was.'

'I figured you were busy.'

'You really didn't have to come and do this. I was going to have a day in the yard before I left.'

'Your gran *did* ask me to come and cut back some of these bushes a while back. I should have made time before this.'

'I'm sure Gran knew you were busy. If it bothered her that much she would have called in a yard service.'

'Yeah, I know, but I feel bad that I didn't get to it before now.' He pulled his shirt back on and Erin tried not to acknowledge how disappointed she felt. He leaned across the back of his vehicle and lifted out a small chainsaw.

'What are you going to do with that?'

'Prune the hedge.'

Prune with a chainsaw? She glanced nervously at the machine.

'Stand back,' he said, moving towards the nearest bush.

'Just take of a few of the longer—' The roar of the saw drowned out her words.

'I can't hear you,' he said, shaking his head before running the blade about halfway through the height of the plant and jumping back as it fell to the ground at their feet, then moving on to the next one.

'What are you doing?' she shrieked, but Jamie was too busy mutilating the shrub to look. At this rate there wouldn't be any garden left. Erin tried to get his attention but gave up after a while once she realised it was too noisy for him to hear her. When he finally cut the engine, the quiet almost hurt her ears.

'There,' he announced, wiping the sweat from his brow with the back of his forearm.

'You sure showed it.'

'It needed a good trim.'

'Trim? You call that a trim?'

'It'll grow back,' he said, switching his gaze from her disbelieving expression to the now waist-high hedge.

Erin shook her head in exasperation. Admittedly it was now a hedge instead of a giant row of shaggy bushes, but still . . . did he have to be so brutal about it?

Gran had always been extremely proud of her yard. She loved pottering outside and had done so until only recently. It was clear that it had begun to get away from her, though. *She would have hated that,* Erin thought sadly.

Jamie began dragging out the bigger branches and heaving them up into the back of his ute. Erin helped by picking up the smaller ones. They worked until the ute was full of the discarded garden cuttings and the lawn was cleared. At least now that the shrubs had been tamed, the yard would get a bit more sun and the constantly spongy ground would have a chance to dry out. Jamie walked around and stomped back the majority of the divots the cattle had churned up in the soft ground. While it wasn't perfect, it looked a lot better than it had early this morning.

Okay so maybe he *was* doing the place a favour by cutting it all back so hard, she had to admit. The improvement was pleasantly surprising.

'Thanks,' she said as he loaded his chainsaw in the back and prepared to leave.

'No worries.'

Erin stood there while an awkward silence fell between them.

'Well, I guess I better get back to work.'

'Thanks for lending a hand. It made a big difference,' Jamie said, not making an attempt to leave.

'Thanks for doing it. You didn't have to.'

'It's for Gran.'

'She's lucky to have you and your family as neighbours,' she said gently, placing her hand on his arm. Gran loved them like her own.

'How do you keep so positive about it all?' he asked unexpectedly. 'She's fading away in that place. I hate seeing her like that,' he added, turning away slightly. 'I half expect her to come out onto the front verandah and call me in for a cuppa. It just doesn't seem right she isn't here where she belongs.'

'I know,' Erin agreed with a small sigh. The place seemed empty without her. The warmth beneath her hand suddenly reminded her that she was still touching him and she quickly withdrew her hand and dropped her gaze, feeling self-conscious.

When something touched her cheek, she flinched and looked up to find Jamie's hand lifted to the side of her face. 'You had a smudge of dirt there,' he said as their gazes met briefly. He lowered his hand slowly.

'I better go and do some work,' she stammered as her insides did the cha-cha-cha. Then she turned away before she could do or say anything stupid. A few minutes later she heard his four-wheel drive start up and drive away. When she realised she'd been staring blankly at the screen for over five minutes, she closed her laptop and went in search of a glass of wine.

Twenty-one

Erin hurried along the hallway that led to Gran's room. When the phone call had come this morning, though not unexpected, it had still been a shock. Gran had not responded to her for some days now and, although she had continued to visit and sit by her bedside and talk, she had known in her heart Gran was slipping away from her.

She paused outside the room and realised she was a little out of breath. *You should come as soon as possible. She's deteriorating quite rapidly.* The nurse's words echoed through her mind.

She'd never lost anyone before and facing the death of a loved one was a lot more confronting than Erin had anticipated. She wasn't ready. Her gran had lived an exceptionally long life, but that did not give Erin much comfort. This was still her grandmother, a beautiful woman who had loved her and been a huge part of her life. It hurt terribly to know she was about to lose her forever.

Erin took a deep breath and forced herself to walk into the room.

Nothing had changed visibly, her gran still looked small and incredibly fragile, but her breathing was laboured. The small chest beneath the light blanket lifted and fell rapidly, and her breathing was far louder than seemed possible for such a small frame. The sound was rattly and harsh, leaving Erin feeling helpless.

She pressed the buzzer and after a few minutes the kindly middle-aged nurse who usually did the day shift came into the room.

'Can't you do something for her? She sounds like she's struggling to breathe.'

'That's because she is struggling. She has a lot of fluid on her lungs.' The nurse put a hand on Erin's shoulder as they looked at the woman in the bed before them. 'The doctors have done everything they can. It's just a matter of time now.'

'Is she in any pain?'

'She hasn't been responding to anything for the last two days. I don't think she knows what's happening. But it's good that you came. She'd like to know you were here.'

Erin blinked and her throat ached with the effort of holding back tears. She didn't hear the nurse leave the room, but she jumped a little when someone took a seat beside her.

'Diane from the front desk called. Do you mind if I stay?' Jamie's deep voice sounded calm and gentle.

Erin shook her head, she couldn't speak, it hurt too much, but she was incredibly grateful that Jamie was here. He didn't talk, he just sat beside her and laid his hand on top of hers and Gran's in a silent show of support.

Twenty-two

There was someone standing in the doorway. It was just a silhouette but there was something very familiar about it.

She pushed back the covers and stood up. It was so lovely to be upright again, she was tired of lying in bed all day. She missed being outside in her garden. Evelyn took a cautious step, fearing after being immobile for so long that her aching legs wouldn't be able to support her any more, but she was surprised when not only could she stand unassisted, she could do so without any pain. *When was the last time that had happened?* she wondered briefly, before a movement in the doorway grabbed attention once more.

It was a man. He stepped out from the shadows and Evelyn caught her breath as she saw the face she'd held so firmly in her mind for the last seventy years and more.

'Jimmy?'

'Hello, Evie,' he said, smiling as he came towards her, holding out his hand.

'What are you doing here, Jimmy?'

'I've come to take you home. Just like I promised.'

'Home?' said Evelyn, automatically reaching for his outstretched hand and gaping at her own. What was going on? This wasn't her hand. Where was the fragile skin that bled and bruised whenever she knocked it? This hand was smooth; it was like her skin used to be when she was just a young girl.

'It's all right, Evie,' said Jimmy, smiling in that lopsided way she loved so much. 'Everything's okay now.'

He pulled her to him and she sighed as his arms held her tightly. She had missed him so much. Every day. And now he was here.

'We have to go now,' he said gently, easing away to look down at her.

Evelyn turned and looked back across the room. In the distance was the bed that had trapped her, and two young people who held an old woman's hand so lovingly. She smiled tenderly at the scene and knew that woman was very lucky to have people who loved her so much sitting by her side in her final moments.

'Yes, Jimmy,' she said, turning her gaze back to the man she'd loved for a lifetime. 'I'm ready. Take me home.'

Twenty-three

Erin heard a car pull up outside and put down the pen she'd been making notes with, walking to the door to see who had arrived.

It had been two days since she'd last seen him and she didn't like the surge of joy his appearance caused. It was confusion she didn't want right now but it was becoming harder to keep pushing aside.

'How was the sale?' she called as he got closer. His jeans and checked shirt were reasonably clean, which was unusual because he'd normally have been out working. She dragged her gaze from the strong, tanned forearms exposed where the sleeves of his shirt were rolled up.

'Not bad. Just got back,' he said, coming to a stop at the

bottom of the steps. 'I had to stay overnight and drive home early today.'

'Didn't think you looked dirty enough to have been working.'

'We can't all go to work in suits,' he said. 'How are you doing?'

Erin suspected he was having a dig at Phillip, but let it go. She really didn't have the heart to engage in their usual banter, and even less enthusiasm to bother defending her soon-to-be ex-husband. 'Fine,' she replied.

'Really?' he asked, attempting to hold her fleeting glance.

Erin shrugged. 'I don't know what I feel. Sad mostly. But a little bit relieved too.' She wasn't sure why she'd admitted that out loud, it was something she'd been feeling terrible about.

'Me too.' He held her reluctant look. 'I really hated visiting her in that place. At least she's not trapped in that damn bed any more.'

Erin swallowed over her tight throat and nodded. 'She was miserable when I saw her that first day . . . and then she just kind of gave up.'

A sad silence fell between them and Erin stared out over the tall treetops in the distance.

'Mum said she and Dad were over earlier today.'

'Yeah. They dropped by to see if I needed any help.'

'So they mentioned. They also said you told them you didn't,' he said in a droll tone. 'You know, you don't *have* to do everything alone. They want to help.'

'I know they do, but there's just nothing to help *with*,' she said and nodded across to a black leather-bound diary sitting on the table.

'The little black book?' he asked.

Gran had always made sure those closest to her knew about her little black book. It wasn't a book of old flames; it was the book where she kept all her important information. She'd paid for her funeral plot and all the burial arrangements decades ago when Pop had passed away; she'd written down exactly how she wanted her service, complete with hymns and music, flowers for the church and readings she wanted. There was really nothing much left to do except notify the relevant places and instigate her pre-organised requests.

'You know Gran,' she said sadly. 'She had everything organised. Cuppa?' she asked as she turned to walk inside.

'She only did it because she hated the thought of being a burden on anyone, you know that, right?' he said gently.

His softer side caught her off guard for a moment. 'Yes, I know,' she replied.

A comfortable silence fell between them as she fixed their coffee and reached for the Tupperware container of biscuits, before handing him his mug and taking a seat at the kitchen table.

Erin passed the biscuits to Jamie and watched him take two large jam drops. He closed his eyes and gave a small moan of appreciation after biting into the first one. 'Gran makes the best jam drops.'

Made. Erin corrected silently. She *made* the best jam drops. These were the last of the batch Gran had stockpiled in the freezer. Her throat tightened at the thought. After this there would never be any more.

'Did you manage to get hold of your mum?' he asked.

145

'No, but I left a message with the airline. I didn't want her arriving without knowing.'

He nodded and they let the conversation drop.

'I know it's the neighbourly thing to do, but you don't have to keep checking on me, you know,' she said after a while. 'I'm okay.'

'You think I'm only doing it to be neighbourly?' he asked, his eyes fixed on the mug before him.

'Well, yes. I know our families go back a long way and everything.'

'*We* go back a long way,' he said, lifting his gaze and holding hers steadily.

'Yes. We do,' she said, clearing her throat. 'All I'm saying is you don't have to feel obligated—'

'It's not an obligation.'

Erin fiddled with the handle of her cup. She wasn't entirely sure what she could add. His tone suggested she'd offended him, but his expression remained outwardly calm. It was strange having known someone as a child, yet time and distance making them relative strangers.

Downing the remainder of her coffee, Erin stood and crossed the kitchen to place her cup in the sink. She heard Jamie behind her and turned to accept the plate he was holding. Something about seeing that empty plate triggered an unexpected reaction. Only a few crumbs remained on the pretty pale pink plate. Gone. Empty. She turned abruptly to add the plate to the dishes in the sink.

A pair of strong hands rested on her shoulders and she blinked hard. Heat shot through her body, the warmth spreading from the hands against her skin, igniting something dormant inside her. Without conscious thought, she turned slowly, keeping her gaze firmly fixed on the front of his shirt.

His hands slid slowly from her shoulders down her arms, to her hands, which he held loosely. Erin felt his gaze on her, watching, waiting for a response. If she looked at him, she knew she would be lost. In her present state of mind, it would be all too easy to give in to whatever this lingering *thing* was between them. She was lonely, damn it. The need for physical contact, to feel desired after having been rejected by her husband, was a powerful force.

He was waiting, she could feel his gaze burning into her flesh, but he made no movement, just stood there like he was built of rock.

Was it fair to use Jamie as a balm for her wounded pride? Would she like to be used that way by him? The thought was enough to instantly strengthen her wavering willpower.

Erin took a sideways step and Jamie released her hands without comment.

After a brief silence, he spoke and his tone sounded surprisingly normal, as though the moment had never even happened. 'There's a bit of a gathering happening at Mum and Dad's tonight. It's nothing fancy, just a barbie and a few beers if you're up to it.'

Up until now she had been somewhat of a hermit, and quite frankly it would be nice to get out of the house for a while. She found herself nodding in agreement. 'What time?'

'Six-thirty, seven, whenever you get there.'

'Okay. Thanks. I guess I'll see you tonight.'

He was already at the screen door when he sent her a wave, but she saw him pause briefly at the threshold.

Erin held her breath, but the moment passed and he obviously changed his mind about whatever it was he had been about to say.

Long after the sound of his vehicle had faded, Erin stood in the doorway looking out. She hadn't counted on anything like this happening. It had been the last thing on her mind when she'd left Sydney, but as hard as she tried to ignore it, something was still there between her and Jamie. Maybe staying on after the funeral for a while wasn't such a great idea after all. Then again, the thought of leaving didn't hold much relief either.

She wasn't entirely sure she was strong enough to keep being the one to step back from the edge every time. Not when a small part of her was urging her to jump.

Twenty-four

Jamie had said it wasn't going to be anything fancy, but it still felt wrong to turn up empty-handed. It was time to get out of her trackies and into something halfway decent and venture into town.

Life in Tuendoc wasn't exactly hectic. Small groups of people stood on the footpath in front of shops in the main street catching up on news. Young mothers pushed prams and called to toddlers who ran ahead. Farmers drove through town, some with produce stacked high in their old utes, others with utes filled with supplies from the local store. People waved and smiled, and strangers nodded as they walked by. Erin had to admit it was nice.

She'd always liked this little town. It had the essentials: supermarket, butcher, baker, takeaway shop, cafes, two pubs, a chemist and doctor's surgery, as well as an assortment of little shops that sold second-hand bric-a-brac and one or two places that stocked clothing. She made a mental note that she needed to come into town more often and take a look around.

Erin parked the car, dropping the keys into her bag, and headed towards the grocery store. As she approached the doorway, she narrowly avoided a head-on collision.

'Whoa. Hey, are you okay?' Jamie asked, stepping back quickly, his fingers looped through a multitude of white shopping bags.

'Sorry, I didn't see you,' Erin said automatically, seconds before her surprised mind registered who it was she'd collided with.

'Careful, babe. Don't break the pastry cases,' a voice instructed. A woman stepped out from behind Jamie and reached for one of the bags he carried. Erin's memory flashed back to a riot of wild red hair caught in the beam of headlights.

'Vanessa, you remember Erin,' Jamie said.

The woman looked across, eyeing Erin up and down briefly. 'Vaguely. How are you?'

Erin opened her mouth to answer, but Vanessa had already turned back to Jamie. 'I've got an hour before everyone turns up for the barbecue. Help me get these into the car, will you.'

Behind his sunglasses, Erin couldn't read Jamie's expression, but the straight line of his mouth told her she hadn't imagined the other woman's cold shoulder.

'I'll see you tonight,' Jamie said, turning away before Erin had the chance to reply. She watched until they disappeared around the corner.

Jamie and Vanessa were still an item? She frowned at that. He'd never mentioned he was seeing anyone, and certainly not *Vanessa*. Had she been imagining the chemistry between herself and Jamie? 'Oh, my God,' she groaned, closing her eyes briefly. She felt like a complete idiot. He was involved with someone. And not just any someone, the very someone from her past who had broken them up in the first place.

∽

Parking her car in the driveway, Erin counted another five cars already there. The entire trip home from the store and the drive here she'd been trying to talk herself out of coming. This was stupid. There was absolutely no reason she should care who Jamie was seeing. They were just old friends. Anything that may have mistakenly felt like something else was clearly just a case of her jumbled emotions from everything she'd been dealing with.

She pushed her car door open with new resolve. She'd been looking forward to getting out of the house and she didn't see why Jamie and Vanessa should ruin that for her. Now she was here, though, she was feeling more than a little nervous.

Almost as though he had been waiting for her, Jamie appeared around the corner of the house.

'You came.'

'I said I would.'

'Yeah, but I kinda thought after this afternoon you might have changed your mind.'

'Why?' She was just going to play dumb and hope to bluff her way out of it, she decided.

'Vanessa,' he said.

'It's none of my business who you're with,' she said, moving past him.

'There you are!' Pat called out, thankfully stalling any further awkward conversation. 'I'm so glad you came. Come on in and we'll get you a drink. Jamie, hurry up, we need that ice.'

Erin saw him roll his eyes at his mother, but he turned and did as he was told without comment.

As they rounded the corner of the house into the backyard, Erin saw fold-out chairs had been set up and two tables laden with food had guests hovering around them, picking at nibblies.

'Jamie said it was just a barbecue and a few beers,' Erin protested when she saw the amount of food laid out. She was glad she'd stopped into town and picked up the chips and a dessert.

'What, this?' Pat exclaimed. 'It's nothing much. You didn't have to bring anything, you know. We have more than enough food. Go find yourself a seat. Jamie will get you a drink in a sec.'

A small group of women sat in a semicircle, most with children on their laps and chatting with a casual air of familiarity that suggested they'd all known each other a long time. Further over, near the large brick barbecue, were most of the men, beers in hand and all keeping a watchful eye on the hotplate. She waved at Jamie's dad who, as host, had the honour of holding the tongs, and nodded at Mick, *from down the road,* when he toasted her with his beer can.

Erin took a seat next to the Chapmans, an elderly couple who had often visited her gran. They were the only people she really knew, other than the McBrides.

'What can I get you to drink?' Jamie asked a few moments later, coming over to perform host duties.

'Wine would be great.'

He came back a few moments later with a glass, handing it to her and surprising her by taking a seat beside her. Jamie and Mr Chapman talked about cattle and feed and a whole heap of other topics somehow relating to cows that she had no idea about, while Erin did her best to strike up conversation with a rather deaf Mrs Chapman, eventually giving up and listening in on the men's conversation.

Out of the corner of her eye she noticed how close Jamie's chair was to her own. His arms, bare tonight in a T-shirt, were braced along the tops of his jean-clad thighs as he leaned forward, nodding occasionally at the older man as he spoke. Her gaze fell on his thick wrists lightly covered in hair and the wide links of the watch that wrapped around it. She'd never thought of a man's wrist as particularly interesting before, but for some reason tonight she found it more than a little distracting.

She shifted a little in her seat, stopping when he looked over at her. Erin quickly averted her eyes, and cursed silently as she felt a blush creeping up her throat. The last thing she wanted was for Jamie to think she was checking him out. *Thank God he can't read minds,* she thought gratefully.

'What do you think?'

'What?' Erin gave a start, almost spilling her drink in the process.

Jamie looked at her oddly. 'Ted wanted to know if he could drop around some orchids for the funeral.'

'Your grandmother loved my orchids,' Mr Chapman said sadly. 'I thought she might like a bouquet to put on the coffin, in the church.'

'Oh. Sorry, I was miles away,' she apologised. 'That would be lovely, Mr Chapman. Thank you,' she said, touched by the gesture.

'Food's ready,' Mr McBride yelled across the yard, and people began to move towards the tables to grab plates and salads.

'Come on, better get in there before it's all gone.'

Erin followed Jamie and took the paper plate he offered her, smiling as he introduced her to a few people nearby as they made their way along the table, adding food to their plates.

When she turned away to head back to her chair, she saw Jamie was right behind her. 'You don't have to babysit me, you know. I'm sure you'd much rather be mingling with other people.'

'Nope. I'm happy here.'

'What about Vanessa?' she asked, taking extra time to organise her plate on her lap.

'What *about* Vanessa?' he asked, sticking a forkful of steak in his mouth and watching her closely.

'Won't she be wondering where you are?'

'I doubt it,' he said. 'She's busy hosting a barbecue of her own.'

'I thought she was talking about *this* barbecue.'

'Well, you thought wrong. About a lot of things,' he added.

Erin eyed him as she chewed her own mouthful of tender meat. She may have been wrong about the barbecue, but she hadn't been wrong about the woman's attitude earlier. There was definitely *something* between those two.

'So how come you've never gotten married?' Erin asked, cocking her head slightly to look at him.

If her question surprised him he didn't show it; he did, however, take a moment to answer, as though considering his words. 'Maybe I'm too fussy.'

Erin frowned at that. It could be that she was oversensitive when it came to the whole 'perfectly packaged' woman when she'd experienced being dumped for not measuring up, but the thought that even Jamie could be that shallow irked her. 'So you're holding out for some Barbie-waisted model or something?'

'Not necessarily.'

'You're telling me that no woman out here measures up to your high expectations?'

'Something like that,' he said, his gaze roaming the yard.

'Not even Vanessa?' She knew she was sounding more like a pouty teenager than a mature woman, but she couldn't help it. There was no way Jamie would be living like a monk, and she'd always wondered why he'd never ended up with Vanessa. During their brief relationship as teenagers, she had made her dislike of Erin painfully clear at every opportunity. She knew that before she'd come along Vanessa and Jamie had been an item, although Jamie had reassured her it had never been serious between them.

Jamie raised an eyebrow pointedly and a ghost of smile tugged at the corner of his mouth. 'You two really hate each other.'

'I don't hate her,' Erin frowned. 'She was just never particularly nice to me on the few occasions we met. So how come you two never ended up together?' If she'd hoped to sound blasé she'd failed miserably, given the smirk Jamie sent her.

'I don't know. I think for a while there she thought it was going to happen, but she gave up in the end and married Muzza, a guy I used to play footy with.'

She was married. The amount of relief which followed Jamie's statement was truly ridiculous, but it soon dissipated with his next words.

'She moved back to town a year or so ago with three kids after her husband died.'

'Oh.'

'We hang out sometimes,' he said. 'It's *still* not serious. Ness and I aren't compatible as a couple.'

Something about her expression must have alerted him to her disapproval.

'You think that's wrong?'

'That you don't consider her serious but you still "hang out"?' she asked. She may not have particularly liked Vanessa, but she had to admit she felt a little insulted on her behalf. 'I'm sure she loves the lack of commitment.'

'She knows the way it is. What would be the point in being with someone if it wasn't perfect?'

'Perfect?'

'Okay, maybe perfect was the wrong word,' he said. 'But when you know what makes you happy and you can't have it, there's no point settling, is there?'

'I'm sure she's completely fine with knowing she's just keeping you amused.'

'Bit judgemental, aren't we?'

He was right, who was she to judge? Her sure thing had turned around and impregnated his child-bride assistant.

'You're right. It's none of my business.'

She saw the tight smile pass across his lips as he gave a small shake of his head. 'Then again, maybe you're right. Maybe I just don't do commitment.'

Yep, there are still sparks there, she thought wearily. Those sparks could either ignite a flame of passion or create instant confrontation. There seemed to never be any middle ground with them.

Twenty-five

Choosing an outfit was harder than she'd expected. It was painful to go into Gran's room when everything still smelled like she was right there. The bed was neatly made, with its beautifully embroidered bedspread that was so much like its owner—made in a time when things were built to last, its quality unmatched today.

But the room felt empty. When she'd first arrived back, Erin had packed a few odds and ends to give her nursing home room a bit of a homey feel, like the photo of Pop that had always been on her dressing table. Those things were still in a box on the back seat of her car after she'd collected them from the nursing home.

Erin moved across the room to the heavy carved-timber monstrosity of a wardrobe Pop had made for Gran on their first wedding anniversary. Opening the doors, she took a step back as the smell of lavender and sandalwood spilled out and enveloped her. She blinked quickly before taking a shaky breath and reaching out to touch the garments hanging inside. Frocks. That's all there were; she couldn't ever recalling a time she'd seen her Gran in anything other than a dress. She had certainly been the last of a dying breed. Gran was from the 'always dress up to go into town' era. Many a time Erin had been sent back inside to change from her house clothes into something nicer to go into town to pick up groceries. 'But Gran, it's only Tuendoc.'

'It doesn't matter if it's Tuendoc or London. You can take pride in yourself and dress nicely wherever you are.'

Choosing a pretty blue floral print dress her gran had always liked, Erin laid it out on the bed and gently smoothed the fabric. 'Pantyhose,' she murmured, turning back to the wardrobe drawers. Gran always wore stockings, summer or winter. 'And shoes,' she added, looking for Gran's good pair of heels and frowning when she only found one. It was not like Gran to not have everything put back where it belonged. Erin knelt down on the floor and reached into the bottom shelf of the wardrobe, feeling around blindly.

Her fingers brushed against something solid, but definitely not shoe-like, and, curious, she grabbed hold of the object and pulled it out. It was a tin box. Putting it to one side she went back in to continue the search, finally locating the missing mate and placing the outfit on the bed to make sure she had everything.

Gathering up the items from the bed, she turned to walk from the room when she kicked her toe and almost tripped.

She swore under her breath, then put her armload down and picked up the tin box, which she'd managed to promptly forget about. She sat on the end of the bed and struggled to prise open the lid. It appeared to be stuck fast, but after a few moments she loosened the lid and it opened with a small pop.

Erin looked inside at the strange assortment of contents, mostly old letters and photos. Carefully she picked up the top few photographs and turned them over. Jimmy was written across the back.

Erin turned it back over and took a closer look at the man in the picture. He was dressed in a military uniform that reminded Erin of the uniforms she'd grown up seeing on *Hogan's Heroes* re-runs. A handsome young man in his mid-twenties, wearing a dark bomber jacket, cap, and uniform trousers, leaning against a plane. She frowned. *Jimmy?* Could this be who Gran had been referring to those few times she'd confused people in photos?

She took out another photo which had a group of young people from the 1940s, judging by the fashion, who seemed to be enjoying some kind of beach party. Pallarenda Beach, 1943 was scrawled on the back. Her gaze moved across the happy faces in the photo, stopping at one which seemed familiar, and then she realised it was her gran. She searched the rest of the faces looking for Pop but he wasn't there. In fact, when she looked closer she saw that the same man, Jimmy, was in this photo too, and he had his arms wrapped around her gran, albeit a very young version of Gran.

Was this before Gran and Pop had met? She tried to think but couldn't work it out.

There were a few letters, their envelopes addressed to Evelyn Ward, Gran's maiden name, and the address was in Townsville where she'd grown up. Taking out the first one, Erin quickly scanned the contents and turned to the last page to see they were from Pop, written while he'd been stationed in New Guinea during the war. Strangely, the date on the letters was only a few months before the date on the back of the photographs.

Had Gran been unfaithful to her fiancé at the time? It was an odd thought. All her life she'd never really thought of her grandparents as ever having been young and in love. She'd never known her grandfather, he was just a man whose photo hung on the wall. Erin knew he'd died in a terrible farm accident, and from an early age she had worked out that talking about him made Gran sad. It didn't stop Gran telling her some stories about him though, mostly about him going to war. She'd always spoken with a quiet kind of pride about his service, although it was always tinged with sadness. He'd seen some terrible things in the war and come back a different kind of man. When Erin was younger she hadn't really understood what that meant, but over the years, reading about the Australians and where they fought, the battles they were involved in and the price they paid, she had a better understanding about what her pop must have gone through over there. He'd had nightmares for years, her gran had told her once when she'd asked about it, and often used to suffer terrible headaches. Erin could only speculate on how much pressure that would add to a family—to a marriage.

Erin put the letters down to read later and sorted through the rest of the tin's contents. At the very bottom, under the various movie ticket stubs and bric-a-brac, she found a ring. It was too big to have been Gran's; it looked like a man's ring, with a huge oval-shaped ruby in the centre and the words US Air Force stamped around the edge. When she turned the heavy piece of jewellery around to look at it, she saw that it had a propeller with wings etched on each side. It was a big clunky piece but obviously very expensive. The ruby alone would be worth a small fortune. Inside was an inscription that read: To J from Mom & Pop, 1940.

Erin frowned as she ran her fingertip across the intricate detail of the design. She rifled through the photographs beside her until she located the one of Jimmy and the big airplane to see if he was wearing a ring, but she couldn't see either of his hands clearly as one was in his pocket and the other was holding onto the wing of the aircraft above his head.

The photograph with his arms around Evelyn was a different story, though. She could just make out a band of oval-shaped metal around his right-hand ring finger. His left hand appeared to be bare, which would suggest that at least he hadn't been married at the time.

She noticed that Evelyn—she didn't feel comfortable calling her *Gran* while looking through her private keepsakes—wasn't wearing any jewellery. *Maybe she hadn't been engaged at the time after all*, she thought, puzzling over the evidence. But then again, she was positive the stories she had been told growing up were that she'd been engaged just before Pop went off to training camp and then overseas to fight.

The clock out in the lounge room chimed and Erin realised she needed to get the clothes back to the funeral home. She quickly gathered together the contents of the tin and pushed the lid back on securely. This wasn't over yet, she intended to come back and get to the bottom of it all later.

As she drove back into town she went over the unexpected discovery in her mind. It wasn't important; after all, it happened a very long time ago. They were just keepsakes from another part of Gran's life, yet they were incredibly intriguing. This was a time in her life where she looked truly happy. *What happened to you, Gran?* she wondered. *Where did that girl in the photos go?* If only she were still here to ask.

Twenty-six

Erin was outside watering the front garden when she heard the sound of an approaching car. Shading her eyes from the afternoon glare, she watched the vehicle pull up and braced herself with a deep, fortifying breath, crossing to the tap to turn off the water.

'Hello, darling,' her mother greeted her, holding her close in a tight hug. From previous experience, she knew she had to be the first one to break the embrace or they would stand there all day. First universal law of parenting: the parent must never be the one to pull away.

'Hello, Mum.' *It was kind of nice to be able to hug her,* she thought, as an unexpected rush of emotion surfaced. She smelled of incense and sandalwood, but she also brought back memories of childhood, when a hug from Mum always made things better. It had been a long time. She missed it.

'Well, this place hasn't changed much, has it?' she said, leaving one arm around Erin's waist as she surveyed the house.

'Nope.' *Thank goodness,* she added silently. In this world where everything was always changing, everyone needed *something* that stayed familiar. 'Come on in, I'll put the jug on,' Erin said, giving her mum's hand a squeeze as she slipped it from around her to move inside.

Erin watched her mother as she took in her surroundings, her gaze moving around the kitchen and taking in the sights and smells. It had been a long time since she'd been here. The thought made Erin sad. She didn't understand the rift between Gran and Mum, but she knew that if it had been her she wouldn't have let it hang between them unresolved. She'd have wanted to make sure her mother knew she loved her, despite everything.

'Coffee?' Erin asked, taking down two cups from the holder.

'Oh, goodness no. I brought my own tea,' her mother said, moving across to the end cupboard and withdrawing an old teapot, then proceeding to prepare a foul-smelling beverage with a concoction of herbs and other things Erin was too scared to ask about. She was only mildly amused that her mother instinctively knew where everything was kept, as it always had been, for the last seventy-odd years.

'How long are you planning on staying for?' Erin asked.

'I'll need to leave after the funeral tomorrow.'

'That soon?'

'I had to leave things unfinished back at the foundation. I'm in the middle of a very important legislative change that could mean a great deal to the entire province where the orangutans are most vulnerable.'

'There are things I thought we should sort out.'

'There's nothing that needs to be decided upon right this minute, and there's nothing that you need to worry yourself about. That's what solicitors are for.'

'Well, I was hoping we could talk about what you're going to do with this place. I'd really like to stay here for a while.'

'Stay? What for? There's nothing here.'

'I've always loved it here, and at the moment I'd prefer to be out of the city. I'd like to take over here as caretaker for six months or so, maybe longer.'

'What does Phillip think about this?' her mother asked, looking around as though she'd somehow managed to overlook her son-in-law until now. 'Where is he anyway?'

'He's . . . back in the city,' she fudged.

'Are you two having a bit of a spat?' she asked, placing a hand on Erin's arm comfortingly. 'I may not be a marriage councillor but, darling, if there's one thing I do know, it's that you cannot hope to work through problems if you're not present. I don't think staying up here is a good idea.'

'Like you were present to work through your problems with Gran all these years?' Erin asked pointedly.

Her mother's concerned expression hardened slightly before she dropped her hand and stepped away. 'I was talking about your marriage. But if you don't want to discuss it, then we won't.'

And that, apparently, was that. As usual her mother shut down whenever it came to her past, and Erin was too tired to bother explaining the fact she no longer *had* a marriage to save. Not for the first time she wished her mother had just a little more empathy for normal *everyday* kind of problems, like cheating husbands and heartbroken daughters. Unfortunately Erin wasn't an orangutan. It was hard to compete with a species facing extinction.

'If you want to stay on for a little while, I guess that's all right, but I had plans to put the place on the market as soon as possible. I could use the cash injection into the foundation.'

'Sell it?'

'Yes, Erin. There's no reason to keep it. I certainly don't need this place hanging over my head. And you should really move on too. Now that Mum's gone, we need to start afresh. Get rid of all this baggage,' her mother said, waving a hand around the room.

What was she talking about? Erin stared at her mother, horrified to hear her talking like this. 'What baggage?'

'Oh, I suppose you're right—it's not yours, it's mine.'

'Mum, what are you talking about?'

'I wasn't close with your gran. Why would I act the heartbroken daughter now?'

'Oh, I don't know . . . maybe out of respect for the dead!'

'She's gone. There's nothing I can say or do to hurt her now.'

'I seriously don't get you at all,' Erin said, standing.

'Well that's another thing you and your gran had in common. You need to focus on your own life now.'

'My own life is falling down around me, I don't actually *have* my own life right now, in case you care.'

'Of course I care, I'm your mother. But I raised you to stand on your own two feet just like I had to. I did what was necessary, I raised a daughter, built up a business and made a lot of money, and you know what I discovered? I should have lived what I preached. I owned a health food store, for heaven's sake, and I lived in a polluted, filthy city! I should have taken you and moved to a place like Nimbin years ago, allowed you to grow up surrounded by nature and people who aren't controlled by the pressures of society.'

'If you hadn't done what you did, you wouldn't have had the money to *start* your retreat. So money's still a necessary evil, isn't it, even for all the free spirits of the world,' Erin snapped, leaving the kitchen.

For a healer, her mother sure as hell could hold onto a lot of bitterness.

Yes, her mother had had a tough job being a single parent, but standing alone had been her decision. She'd pushed Gran away, and as for Erin's father, well, she'd never intended on having him around.

At fifteen, Erin had confronted her mother and demanded to know who her father was. She didn't want to hear her mother's excuses any more: that he wasn't interested in a second family, that she'd been trying to protect Erin from the rejection she was sure she'd receive from him. She'd given her the name and Erin had ignored her warnings and tracked him down by herself.

She'd approached him one day as he left his office to go home. She still remembered that moment of nervous antici-pation as she waited for the well-dressed businessman to turn and acknowledge her. For years she'd dreamed of that first moment when she'd meet her father. Their eyes would connect and instantly he would recognise her—he'd smile and open his arms to her, the child he always thought he'd never see, and he would welcome her into his family.

None of that had happened.

Her father had turned around when he'd sensed someone standing behind him in the underground car park of his office. Erin had smiled, waiting for that lightning strike of recognition to hit him.

'Yes?' he'd said in an impatient tone.

Momentarily thrown off balance that things didn't seem to be following the script she'd written in her head, Erin continued to stare at the man silently.

'This is private property. How did you even get down here?'

'I came to see you,' she stammered.

'Look, I don't have time for this today. You shouldn't be lurking around in dark car parks.'

'I'm your daughter,' she blurted, then bit her lip uncertainly when the man continued to stare at her with a forbidding frown.

'What's your name?' he demanded roughly after what seemed an eternity.

'Erin Macalister.'

His gaze narrowed at the mention of her name and he looked around behind her. 'Did Irene send you here?'

'No. She doesn't even know I found you.'

'Do you know that you're breaking the terms of our contract? I could take your mother to court over this.'

'What contract?'

'You tell your mother that if I ever see her or you anywhere near me or my family again, I'll have her in court.'

'She doesn't know I'm here, she knows nothing about this. I wanted to find you.'

'She should have told you to stay away,' he said, reefing open his door before pausing and looking at Erin. For the briefest of moments she thought he was about to change his mind. 'Look, I'm sorry, okay? But I didn't even want her to have—' he started, then stopped abruptly. 'I already have a family. She knew that. Just go on home.'

Erin watched him drive away, frozen to the spot. It took a while for his words to sink in. The whole way home she replayed them over and over in her mind, all the while wondering how this meeting could have gone so terribly wrong.

She hadn't intended to tell her mother, but when she got home Irene took one look at her and instantly knew something was not right. The whole story came tumbling out as she sat on the end of her bed, eyes red and puffy from crying.

'I'm sorry you had to hear it like that. I thought I was protecting you by not telling you.'

'He said he could take you to court. Did he really *pay* to get rid of us?'

Her mother gave a bitter snort. 'More like he paid me to keep it quiet from his wife. Anyway, it doesn't matter, I got you and that's all I wanted. He won't risk taking me to court, his family would find out.'

'Did you think he'd leave his family for you?'

Her mother shrugged. 'Not really. I wasn't looking for a relationship. I'm not sure I went into it planning to get pregnant, but I certainly wasn't devastated by it. I don't regret it—not for a second,' she said fiercely, returning her daughter's gaze steadily. There was so much love burning there that Erin's indignation died down.

'How can he love some of his children but not all of them?'

'Oh, baby,' her mother sighed, hugging her tightly.

Things had changed between mother and daughter after that. Erin hadn't said it out loud, but part of her had always blamed her mother for having an affair with a man who was not only married but also selfish and cold-hearted enough to turn his back on his child. Now she understood things with a little more clarity. Her mother was human. She'd made mistakes. She'd waited a long time for a child and, when she'd finally fallen pregnant in her forties, she'd been determined to keep the baby, whether the father wanted to be involved or not.

Erin went into her bedroom and sat on the edge of the bed. She looked over at the night stand and saw the tin box. Technically everything in the house belonged to her mother now, to do with as she saw fit. But her mother held no sentimental value for anything belonging to her past, and there was no way Erin was going to risk any of her gran's personal belongings being thrown out, so she tucked the box into her suitcase in the bottom of her wardrobe and gave it a comforting pat before closing the door.

Twenty-seven

Erin hated when things got strained between her and her mother—it was probably why they avoided long visits—but if her grandmother's death had reminded her of anything, it was that leaving things unsaid wasn't the way to get things sorted.

Finding her mother on the verandah sitting cross-legged and eyes closed, meditating, Erin turned to walk away so as not to disturb her.

'I heard you coming, I'm almost done,' her mother said, stopping her in her tracks.

Erin only hesitated briefly before pulling out a seat and placing the tray and photo album on the outside table.

After a few moments of humming and chanting, her mother stood up and took a deep breath before opening her eyes and adjusting to her surroundings.

'I made some lemon water,' she said, reaching for a glass to pour her mum a drink.

'Are they organic lemons?'

'I guess so, they're from Gran's tree.'

'That doesn't mean they're organic, darling, but close enough. I guess I'm spoilt for choice. Nimbin has the most beautiful organic farms and produce.'

'How nice,' Erin murmured. She was fairly confident a fifty-year-old lemon tree was as organic as it damn well got.

'You look tired. Are you getting enough sleep?' her mother asked, eyeing her critically. 'How's work going?'

'It's fine. We've got a big deal with the Grand Pacific in the pipeline. It's keeping everyone busy.'

'Too much stress isn't worth the damage it does to your body, darling, just remember that. I learned the hard way. When I left the company I was so rundown and tired, but now I have energy to burn. Maybe you should look at cutting back your workload?'

'I love my job, Mum. Things will get back to normal once this deal's finalised.'

'Until the next deal comes along, and the next, and then the one after that. It'll be too late one day. You'll be on prescription pills and headed for a heart attack.'

'Gee, I can hardly wait,' Erin murmured.

'I'm serious, darling. I've been there. You need to take better care of yourself.'

'I'll try harder to get some more sleep,' she promised.

'What have you got there?' her mother asked, noticing the photo album on the table, and Erin was more than happy to change the subject.

'While I was visiting Gran, I took this up to give her something to look through. She told me lots of stories. It was fascinating. She talked a lot about the war.'

'Did she now?'

'She mentioned a man. Do you know anyone named Jimmy?' Erin watched as her mother's expression became guarded.

'No. I wouldn't go thinking too much about it. She was old and probably had no idea what she was saying towards the end.'

'That's not true at all. She was a little bit confused now and again, but when she talked about the war you should have seen her face light up. I think whoever this Jimmy was, she loved him very much. I'm just trying to place where she would have met him. Do you remember when she and Pop got engaged? I thought it was before he went to New Guinea, but maybe I got it wrong. Maybe it wasn't until after he came back.'

'Why could it possibly matter now?'

Erin frowned at her mother's dismissive tone. 'Because it's interesting. It's our history. Don't you care about where we came from?'

'No, I don't. The past doesn't matter. It's the future you need to concentrate on. We choose our own path in life and we learn to accept the things we have no control over.'

'Aren't you curious?'

'I think you should concentrate on your own life.'

She couldn't recall her mother ever being quite this blunt before. She'd become very self-centred or, as she liked to call it, 'self-aware' after she'd sold off her share of the business and gone in search of enlightenment. Erin had accepted that her mother needed time to find herself, or whatever she wanted to call it, but it sometimes felt as though this also meant rejecting everything from her old life.

'I know you and Gran had your differences, but I don't understand why you're being like this.'

'Why is it that I'm the one who is suddenly being selfish or unreasonable simply for leading a life that makes me happy? Your gran never understood that either, and that was hypocritical coming from her.'

'I just don't understand where all this anger towards Gran *comes* from. Surely you two could have got past it at some point?'

'Apparently not.'

'Well, I would very much like to understand why.'

'It doesn't matter now, it's in the past. My mother made her choices and I made mine.'

'What choices?'

'I don't want to discuss it any more, Erin. I just want to get this funeral over with and move on. And I would appreciate you not making this more painful than it already is.'

She watched her mother walk inside and her heart sank. All she'd wanted to do was to get to the bottom of whatever had hung between her gran and her mother all these years. Whatever it was, it seemed it wasn't going to be discussed any time in the near future.

Twenty-eight

The funeral was everything Gran would have wanted it to be: elegant, simple and low-key. All her favourite hymns were sung, some of them bringing back memories of her gran singing her to sleep when she was little, or listening to her hum the tunes under her breath as she did the housework. It was a large turnout with lots of people Erin had known growing up, but it was sad to see so few of her grandmother's generation in attendance, and those who were there sat through the service with a weary kind of acceptance. How many times had she listened to Gran telling her about another long-time friend passing, that same kind of expression on her face?

Her mother sat through the service with a straight back and dry eye, while Erin struggled to keep her composure, failing miserably when the pallbearers prepared to carry the coffin away to Gran's final resting place beside Pop.

Jamie took his position behind his father on one side of the coffin, opposite two men from Gran's church group. Through her tears, Erin saw that he wore his sunglasses, shielding his emotions from the rest of the congregation. She wished she'd remembered to bring hers along.

On the short trip to the cemetery in the funeral car, Erin tried not to let her mother's demeanour upset her, but it was difficult when she refused to so much as try to look as though she were mourning.

'Are you all right?' Erin asked, when she was unable to stand the silence for another second.

'I'm fine.'

'Really?' Erin snapped.

Her mother turned her head from the window and looked at her. Erin searched her eyes but there was nothing there to suggest her mother was simply putting on a brave face.

'It's okay to cry,' Erin said quietly, hoping that she could somehow break down that stubborn barrier her mother had built over the years.

'Death isn't something you have to mourn.'

'You sound like that minister back there.'

Her mother shrugged a little. 'I guess all spirituality is similar. It's just the entity that we disagree on.'

'Mum, I don't feel up to a debate about your beliefs right now.'

'You brought it up.'

'I said it was okay to cry, I didn't say I wanted a lecture about it.'

'You're upset because I'm not showing enough emotion?'

'I'm upset because it's not normal to be so damn serene about the death of your mother,' she said, making an effort to control herself when she noticed the driver from the funeral home turn his head slightly.

'Well, I'm sorry that you can't accept my beliefs. I choose not to grieve but to rejoice in the journey my mother has now begun. It's not a time for sadness, it's the circle of life moving as it has done since the beginning of time.'

How could this woman even *be* her mother? Erin shook her head and turned to look out the window to find they were already pulling up outside the cemetery.

As they gathered at the gravesite, Erin swallowed hard against a lump of emotion as the coffin was lowered into the ground. She closed her eyes, then opened them a few moments later when she felt a warm hand circle her arm. It was Jamie. He didn't look at her, but continued to keep close by her side. She was too stunned to do much about it, but after the initial surprise wore off, she realised she was touched by the gesture. It felt good to have someone to lean on, even if only for a little while.

The funeral director offered her a flower to place in the grave, and for a moment Erin froze. She didn't want to throw that beautiful, vibrant rose into that dark, cold hole in the ground. She couldn't do it.

Jamie reached out and took the rose from the man's hand and thanked him, nodding that he should move on to offer the flowers to the rest of the mourners. Erin felt her lip tremble and clenched it tightly between her teeth, fighting to keep herself composed.

Jamie gave her arm a small squeeze, moving in close to ask if she was okay. Erin looked up and nodded to reassure him that she was fine.

'Are you ready to leave?'

With one final glance at the hole, she quickly nodded and allowed him to lead her away. She heard him tell the funeral director that he would take Erin to the wake, and then they were walking across the cemetery towards the car park.

She took a deep breath and let it out slowly. That final goodbye was too cruel. There was nothing comforting about watching a loved one being lowered into the earth. She didn't want that to be her last memory of Gran; she tried to replace it with something happier, determined to shake the feeling of bleakness.

As they approached a sleek black ute, Erin looked at Jamie, puzzled.

'This is my baby,' he said with a sheepish grin.

She looked back at the high-powered machine and had to admit there was something awe-inspiring about it. Although it was technically supposed to be a working vehicle, there was nothing utilitarian about it. It was too low to the ground to be practical, and the gleaming paintwork suggested it didn't leave the bitumen. It was the complete opposite of the big, dusty four-wheel drive Erin had seen Jamie in until now.

Jamie opened the door for her and she slid into the leather upholstered seat, admiring the dark interior and the new car smell that went along with it.

The dashboard that lit up once Jamie turned the ignition resembled the flight deck of an aircraft, and she couldn't help but be a little bit impressed. She'd never considered herself a car fanatic, but she could make an exception for this one.

'How long have you had this?'

'Bit over twelve months now,' he said, reversing from the car park.

She was surprised it had been that long, it looked as though it had just been driven off the showroom floor.

'It's my one indulgence. It's completely impractical, and I only drive it on special occasions, but we've all gotta have one vice, right?'

'Hey, I'm not judging,' she said lightly.

The low purr of the engine filled the cabin as Erin watched the passing scenery outside the window. 'Thank you, for back there,' she added quietly.

'No problem.'

'I probably should have stayed and made sure Mum was okay.'

'She looked like she was handling it just fine,' he said.

'Yeah,' Erin agreed. 'Apparently it's only the *unenlightened* who find death sad.'

Twenty-nine

They pulled up back at the church where the ladies from Gran's congregation had organised a morning tea for the wake in the small hall off the side of the old brick church. There were already a few people dribbling into the hall by the time Jamie parked the car and they made their way inside. Erin thanked the church women, who went around carrying platters of little sandwiches and delicate tarts, scones and quiche. *There were no jam drops though*, she thought sadly.

She shook hands, greeting people she hadn't seen in years, and smiled through a sheen of tears when people mentioned how much they'd admired her gran.

The last of a dying breed.

There were so few of her generation left. It was hard to accept. Grandparents weren't supposed to die, they were just *there*. The ones who sat smiling from the sidelines as they watched their children, grandchildren and great-grandchildren on their journey through life.

Erin noticed her mother was also mingling. For all her eccentricities, she was still a daughter of the community and people here seemed to overlook the bright purple muumuu dress, and the woven headpiece she wore in her salt-and-pepper coloured hair. Over time her mother's once dark head of hair had begun turning grey, and the resulting, stubborn streaks of darker hair that remained added a striking colour intermingled with the shades of grey and white. She was still a very good-looking woman, even though she was now in her seventies. It seemed hard to imagine that seventy was once considered so old. Her mother showed no intention of slowing down, and obviously her lifestyle agreed with her—she did not look her age. She seemed completely at ease in a room predominantly made up of graziers, farmers and church women. Maybe they saw through the exterior and could still recognise the little girl who was born and raised here all those years ago. Erin wished she could see through it and find the mother she'd known before her big journey to self-discovery.

In truth, her mother's attraction to an alternative lifestyle hadn't been a huge leap—she'd always been a little inclined that way. At a young age Erin had realised most kids didn't have tie-dyed school bags, alfalfa on their sandwiches and organic black bean chips in their lunchboxes. Her mother's passion for healthy food and lifestyle had been the driving force behind starting the Health Hut. She had just got lost for a while once the business became a success, before finding her true self later in life. While Erin might not understand this new version of her mother, she didn't doubt her mother loved her. It was just hard having to wait in line for her attention.

Jamie appeared beside her, carrying two cups of coffee. Erin smiled her thanks and took one. 'Funerals tend to bring out the gentleman in you, I see,' she said over the top of her cup.

'I've always been a gentleman,' he corrected her. 'I just don't like people knowing about it. Ruins my reputation,' he added with a wink.

Erin gave a soft snort of disbelief. 'Yeah, right.'

Across the room, Erin saw that her mother was now talking with Jamie's father and giggling like a schoolgirl. Giggling! *Her* mother?

'Uh-oh,' Jamie's low warning came as his mother made a beeline for her husband from across the other side of the hall.

'What?'

'We better go intervene.'

'My mother's harmless, really,' she said.

'Yeah, well mine's not.'

'What? Why?' she asked as she followed Jamie, confused.

'Because of their history,' he said, turning to look at her, before frowning. 'You knew your mother and my old man dated when they were younger, didn't you?'

'*My* mother?' she said, stopping short.

'Yeah. Why do you think my mum can't stand her?'

She'd never really thought about it. She knew the two women had never been particularly friendly, but she'd never known *why*. 'Well. I guess that explains a few things,' she muttered.

'You're looking well, Irene,' Erin heard Pat say politely as she snaked her arm through her husband's and smiled.

'It's Serenity, and thank you, Patricia.'

'Oh, that's right, I'd forgotten you'd gone and changed your name.'

Erin saw her mother's smile tighten a little at that, but she continued to smile calmly, living up to her new name.

'It's been a while since we've seen you back here.'

'My retreat and wildlife foundation keep me very busy.'

'Apparently,' Pat sniffed, dusting an imaginary piece of lint off the front of her husband's shirt.

Tension, thick and heavy, hovered over the small group.

Erin stopped a lady with a tray of sandwiches, waving her over hastily. 'Sandwich anyone? Mum?'

'You know I don't eat meat.'

'I think there's some egg and lettuce ones,' said the lady bearing the tray.

'I'm a vegan,' her mother replied curtly.

'What does that mean?' Pat asked.

'It means I don't eat anything animal derived.'

'Animal derived? So what do you eat?'

'Grains, legumes, vegetables . . . fruits.'

'You sound more like a cow than a person,' Pat chuckled.

'I choose to live a lifestyle that doesn't cause animal suffering.'

Erin winced. They were standing in a hall full of farming families.

'Suffering,' Pat scoffed. 'I can't tell you how sick I am of hearing everyone jumping up and down about Australian farmers and how cruel we all are. It would be nice if just once some of these people actually came to a farm and had a look for themselves at how terribly our livestock are *suffering*,' she snapped, 'instead of blindly believing everything they hear in the media. Our livelihood depends on the quality of our stock, no one in their right mind would ever do anything to cause stress and harm to their animals.'

'I don't agree with any industry that kills animals for meat.'

'Our industry supports Australian jobs and livelihoods right across the country,' Pat said, folding her arms across her chest.

'I simply choose not to support that way of life.'

'So how's things up in Nimbin?' Neville cut in quickly, and Erin breathed a silent sigh of relief.

'Beautiful,' her mother said, smiling at Jamie's father. 'You should come and visit my retreat. It would do you both the world of good.'

Pat gave a small snort. 'Oh, yeah, I can see the two of us in a hippie commune.'

'It's not a commune,' her mother explained, pointedly ignoring the other woman's sarcasm. 'It's a place where groups of similar-minded people come to focus and revitalise their lives. You might have more in common with my guests than you realise.'

'I doubt it,' Pat said.

'Many of them earn their living as farmers.'

'Not in beef, I take it?' Neville added with a slight grin.

'No, not in beef,' her mother said, and Erin was surprised by the gentle look the two shared. Pat also caught the under-tones of something and straightened next to her husband.

'I think it's time we were heading home,' she said briskly.

'No rest for the wicked,' Neville agreed affably.

'It was very nice seeing you again after all this time, Neville,' her mother said quietly, before nodding to Jamie's mother. 'Patricia.'

Patricia ignored her mother's farewell, turning instead to Erin and hugging her briefly. 'I'll see you soon?'

'Yes, I'll drop by tomorrow,' Erin promised.

'I think I had better head off too. It'll be late enough already by the time I get home,' added Irene.

'Why don't you just stay tonight and start off early tomorrow?' Erin suggested.

'No, I need to be back tomorrow morning to catch the sunrise,' her mother dismissed.

Of course. How silly of me. The sunrise. It's not like it happens every day, she thought sarcastically.

'We can give you a lift back to Tallowood, we're heading that way anyway,' Neville offered.

'That would be lovely, thank you, Neville.'

Patricia was clearly not keen on the idea, but she restrained herself from protesting.

'Goodbye, darling,' her mother said, kissing Erin soundly on the cheek and hugging her briefly.

'Bye, Mum.' As she watched the trio walk away, she felt a strange lurch that felt a lot like abandonment. She quickly pushed aside the feeling and reminded herself she was a grown woman, not a five-year-old watching her mother leave her on the first day of school.

'Okay?' Jamie's deep voice cut into her thoughts and she managed a faint smile.

'Yeah.'

'I think this thing's wrapping up.'

Erin noticed people beginning to follow her mother's lead and she straightened her shoulders as a couple she knew approached to say their goodbyes. Twenty minutes later, the hall was all but empty, with only the church committee women remaining behind to clean up. After making a donation to the church and saying a heartfelt thankyou to the women for making her gran's send-off so lovely, Erin allowed Jamie to lead her back to his vehicle and drive her home.

Thirty

They pulled up outside the house and Erin saw that her mother's car was gone. She'd been hoping her mother might have changed her mind and decided to stay a while, but it seemed whatever happened at Tallowood was still too painful for her mother to stay and face. Or perhaps Erin was just being overly dramatic. Maybe her mother had simply moved on and had no feelings whatsoever about Tallowood. The one thing she *did* know for certain, if her mother didn't want to talk about it, there was no way Erin was ever going to understand it. She reached out to open the door but paused. 'You know what I feel like?'

'I have no idea,' Jamie answered, eyeing her with an amused smirk.

'A homemade hamburger.'

'I take it red meat was off the menu while your mother was here?'

'*Everything* was off the menu. Come on, those little sandwiches wouldn't have even touched the sides with you.'

'You twisted my arm,' he said, opening his door and following her inside.

Erin left him and went to change out of her heels and simple black dress and into a pair of jeans and a T-shirt. She wriggled her toes in the carpet and sighed in relief. She'd never been a shoe person, usually kicking them off the moment she came inside.

In the kitchen, she reached into the back of the fridge and pulled out the wrapped mince she'd disguised to avoid a lengthy lecture on the evils of eating the flesh of God's creatures. It needed using and she'd been dreaming of a juicy hamburger ever since last night's meal of lentil patties.

Mixing the meat, herbs, spices and breadcrumbs together, she made up a plate of hamburger patties and handed them to Jamie to cook out on the verandah. He'd taken his suit jacket off, hanging it on the back of the chair, and rolled up the sleeves of his dress shirt. She took out two wineglasses from her gran's china cabinet and smiled. The small glass-fronted cabinet held a treasure trove of small crystal animals her gran had collected, many of them birthday and Christmas gifts from Erin over the years.

By the time the meat was cooked, she had the buns and salad ready and they carried it all outside to eat.

'I wonder why I never knew about my mum's history with your dad?' Erin said as she watched Jamie devour his burger.

'I don't think it was anything too serious. They just grew up together.'

'Your mum must think it was fairly serious. She really doesn't like her, does she?' Erin said with a shake of her head.

'Mum's always been a pretty opinionated woman,' he said, smiling. 'I think it's more of a personality clash.'

Erin looked thoughtful. 'I can't imagine my mother and your dad together. They're so . . . different.'

'Maybe she was less "out there" when she was younger?'

'Maybe.' She wondered what her mother had been like as a teenager. From the snippets she'd heard over the years, she knew she'd been something of a rebel or, as Gran sometimes said, 'a bit of a handful'. She knew she'd always clashed with her father. Erin felt sad for her grandmother, caught between her husband and her daughter. What had happened? How had things gotten so bad? Why couldn't she have had a family like the McBrides? They argued all the time, but they never stopped talking or gave up on each other. What was wrong with her family?

As she and Jamie cleared the table and stacked the plates into the sink, Erin found herself enjoying the quiet way they worked together. Somehow over the last few days she'd begun to let down her guard with Jamie. There was still an undercurrent that flowed between them, or at the very least it did on her part. It was hard to tell with Jamie. He'd been baiting her for so long, she sometimes wondered if maybe for him it was just a habit.

She looked at him as he washed the dishes, her eyes following the cut of the dress shirt across his broad shoulders, and tried to ignore the stab of awareness. The sink was an old-fashioned one with a single basin, which left little room for two people standing side by side to wash and dry dishes, and his arm brushed hers as he reached across to sit the plates in the dish drainer.

She felt his gaze on her but couldn't meet it with her own. She held her breath as he turned slightly, then she felt his thumb lightly brushing against her cheek, and her eyes darted to his at the unexpected touch.

He held up a small clump of foam from the suds in the sink. Her heart was beating faster and for some strange reason she could not make herself drag her gaze away from his. She wasn't sure how long they stood there, but when he lowered his head she felt the warmth of his breath against the side of her neck and goose bumps broke out across her arms. For the briefest of moments she leaned into him, her body craving his touch. Feeling her reaction, his arms slipped around her waist and he increased the pressure of his lips against the soft skin of her neck, drawing a small moan from Erin that shocked her enough to break away from his embrace.

'Erin,' Jamie started, but she stepped back.

'It's been a really emotional day.'

'What's that got to do with anything?'

'It's probably why . . .' She faltered a little as he pinned her with a heated look that made her lose track of what she'd been about to say. Clearing her throat, she hung up the tea towel. 'Just leave the rest, I'll do them later.'

'It's still there,' he said quietly.

'What is?' she asked, although part of her already knew what he was talking about.

'What we had before. It's still there.'

'I buried my grandmother today, Jamie, this is not the time—'

'You know as well as I do she would be the first person to give us her blessing if we jumped into bed right now,' he said.

Erin gaped at him as an image flashed through her mind of her grandmother ushering them into Erin's bedroom. She quickly tried to *unimagine* it. '*No one* is jumping into anyone's bed,' she said curtly.

'Why?'

'Excuse me?'

'Why are you fighting it? What's the big deal? You're not married any more.'

'I am married.' *Technically anyway*, she added in her head.

'Until the divorce goes through,' he replied. 'You're running out of excuses, Erin.'

'I don't need an excuse. Is it so hard to accept that maybe I'm just not interested in sleeping with you?'

'If that were true, I'd accept it, but we both know it's not, don't we?' He cocked one eyebrow in challenge.

He's got you there, a little voice chortled in the back of her mind, sounding suspiciously like Gran. She shook her head quickly to dismiss it. Damn Jamie for bringing her grandmother into this.

'Come on, let's get out of here,' Jamie said, surprising her with his sudden change of tack.

'What? Where?'

Her protest seemed to fall on deaf ears as he just shook his head and pointed to her feet. 'Get some shoes on.'

'But—'

'Shoes.'

Grumbling, she walked to the back door and slipped on the canvas shoes she'd kicked off there yesterday. At least going somewhere would distract him from their previous conversation. 'Fine. Shoes are on. Now what?'

He didn't bother replying, just gave her a mysterious smile and took her hand, leading her out to his ute.

'But I haven't locked the house,' she protested.

'It'll be fine, we're not going far.'

Opening the passenger door, he waited until she was settled in the seat before shutting the door firmly and going around to the driver's seat.

'Where are we going?' Erin asked after they pulled out onto the road and headed in the opposite direction to town.

'Do you have to know everything? Can't you just for once sit back and just stop thinking?'

Well, maybe if she wasn't being whisked away by a man who threw her into a spin whenever he came within ten feet of her, maybe she would be able to stop thinking.

Giving up on getting any answers, Erin looked out her window instead and watched the farmland roll by. It really was pretty; the further out you drove, the smaller you felt, dwarfed by the large rolling hills. They turned off the road and drove along a dirt track that wove in through pockets of uncleared bushland, past fat, lazily chewing cattle who looked up at them with bored expressions.

All too suddenly their destination became clear and she saw a slow grin spread across Jamie's face when he realised she'd worked it out.

Thirty-one

Was he crazy? It had been years since she'd been here. Too many years. She closed her eyes briefly as memories clambered over the top of each other. Hot summer days and long lazy hours of lying in the sun making plans about big futures.

They pulled up and Erin stared out at the view before her.

'You remember this place?' Jamie asked quietly.

She didn't trust her voice to answer but gave a slight nod. Remember? Did he think she could forget something like that? You simply did not forget the place where you lost your virginity. 'It's changed a bit,' she managed when he didn't say anything else.

'Floods eat away at the banks over the years, and I guess there's not that many teens around to come down and keep it cleared.'

Lantana grew wild, choking the undergrowth and covering all the way down to the creek in places. The wide, white pebbled beach on which they'd built campfires to cook damper and toast marshmallows was gone; only a narrow dirt track down the riverbank leading straight into the water below remained.

It was still beautiful though. Silent, too, except for the sound of trickling water and the odd cow mooing in the distance. Erin closed her eyes and dropped her head back against the headrest. She'd missed this. She hadn't even been aware how much until this moment. Being back here caused an ache deep inside her soul. This place held some of her most precious memories; it represented a time in her life when she had been at her happiest—those few short years on the brink of leaving childhood behind forever and venturing into the world of adults.

'Come on,' Jamie said to her as he got out of the ute.

Erin reluctantly pushed her door open and slid out, then followed him to the edge of the bank.

He spread out a blanket and took her hand as she sat down, then sat down himself, stretching out his long legs, crossing them at the heels and bracing his weight on one elbow as his gaze wandered lazily over her face.

'I still come here sometimes, you know,' he said, breaking the silence.

'It's a great swimming hole,' she said, looking out over the gently swirling water.

'Not to swim, I come here to think.'

'Oh. Well, I imagine it's a good place for that too,' she said.

'I've made some of my biggest decisions here,' he went on, dropping his gaze to the grass. 'I come here because everywhere I look reminds me of you.'

Erin swallowed nervously. She felt the same. When she looked at the big tree with its massive draped branches hanging over the water, she remembered him at nineteen, showing off and swinging from the old rope. It was still there, broken and rotted now, strands blowing gently in the breeze.

She looked at the patch of green grass below the tree and instantly recalled sun-warmed skin against her own, the smell of coconut-scented sunscreen and long, hungry kisses. God, she'd been so madly in love with that nineteen-year-old Jamie. Totally, madly, insanely in love. She'd been seventeen and he'd been her older, far more experienced first love. That whole Christmas holidays they'd spent every spare second they could find together until it was time for her to go back home and start the last year of high school.

They'd called often and she'd tried her best to get back to Gran's to visit, but hadn't been able to manage more than a weekend here and there. She should have realised that long-distance teenage romances were doomed, but she hadn't given up. The phone calls had eventually grown few and far between, but she still hadn't stop believing. Not until she'd arrived at Gran's, having just turned eighteen, with a brand-new driver's licence, planning to surprise him and spend two whole weeks together. Only she'd been the one surprised when she'd dropped by the McBride house to discover Jamie was out and had gone down to the pub to find him.

She'd swung into the car park and, with headlights still on high beam, she'd caught him, quite literally like the proverbial kangaroo in the spotlight, pressed up against Vanessa, the pair making out like two crazy people in the car park. Thankfully, in the darkness of her car, they hadn't been able to see her, and she'd quickly reversed and driven back to Gran's, shaking like a leaf and devastated.

She'd left a note the next day under the wiper blade on his windscreen on her way back to the city. She'd ignored his calls, and even when he'd resorted to enlisting Gran to pass on messages, she'd refused to speak with him. She'd learned the hard way that summer romances are a double-edged sword—with all the beauty comes pain. They have to end, and it would have been better to have ended it when she said goodbye at the end of summer than to drag it out and nurture dreams that would never have had a chance to eventuate. Of course, over time she'd moved on, but she'd never forgotten.

Faced with a divorce, she really shouldn't be remembering a teenage broken heart, but it suddenly struck her that despite the hurt Phillip's betrayal had caused, the memory of Jamie's hurt so much more. How could that be? They'd been teenagers. *Kids.* Her grown-up marriage to a grown-up man should outweigh the hurt a thousandfold . . . shouldn't it?

'Good times,' she finally said.

'That night—'

Erin cut him off quickly. 'No. I don't want to talk about it. Seriously, it was a lifetime ago.'

'I screwed up, Erin. I had no excuse, I was drunk. She was there. I should have known better.'

'You were a kid,' she replied.

'I was almost twenty and I should have known better. I was missing you so damn much that most weekends I usually forgot about it by getting plastered. It was the only thing that helped. That was the first time I'd ever cheated on you, though. I swear it. I know it doesn't make any difference. I just wanted you to know that I wasn't here screwing around on you all that time. I was in love with you.' He lowered his gaze. 'It's probably stupid, but it's always bugged me. I've wanted to tell you, but it's just never been the right time.'

A lone bird called to its mate high above in a tree and the wind blew gently through the leaves. 'I guess I didn't make it easy for you to tell me.'

'You were pretty good at avoiding me,' he agreed. 'Your gran was the one who helped me put in perspective though. Did you know that?'

Erin shook her head.

'She called me inside one day and sat me down at her kitchen table with a cup of tea and told me straight out I was an idiot.'

'She did?'

'Yep. But after that, she said that sometimes life has to take its course, just like the creek. She told me that I had to be patient, and if it was meant to be, then it would be. It didn't matter what hurdles were thrown in our path, that if it was destiny then it would happen one day.'

'Gran said that?'

'She sure did. I don't know if it was just wishful thinking on my part, but it gave me the kick in the pants I needed. Don't get me wrong,' he added quickly. 'I didn't sit at home and twiddle my thumbs, waiting for the day you came to your senses,' he grinned. 'I stopped moping around and I got on with my life. Maybe she was just saying it to make me feel better, but it worked. In the back of my mind, I never stopped believing it.'

Erin wasn't sure what to say.

'But when you married that . . . married *Phillip*,' he amended with a slight growl, 'I pretty much gave up hoping. But your gran didn't.'

Erin frowned at that. She thought back to her wedding day and remembered Gran being supportive and happy, but now that she thought about it, she hadn't exactly said much. Had she seen something in Phillip that Erin hadn't? Had she somehow known it wouldn't last? Why wouldn't she have said something?

Would you have listened? came a little voice.

Probably not, she had to concede.

Gran's advice had always been given gently and almost without sounding like advice at all. She had a way of putting things into perspective. Those cool, soft hands, withered with age but still offering so much comfort. Erin felt the prick of tears sting her eyes at the memory. She could almost feel Gran's hands now, placed against her cheek, assuring her everything would work out.

It didn't feel like everything was working out. 'I feel like I've completely failed,' she admitted quietly.

'Because of your divorce?'

'Because I thought I was enough. I wasn't.'

'Then he's a bigger fool than even *I* thought,' Jamie said, ducking his head to get her to look at him. 'He had to be to give you up.'

Erin shook her head sadly. 'He just wanted what every man wants. And I couldn't give it to him. I guess I can't really blame him . . . except that I thought he was different. I thought he truly believed it when he told me he didn't want children.'

'That's why he left? Because you can't have kids?'

Erin nodded, but didn't look at him.

'And he *told* you that?' he asked not bothering to hide his incredulity.

'Yes, although the pregnant girlfriend would have been a pretty big clue anyway.'

'He got some other woman pregnant? While he was married to you?'

Erin did look up at him then. His voice had risen an octave and she could see the veins in his neck standing out.

'That prick had better not show his face around here any time soon,' he muttered. 'I can't believe it took you this long to see through that bastard.' He got to his feet and walked to the edge of the creek.

'Gee thanks, that's just what I needed to hear,' she snapped, also getting to her feet, but storming off in the opposite direction. She walked along the creek bank until lantana grew too thick to continue.

'Erin. Wait,' Jamie called from behind her.

She turned reluctantly, waiting for him to catch up, half expecting him to launch into a new tirade.

'Sorry. I didn't meant for that to come out the way it did. I just can't believe he'd do something like that.'

'Yeah, well, that makes two of us,' she said wearily, all the fight leaving her. 'It's not the end of the world, it's just been a lot to deal with on top of everything with Gran. I'll be fine.'

'You will be, you know,' he agreed, holding her reluctant gaze. 'You're like your gran. Tougher than you look.'

She smiled a little at that, grateful for his attempt to reassure her. 'Sometimes I don't feel all that tough.'

Slowly he took a step towards her and Erin caught her breath, wondering what he was going to do. He raised his hand and cupped her cheek, watching her carefully as though he expected at any minute she would run. *That's what I should do*, she told herself sternly, but another part, the part that longed for someone to hold her and tell her everything was going to be all right, held her firmly in place.

He waited for her to object and, when she didn't, moved a little closer and this time he didn't stop until his lips touched hers, gently at first, before deepening and pulling her tightly against his body.

What started out as comfort soon became urgency. It was as if he'd flicked an invisible switch and her body instantly responded, as though recognising some long-forgotten part of herself. It wasn't like kissing a stranger, even though that's practically what they were after all these years. There was something familiar, as though they'd never been apart.

Jamie pulled away to gaze down at her, looking almost as dazed as she was feeling. 'Holy crap,' he whispered.

Yep, that pretty much summed it up, she thought, trying to catch her breath. 'We should probably get back.'

'We're not kids any more, Erin. We don't *have* to get back to anything.'

'I was going to say,' she told him calmly, 'we should get back, because if you think I'm going to continue making out with you out *here* like a horny teenager, you're in for a big shock.'

His smile spread slowly as her words sunk in. 'You think I'm that easy? That I'm just going to let you have your way with me? What kind of guy do you think I am?'

'You probably don't want me to answer that.'

'I'm not just a slab of meat to be used for your enjoyment, you know,' he said as he walked with her back to his ute.

'Right,' she agreed. 'Though I notice you're almost breaking both our necks to get home.'

'I'm not easy but I'm not stupid either. I don't want to give you time to change your mind,' he replied, smiling as he opened her door.

Thirty-two

When they pulled up at her gran's house, Erin felt a bubble of joy as Jamie met her at the back of the car and pulled her against him in a deep, heady kiss. They'd barely made it onto the verandah and inside the front door before he began unbuttoning his shirt, never lifting his lips from hers as he did so.

Erin let out a painful gasp as her hip connected with the kitchen bench as she walked backwards, but she didn't stop to rub it. Jamie's kisses were burning liquid desire through her veins.

She tried not to think how long it had been since she'd felt this kind of fervent yearning. She remembered attraction with other men before Phillip, and while Phillip himself had been a generous and satisfying lover, she didn't recall ever feeling this out-of-control urgency with anyone else. In fact, the last time she had felt anything similar had been when she'd been a teenager . . . with Jamie.

They bumped into the hallway wall, and kicked toes on tables and bedposts, until eventually Erin felt the edge of the mattress behind her thighs. *We're both going to be covered in bruises after this*, she thought vaguely, but then lost all cognitive ability completely when Jamie's warm hands moved to the button of her jeans and slowly began sliding them down over her hips.

She allowed him to gently lower her onto the bed, watching him stand before her and remove the remainder of his clothing before helping with hers and lowering to brace himself on strong arms above her.

For a moment they didn't move. Erin watched as his gaze roamed her face, throat and breasts, before he swallowed hard and lifted his gaze once more to meet hers. The intensity of his expression sent a quiver of longing through her already inflamed body. Gone was the gentle teasing, in its place was hot, burning lust, and this Jamie was not the *boy* who had once been her lover. He was a man.

Slowly he lowered his head and kissed her. Unlike the previous kisses, desperate and needy, this one was slow and deep, plunging and pulling at her very core until she was left a hot, withering mess and desperate for more of him.

She wanted to trace every delicious inch of his hard body, and take her time discovering this new, mature version of the boy she'd once known, but she'd been too long without the touch of a man, too long without feeling desired and wanted. There was no time for slow and thorough. She needed hard and fast. Threading her hands through his short hair, she pulled his face down to meet hers. That one sizzling look was all he needed to get the message. When he slid inside her, Erin arched her back and took what he gave with greedy abandon. She didn't want to think any more, only to *feel*, to allow Jamie to take her away from everything for just a little while. To lose herself in the heady sensation of falling over the edge of a giant cliff.

⁓

It was late afternoon and shadows were falling across the hills in the distance. Erin stared out through the window from bed. Beside her Jamie lay on his back, one arm thrown across his eyes, appearing to be taking a well-earned nap.

Erin fought back a small gurgle of disbelief. It seemed more than a little surreal to find her adult self lying next to the boy she'd loved all those years ago. Although there was nothing boyish about him, she had to concede as she took in his masculine form.

She itched to reach out and run her hands across his warm skin, to explore his strange yet familiar body. At nineteen, he'd seemed like a man to her, so different to the boys she went to school with. There was something about him back then . . . Maybe country boys developed faster than city boys. Maybe those two years of maturity he had on her really did make a difference. While she'd been in her final year of high school, he'd been out working on his dad's property: a working man.

God, she thought, feeling melancholy, *at seventeen I didn't stand a chance.*

'You're thinking too loud,' he muttered.

Erin smiled at his drowsy voice. It was rare that she'd ever heard him so relaxed. 'Sorry. Go back to sleep.'

'I wasn't sleeping. I was recovering,' he groaned. 'You wore me out, woman.'

She gave a small snort. 'Wow, I thought you had more stamina than that.'

He moved faster than she'd expected. One minute he was on his back, the next he was above her, pinning her to the mattress. He swallowed her gasp as warm lips covered her own, silencing further comment.

'I'm sorry I ever doubted your stamina,' Erin demurred when he finally lifted his head, eyeing her with a satisfied grin.

'That's better,' he said, lowering his head to nuzzle her ear. 'You are a bad influence.'

'Me? What did I do?'

'You're keeping me in bed all afternoon.'

'I'm not keeping you here,' she said, smiling as she ran her fingernails along the smooth, warm skin of his back and grinning when she felt a quiver run through his body. The low groan that followed wiped the smile from her face and a primal response overtook her.

Later, as they lay side by side breathing heavily, Jamie turned his head on the pillow to face her. 'You were saying?'

Erin gave a weary chuckle before throwing back the cover and reaching for his shirt on the floor. 'I'm not saying a thing. You're far too easily corrupted. I'm getting us something to eat to replenish our energy.'

'Good thinking,' he nodded, reluctantly letting the hand slip away that had automatically reached for her when she'd moved to get out of bed. 'We're going to need it. We've got a lot of catching up to do.'

'Oh, really?' Erin said lifting an eyebrow. 'That's pretty ambitious. You're not exactly nineteen any more.'

'Are you saying I'm too old? Is that doubt I hear in your tone, young lady?'

Erin chuckled as she backed away from the bed. 'No. No. I promise, I'm not doubting your prowess. Silly me,' she grinned and left the room.

Later, after they finished the bacon and egg sandwiches she'd hastily thrown together, Erin's gaze fell on the wardrobe across the room. 'I want to show you something,' she said, sliding from the bed.

Jamie grinned and folded his arms behind his head, his biceps bulging rather attractively. 'I think I've seen just about everything, not that I'm complaining. In fact, I don't think I'll ever get tired of seeing your *something*.'

'Will you stop thinking about sex for one minute?'

'A whole minute? I dunno . . . that's a pretty big stretch.'

Erin shook her head as she crossed to unzip her suitcase and take out the tin box.

'What's that?'

'*Something*,' she told him drolly.

He faked a disappointed sigh before pushing himself further up against the headboard.

Erin dragged her gaze away from the sheet that had slipped rather low on his hips and forced herself to focus on what she'd wanted to show him. She prised off the lid and withdrew the photos, handing them to Jamie. 'I found this box in Gran's wardrobe. It's full of stuff from around the time she was in Townsville, during the war.'

'Oh, man, no problem working out which one she is,' he said, looking at the group photo on the beach. 'It could be you in this photo.' He turned it around, pointing at the smiling woman in the image.

'You think?' Personally she didn't see the resemblance, other than the dark hair maybe, but it was hard to tell what colour it was exactly, since the photo was in black and white.

'You're the spitting image of her back then. So who are the Yanks she's with?' he asked, turning his attention to the men in uniform.

'I'm not sure. But I think the man she's with is this Jimmy guy.' She leaned over and leafed through the rest of the photos he was holding until she found the one she was looking for. The man with the easy smile and good looks stared back at them.

Jamie put the two photos side by side and compared the men. 'Yeah, it's definitely him. So Gran was pretty hot stuff back in the day, huh?' He wiggled his eyebrows suggestively.

Erin bit back her grin and levelled a stern look at him. 'It would be rather cool, if there wasn't this weird niggle in the back of my mind telling me something is wrong with this whole picture.'

'What do you mean?'

'I'm positive Gran was engaged to Pop before he went away to fight. But everything in this tin suggests otherwise.'

'So your gran was, what? Eighteen? Nineteen here? So she had a bit of fun. Can't blame her. There was a war going on. She wouldn't have been the first to have a fling with a Yank.'

'It's not that, exactly.' Although she had to say the thought of her gran having cheated on her pop was a little hard to imagine when they'd been married for so long. 'When Gran was in the nursing home, she started reminiscing. She kept mentioning Jimmy and Dolly and a whole heap of names of people I'd never heard of before. It wasn't until I found that,' she nodded down at the tin box, 'that I realised these people had been important to her. You should have heard her talking about them. Her eyes lit up and she had this *smile*,' Erin said softly, unable to put into words how beautiful it had been. 'And then I found this.' She took out the ring and dropped it into Jamie's hand.

She watched as he turned it around and read the inside inscription. 'US Air Force. It looks kinda valuable.'

'I know. So why would Gran have it? It's not something a person would give lightly. It was from his family.'

'I don't know. Maybe it *was* serious.'

'I can't help but wonder what happened. I've read through the letters, a few from girlfriends in other places, but they're mostly from Pop, and they don't mention anything too personal, or say anything about when they'd get married, but they're dated around the same time as these photos were taken, judging by what's written on the back.'

'Does it matter? It happened a long time ago. Your gran lived a hell of a long time, but she was the exception to the rule and there's not much chance anyone else from then is still around.'

'I think I'm going to try to track this guy down. He may not still be alive, but I think his family should have this back,' she said, taking the ring from Jamie and turning it so the ruby caught the light and burst into a kaleidoscope of colour.

'Might be a good idea. You could probably use a bit of a distraction after everything else that's been going on lately. Although,' he said, taking the ring and placing it back in the tin along with the photos, 'I've been known to come up with some pretty good distractions myself.' He ran a hand up her thigh and smiled as he felt the slight tremor that ran through her at his touch.

'Oh, I *know* just how distracting you can be,' she said, relaxing into his gentle stroking.

'What can I say? It's a gift.'

Who was she to knock back a gift? She smiled as he lowered his head and all thoughts of mysterious strangers vanished from her mind.

Thirty-three

Life had taken on a strange kind of normal after the funeral. Jamie had stayed the first night, leaving early in the morning to start work, and had spent every night since with her. It wasn't an unpleasant turn of events, but it was definitely throwing her a curve ball.

She wasn't game to try to define their relationship. Each time she tried she felt herself beginning to panic. What was she doing? Her husband had left her less than four weeks earlier.

There was no denying the feelings she'd had for Jamie as a teen were still there, but did that mean they should be reliving the whole affair? What if they were just remnants of a past love? What if she was confusing the boy he was back then and the man he was now? What if he was doing the same with her? They'd both changed so much.

This was clearly some kind of rebound thing. Her pride was hurt, she felt betrayed and her confidence had taken a solid knock, it was just natural that a guy like Jamie, a natural charmer who knew all the right buttons to push, would be a logical safety net. With her emotions so frazzled, she'd had little hope of resisting a good-looking man who was offering a little comfort and some mighty fine sex to boot.

She had to admit he'd sounded pretty believable when he'd confessed about his and Gran's little talk, though . . . But surely he hadn't been secretly pining away all this time, waiting and biding his time on the off-chance that she and Phillip wouldn't last? He was a virile man in the prime of his adult life, he could have any woman he wanted; why would he waste his time waiting on her? *And he doesn't do commitment, remember?* a little voice reminded her.

Erin pushed away that train of thought. It just made her head hurt throwing around all the what-ifs and whys. It would probably fizzle out in due course. Maybe after he realised they weren't the same two people they were back then. And if that happened, she was prepared. At least it wouldn't catch her unaware this time.

She made a few phone calls to the office and did a couple of hours' work on the computer before closing down the spreadsheets and bringing up her search engine. She stared at the search box before her and thought about what to type. She only had a first name to go on; that wasn't going to be much help.

Dragging the box across the table towards her, she opened it and idly went through the photos once more. She needed to think like a detective. If she could find some kind of information, a place to start, she was confident she could figure this out. But *where* to start, that was the question.

She pulled out the one with Jimmy and the plane. Behind him, a 1940s pin-up girl sat in a provocative pose. The name, *French Quarter,* could be seen on the fuselage on the front side, slightly below the pilot's window. She'd seen similar artwork on planes in old black and white war movies.

Erin put the photo down and quickly typed the words 'French Quarter' into the search engine, along with 'World War Two'. The search turned up numerous pages on New Orleans. She hit the images box, and along with pictures of the beautiful terraced architecture of Bourbon Street came some images of World War Two vehicles in a military museum.

Erin scrolled down the page and stopped as two images of a beautiful redhead dressed in skimpy green shorts, high heels and tight T-shirt came up. They were exactly the same as the one in the photo. She lifted the image to hold alongside the screen and compared the two to make sure. The first image on the computer took her to the website of the war museum in New Orleans. There on display was a plane that looked exactly like the one in her photo. Surely it was too much of a coincidence? She went back to the other image and found that this took her to a page with a photo gallery of multiple other aircraft with noses decorated with artwork, including the *French Quarter.* Excitement began to creep through her as she followed links and read up on the history of the aircraft.

The plane was a B-25 Mitchell aircraft and a member of the 345 bomber group involved in operations throughout the Pacific and during World War Two. Its crew had primarily consisted of men from Louisiana, who had named the aircraft in honour of their home state. Erin sat back in her chair and studied the photo on the screen thoughtfully. Was it the same plane? It certainly looked like it.

From her reading it seemed that a pilot or crew could put whatever they wanted on their aircraft, and that although images of semi-clad women were not endorsed by the air force, they were overlooked because they were said to boost morale amongst the men. But if the men name the aircraft themselves, were the names of the planes recorded officially? What were the chances of two aircraft being given the same name and having the same image painted on the fuselage?

Even if it was the same plane, how was she now going to use that to find Jimmy? She decided to type in the bomber group number and see if that gave her any more information. It did. There were Wikipedia pages, online shops, reunion groups, history information, the list went on; pages and pages of information.

As she opened one of the pages on the history of the unit one sentence caught her eye. *The unit arrived in Australia in August 1943 to be modified* . . . and not just anywhere in Australia, in *Townsville, Queensland.* She grabbed the photo and turned it over, and sure enough the date corresponded with the time frame. A tingle of excitement rippled through her. Had Jimmy been part of this unit? She had to consider the possibility that he could have just been posing in front of that plane and had nothing whatsoever to do with the group. If that were the case she might never find any leads to help her track him down.

Her ringing mobile interrupted her research and she quickly bookmarked the pages she'd found to return to later.

'Hi, chicky,' Roxy's voice greeted her.

'Hey yourself. Did you get that email I sent through earlier?'

'Sure did. I'm at lunch and just thought I'd give you a call. You've been quiet lately. I was worried something might have gobbled you up out there in the back of beyond. When are you returning to civilisation?'

Erin smiled slightly at her friend's concern. 'Nope, still in one piece. I don't know when I'll be back. I really like it out here.'

'You can't hide forever, you know,' Roxy pointed out.

'I'm not hiding,' she protested, but they both knew there was some truth in Roxy's warning. 'I forgot how nice it was. How quiet.'

'But I miss you, and I have no one to go shopping with,' Roxy said with a pout in her voice.

'You should come out and visit,' Erin said, packing up her paperwork which was laid out on the table.

'No offence, babe, but it sounds really boring. Are there any shops? Any hunky country men in tight Wranglers and no shirts?'

'I hate to break it to you, but I haven't seen any bare-chested guys strutting around here in jeans and riding chaps.' *Well, if you didn't include Jamie*, she added silently. Although there hadn't been any chaps involved.

'Then there's nothing much out there for me, is there?' she said.

The screen door banged shut. 'Honey, I'm home,' Jamie's deep voice called out playfully, moments before he entered the room.

'Who's that?' Roxy asked suspiciously.

'No one,' Erin said hastily. 'I gotta go.'

'Wait!' Roxy said loudly and Erin groaned. '*Honey? Have you got yourself a bit of fluff on the side?*' her friend demanded.

Bit of fluff on the side? Erin rolled her eyes at the outrageousness of the thought. There was nothing fluffy about the man who was now leaning against the doorway, one hand braced above his head on the doorframe. Erin's eyes traced the outline of his chest under the soft cloth of his T-shirt and swallowed hard when she reached the hem which had risen up to expose his abdomen and a trail of dark hair that disappeared beneath the button of his jeans.

'I gotta go, Rox,' she murmured, suddenly remembering her friend was still on the other end of the line and disconnecting the call.

'No one?' he asked, watching her.

'Trust me, you do not want Roxy getting wind of your presence.'

'Are you keeping me a secret, then?'

'No.' Secret was going a tad far, but she didn't really want to have to start explaining their relationship to anyone just yet. She wasn't sure why, maybe because she hadn't figured out how to explain it to herself.

Her phone beeped a message and Erin ignored it, standing up to greet him. 'I didn't think you'd be finished in time for lunch.'

'Neither did I, but things went smoothly for a change,' he said, coming across to slip his arms around her waist and kiss her.

Erin felt her bones turn to jelly and was helpless to fight her body's reaction to this man. He had always been a good kisser, even in his teens.

The phone beeped again and Jamie pulled away. Erin felt his deep chuckle and followed his gaze to where the screen of her phone was lit up and a photo of a sexy, bare-chested man wearing a cowboy hat and carrying a saddle over one huge shoulder stared back at her. *Does he look like this?!* was written beneath it and Erin groaned.

Another text followed with a sign saying, Keep Calm and Do a Cowboy.

'I think I like this friend of yours,' Jamie grinned.

'Just ignore her, her lunch hour will be up soon and she'll have to get back to work, *or I'll fire her,*' she added under her breath. 'Want me to make you a sandwich?' she asked, pulling from his arms and heading into the kitchen.

'That would be great, I'm starving.'

Erin gathered what she needed from the fridge and placed everything on the benchtop.

'Seriously, though,' Jamie said as he rested one hip against the sink. 'Do you have a problem with us?'

Erin concentrated hard on putting together the sandwich and tried not to squirm beneath his probing gaze.

'I just . . . I don't even know what it is . . . there's no point announcing it to the world when . . .'

'When what?' he asked, narrowing his gaze.

'Well, it's not like Mr Sow His Wild Oats, most eligible bachelor of Tuendoc, is suddenly off the market just because we've hooked up for a while, is it?'

She was trying to be light-hearted but she knew as soon as the words came out that they were wrong. His jaw clenched tightly for a minute, then he pushed away from the sink and walked around her, heading for the door.

'Where are you going?' she called after him.

'Don't worry about lunch, I've got work to do. Sowin' more oats and stuff,' he added just before the screen door slammed behind him.

Erin stared down at the food on the bench sightlessly. She hadn't expected that kind of reaction at all. Damn it, she hadn't asked for a relationship with him; why was he acting as though she had? Was he seriously thinking they could somehow make this work . . . permanently? They were practically strangers after all these years; they'd known each other as kids, before the pressures of adulthood had moulded them into the two very different people they were today.

Slowly she packed away the food. She'd lost her appetite as well. She needed to get back to work. At least that would keep her from thinking about things that were just too confusing to understand right now.

Thirty-four

Erin curled up on the lounge with her laptop. This was the first opportunity she'd had to get back to her sleuthing in almost two days. She'd had a stack of work come through that couldn't be put off. Jamie had returned the evening of their disagreement, and neither of them had brought up the subject of labelling their relationship again. She knew she was being a coward, but she didn't care, she was enjoying being with him too much. It was different this time around; they were older, and yet there was that easy sense of familiarity. It wasn't a new relationship, and yet at times it was. They'd discovered everything they could about their younger selves, but there was so much still to discover about their older, thirty-something selves.

She still had no idea what she wanted to do about her future. Ever since Gran's funeral, she'd been happy to stay here in her quiet little bubble. It was nice, but she knew it couldn't last. Sooner or later she'd have to return to her old life in the city.

But right now she wanted to work out who Jimmy was. She'd gone through the contents of the tin box thoroughly, examining everything inside. There were movie stubs and keepsakes from dances, and she suspected these activities had been done with Jimmy, and not her grandfather, Roy. The few letters from Pop didn't express the chemistry that was so apparent in the photos of Jimmy and Evelyn. Pop's letters were almost platonic.

Erin returned to the sites she'd been reading through the other day. She tried narrowing her search with a combination of the bomber group number, Townsville and the year on the back of the photo, and then hit the images button. A handful of sites came up with old photos and she decided to scroll through these and see what she found.

Going from the information she'd gathered so far, she suspected Jimmy had been a member of one of four squadrons, the 489th, 499th, 500th and 501st that made up the 345 bomb group that arrived in Townsville to have their aircraft converted to low-flying strafers—*whatever they were,* she thought, skimming over the notes she'd jotted down. This was the most likely explanation of why he was in Townsville at the time, since the time frame fitted. She spent an hour looking through the photos she'd found, and while she found them fascinating, she was growing increasingly frustrated that she wasn't making any headway working out how she would find a soldier using only a first name when 50,000 troops had come to Townsville over the war years.

She was considering a search of US military databases when she came across a series of photos. Clicking on a group photo of eleven men she waited until the image enlarged and then grabbed the photos of Jimmy she had in the tin box, bringing them up to hold beside the photo on the screen.

She'd found him.

The man squatting in the front row was Jimmy. The plane behind them wasn't the *French Quarter*, it had some other red-lipped, short-skirted vixen painted on the nose, but it was definitely Jimmy.

She scanned the bottom row where names had been typed and couldn't stop the small smile of triumph that escaped as she found the third name on the bottom row: Jimmy Crenshaw. Sitting back in her chair she stared at the face of the handsome young man on her computer screen and sighed.

'Did you have a hand in this, Gran?' she murmured out loud. She must have, there had to be some kind of divine intervention to have unearthed a photo with a name, out of the gazillion and one images on Google.

Now what? she wondered. She had no idea.

She saved the image on her computer, cropping and enlarging the section with Jimmy.

He really was a good-looking man, she thought, studying him. In the photo the men were dressed in a light-coloured uniform, many wearing the sleeves rolled up—no doubt due to the humidity. They looked happy and relaxed.

Erin typed in *Jimmy Crenshaw,* along with the bomber group number, and hit enter. The link where she'd found the photo came up, but there were a few other links and she went to the next one and stared in disbelief at the headline on the web page that appeared.

CRASH OF A C-47 DAKOTA INTO CLEVELAND BAY, TOWNSVILLE, QLD ON 7 AUGUST 1943.

She quickly scanned the list of names set out below the headline and her heart sank. There amongst the list of twenty-seven dead was Jimmy Crenshaw, 1st Lieutenant of the USAF. Erin felt the air rush out of her lungs in a long, deflated breath. She didn't even know this man, but her heart ached for him and the rest of the men on board that plane. She dragged her eyes from the list of names and found a brief story about the crash.

Twenty-seven people dead after a C-47-DL Dakota from the 40th Troop Carrier Squadron of the 317th Transport Group Transport crashed into Cleveland Bay south-east of Townsville at 5.20 am on 7 August 1943, shortly after take-off from Garbutt airfield. Their destination was the Archerfield airfield in Brisbane, where they were scheduled to refuel before heading on to Sydney for some R&R.

For a long time afterwards, Erin remained gutted. Obviously Jimmy had meant something to her gran, and his death would have been a terrible blow. Had she known? It seemed likely she would; the accident had happened around the same time the photos had been taken on the beach and at the dances. What if she hadn't known what had happened to him? Maybe he'd gone on his way and she'd never heard from him again. Had she been waiting to hear from him and, when she hadn't, thought he had simply forgotten about her? She didn't like to think of that happy young woman in the photos waiting for a letter that would never come. 'Oh, Gran,' she whispered softly. She wished she'd known this story of Jimmy and Evelyn whilst her grandmother had been alive. Maybe even after all this time, the pain of losing Jimmy had been too great to talk about. The thought made Erin sad.

Thirty-five

'I'm going away for a few days,' Erin blurted, feeling strangely nervous about bringing it up with Jamie that afternoon. 'To Townsville.'

'Townsville? Why? What's up there?'

'I want to try to trace someone who knew Gran during the war. I tracked down the daughter of an old friend of Gran's from when she lived there. Maybe I can find out something more about her and Jimmy. Besides, I haven't been up to North Queensland in years. It'd be a nice break. You wanna come?'

'To Townsville?'

'Yes,' Erin said impatiently.

'I can't just up and leave this place.'

'I'm not asking you to *move*,' she said, frowning. Seriously? What was the big deal? She only planned on going for three or four days.

'I have animals to take care of. I'm in the middle of fencing right now and soon I'll have to start drenching, and marking.'

'Okay, forget I asked. It was just an idea.'

'Why are you getting angry? You only hit me with this five minutes ago as I walked in the door.'

'I'm not angry, I just didn't realise it was such a drama to get a few days off. It's fine. I'm happy to go on my own.'

'It's a long way to go and an expensive trip just on the off-chance you might find out something about some guy your gran may or may not have had a fling with seventy-odd years ago.'

Erin took out the wine bottle from the fridge. 'I have the time and I have the money,' she said.

'Must be nice,' he muttered.

Erin stopped pouring her wine into the glass to look up at him. 'Is this about money? Is that why you're getting so snarky?'

'I'm not snarky,' he snapped. 'I just find it strange that you want to waste money on something like this.'

'I want to find out who this guy was. I want to return his ring to his family. I don't see that as a waste.'

'There's probably no one left in his family who even knows about the ring. Why would you bother returning it?'

'Because it has sentimental value. Not everything is about money.'

'Spoken like someone who's already got plenty of it.'

'Would you stop doing that! Why are you suddenly so touchy about money?

'Maybe because I have to work my arse off every day to try to make a living, but I never seem to get anywhere. Not everyone can just decide to drop everything and go on a holiday out of the blue,' he said. 'You can't understand not having it. You've always had it.'

'I do have a job, you know. I earn the money I have and I work damn hard for it too.'

'In your *mother's* company,' he pointed out with a touch of cynicism.

Erin stared at Jamie and was pretty sure her jaw had dropped open. She could not believe he was acting like this. 'My mother helped build a franchise business that did incredibly well. It's no different to you taking over your father's damn farm!'

'No different if you ignore the few extra zeroes at the end of the numbers we're both dealing with.' He turned on his heel to head for the back door. 'This was a mistake tonight. I'm too tired to deal with this right now. I'll see you tomorrow.'

'Don't bother,' she yelled behind him as the screen door banged shut. She wouldn't be here. She planned on catching the first available flight north. There was no point putting it off now that he was clearly not interested in coming with her.

By the time she'd drunk her glass of wine, her anger had worn off, leaving her feeling miserable and teary. Their fight had escalated so quickly there hadn't been time to take a step back and think through her words. She tried to understand what might have set him off about the whole money issue, but she couldn't work it out. This was just like old times: Jamie getting angry about something and storming off; only they were supposed to be adults now, not kids fighting over whose turn it was to go first in some game.

She *had* realised that whenever they did talk about finances the tone of the conversation always changed. He'd gone quiet when she'd paid for their meal the night before at the pub, and there had been more than one dismissive look when she'd mentioned overseas holidays she'd been on, but she hadn't realised that this was an issue between them until now. She didn't live beyond her means and she didn't splash her money around; she was in fact very careful with her income and the various funds her mother had invested for her throughout her childhood. She gave an annoyed huff. Why was she defending herself? She hadn't done anything wrong.

She poured a second glass of wine and took it outside to the verandah, sipping it as she looked out over the lush green grass of the bottom paddock and allowing the serenity of the view to help wash away the tension.

Jamie did have a point though, she conceded reluctantly. Why *did* she want to find out about Jimmy Crenshaw so badly? And it was true that his parents who had engraved the ring for him would have been long gone, and yet something kept urging her to continue. Maybe it was just a way to keep herself occupied and to stop thinking too much about the big empty apartment that awaited her back in the city. The similarities of it to her future was a little unsettling: empty and lonely.

The grief she'd managed to keep at bay for so long surprised her with its ferocity. She was tired of being such a failure;

she couldn't have children, she couldn't hold on to her husband. She'd lost her gran too, and just when she needed her the most. Everything was falling apart right before her eyes. She hated that feeling of not being able to control her environment; her inability to conceive a child—the simplest thing a woman was supposed to be able to do, and she couldn't. She'd hated the taste of defeat, but there was only so much disappointment and heartache that her battered emotions could cope with, and it seemed she'd reached the end of that limit. Tears she'd tried to hold off leaked a scalding path down her face. She'd give anything for Gran to be here now, to feel those cool, soft hands smoothing back her hair and reassuring her that everything was going to work out in the end. Erin desperately needed to hear that. She wasn't sure she believed it, but it would be really nice to at least hear it. For a moment she swore she smelled a faint whiff of lavender and sandalwood, which brought on a fresh onslaught of tears.

The evening had cooled off by the time the tears subsided and long shadows now fell across the bottom flats as she tipped her head back, drained by her grief, to stare out over the view. *Well*, she thought with a resigned sigh, *wallowing in self-pity wasn't going to change anything.*

She finished her glass of wine and went back inside to her laptop. Bringing up flights, she booked a ticket to Townsville for the next day.

Thirty-six

It was four-thirty in the afternoon when her flight touched down at Townsville airport. The blue sky and deep green palm trees almost hurt her eyes. The colours were so intense in the tropics, making everything seem brighter.

The heat in March wasn't as bad as it would have been a few months earlier, but for a southerner the humidity still came as quite a shock. Everywhere she looked, brightly coloured hibiscus blossomed, and as she left the terminal in her hire car, she looked up and saw the imposing red rock of Castle Hill. It jutted high above the city, standing out in stark relief, dry and ancient against the tropical the city below.

Her motel was situated on The Strand, not far from a water park where children played beneath a huge water bucket that tipped at frequent intervals, inciting squeals of delight from children and adults alike. Long winding paths hugged the foreshore and a multitude of joggers, bike riders and strolling couples all shared the picturesque atmosphere of this beachside city.

She checked into her room and walked out onto the balcony that overlooked the water and, in the distance, Magnetic Island. She took a deep breath and closed her eyes, filling her senses with the warm, sweet-smelling scent of the tropical north. She'd always meant to visit Gran's hometown but somehow had never made it up here.

Her phone beeped from inside the room and she reluctantly turned away from her surrounds and went inside. It was a text message from Jamie and she opened it, smiling a little when she saw it. A photo of the saddest looking kitten in history stared back at her with the words *I'm sorry* written across the bottom.

She was miserable about the way she'd left things between them and she realised that she missed him terribly. Erin listened to the phone dialling in her ear and when the deep voice answered, those familiar butterflies began fluttering wildly inside. 'I'm sorry too,' she said softly.

'I came back to apologise and you were gone.'

'I may have left a little earlier than I'd been planning to.'

'I shouldn't have walked out like that.'

'I probably overreacted myself.' Erin heard him chuckle and joined in. 'Are we done apologising now?'

'I don't know, have you forgiven me?'

'Yes.'

'I can get Dad to cover for me for a few days. That's what I was coming over to tell you.'

'This whole thing started because of money. I don't want you to go wasting yours on something that's not even important to you.'

'Finding this guy *isn't* important to me,' he corrected calmly, 'but *you* are. *We* are,' he added.

'Thank you for making the offer, but honestly, you'd be bored out of your brain and this is probably something I need to do by myself. I'm not even sure what I'm looking for. I'll be done here in a few days and when I get back . . . we'll talk.'

'Okay, fine,' he said wearily.

'Why do I feel like I'm in trouble again?' she said.

'You're not. You're just so . . . I don't know.'

'I think the word you're looking for is independent?'

'No, I was thinking more along the lines of a stubborn control freak, actually.'

'I am not a control freak.' Was she? Control freak? She was used to taking charge and making things happen, it was part of her job. And if she'd waited for Phillip to make arrangements or book something, she'd have been waiting forever. He had always been preoccupied with his work, too busy to pay bills or book an electrician to fix a broken light fitting; these were the things Erin had quickly realised she would have to do herself unless she wanted to live with constant frustration. She was used to doing things without consultation.

'Forget it,' he dismissed. 'I miss you.'

Erin closed her eyes briefly at his softly spoken words. 'I miss you too.' More than she expected to. 'I just need a few days.'

'Take your time, I'm not going anywhere.'

They talked for a little while longer before saying their goodbyes and Erin felt better that they'd cleared the air. While it hadn't exactly solved their problem and they hadn't really discussed the money issue, at least they'd both acknowledged that they were sorry.

It gave her a lot to think about that night. Was a future with Jamie possible? It would involve a lot of adjustment. Would he be willing to let go of some of that pride when it came to money, or would she be forced to tiptoe around any financial issues? Was she supposed to run everything she did past Jamie from now on? Clearly he had different expectations. It seemed they did need to talk about things, and maybe establish a few boundaries. She wasn't sure if she was happy or annoyed by this turn of events. On one hand it was nice that Jamie wasn't growing tired of her just yet, but on the other hand, she wasn't sure she was ready to jump feet first into another relationship when she was just beginning to regain her independence. She had to admit, in the last few weeks she'd liked not answering to anyone other than herself. Not that Phillip had ever lived looking over her shoulder; in fact, he had rarely showed any interest in anything other than his work and his research. He was oblivious to how much they had in their bank account, or how the power bill got paid.

Did Jamie really want a serious relationship? Maybe he thought he was ready, but would he be truly happy with someone he could never have children with? Sure he could dismiss it now, but what about when he reached Phillip's age and realised he'd lost his chance to be a father?

The thought depressed her more than she cared to admit, and for a long time she sat on the balcony, staring thoughtfully out over the magnificent view, trying to ignore the drums of doom she could hear beating in her head.

Thirty-seven

The gentle lapping of waves against the sand was soothing, and Erin stopped and breathed deeply, filling her lungs with the warm salty tang of the ocean. She'd watched the sun rise from her balcony this morning before a quick run along the foreshore, mixing in with a surprising number of other exercise junkies and early morning strollers enjoying the cool morning air before the heat of the day settled in.

There were no crashing waves pounding the shoreline here. The bay, sheltered by Magnetic Island, was an ideal spot for swimming—if you didn't count the threat of stingers that inhabited the warm tropical waters of far north Queensland.

Her first port of call today was the RAAF museum and, armed with the notes she'd made so far, she drove to the large air force base where the museum was located and parked her car.

Pete, who was an ex-air force pilot and part-time museum guide, proved a wealth of information about everything related to World War Two. Erin explained that she was trying to piece together the connection between a US Air Force pilot stationed in Townsville in 1943 and a family member. She showed him the information she'd brought with her, the list Jimmy appeared on and his unit number, which Pete read with much interest. As soon as she mentioned the crash, though, his face changed dramatically.

'Jimmy Crenshaw? You want to find out about Jimmy?'

'Yes,' she eyed the man curiously. 'You know him?'

'Well, no, I'm not *that* old,' he said with a wink. 'But a few years back we had an original member of the 345 bomber group come back for a visit and he told us some amazing stories—stuff no one had heard about before.' Walking over to a big board on the far wall displaying photographs and newspaper clippings, he pointed to the image of an older man who was obviously being interviewed by a reporter. 'You might find this article interesting,' he said, stepping back so she could move close enough to read the clipping.

A night out on the town cost a young US pilot his chance to explore Sydney on a week's rest and relaxation, but you won't find Chuck Williams complaining about it now. Having drunk too much and gotten himself into an argument with two Australian serviceman while stationed at Garbutt in August 1943, Staff Sergeant Williams spent the night in a holding cell and missed the early morning flight to Sydney. While many would consider this a disappointment, for Mr Williams it was a huge wake-up call and a very lucky escape. Shortly after take-off, the C-47 crashed into Cleveland Bay, killing all those on board.

In an interview with Mr Williams when he returned to commemorate the sixtieth anniversary of World War Two, he spoke about his narrow escape to a group of local school-children at the museum.

'I should have been on that plane. I lost many good friends that morning, but if I hadn't been in that bar fight, I wouldn't be here today to tell you this story,' Mr Williams said. 'Not that I condone fighting,' he added with a twinkle in his eye, to the amusement of the children gathered.

'While I was lucky and missed the flight, the guy who took my place wasn't.'

Mr Williams went on to say, his voice breaking, that his last-minute no-show freed up a seat and a young pilot by the name of Jimmy Crenshaw took his place. Later he learned that Jimmy had been trying for days to get on a flight to Sydney where he intended to get married. 'He never made it and I can't help but wonder what might have been for so many people if I had gotten on that plane instead of him that day.'

Erin turned to Pete. 'Is this true?'

'I have no reason to doubt it. Mr Williams was sharp as a pin.'

Had Jimmy been engaged to someone from Sydney? Had he broken Gran's heart and been on his way to marry someone else?

Erin spent a few more minutes viewing the display of wartime aircraft disasters in the area. She was shocked to read that there had been two hundred or more military aircraft crashes or mishaps in the Townsville area during World War Two.

'Pete, this photo,' she said, pointing to one that showed a long row of coffins lined up side by side, draped in American flags. 'Where is this cemetery? Is this where the airmen were buried? Would Jimmy be there?'

'That's the old US Military cemetery. It's not there any more. It was closed in 1946. All of the deceased were exhumed and returned to the US for burial in their hometown cemeteries.'

❦

Back in her car, Erin scrolled through her phone messages and copied Dolly's daughter's address into the phone's GPS.

At her destination, Erin walked up the front stairs and knocked on the door of the beautifully restored Queenslander. She heard footsteps approaching and then saw a silhouette through the leadlight window of the front door.

'Hello, you must be Erin,' said a woman she judged to be somewhere in her mid to late sixties. 'I'm Cheryl. Come on in.'

'Thank you so much for seeing me. It must have been a bit strange getting my call out of the blue the other day.'

'No, not at all. I was thrilled, actually,' said the woman, smiling over her shoulder as she led her down a long hallway through the house and out onto the rear verandah. 'As I mentioned on the phone, Mum's been gone almost twenty years now, so I was really excited to hear from someone connected to Evelyn after all this time. I'm researching my own family tree, so I understand all about following up leads.'

'Your house is beautiful,' Erin said, taking in the lattice-work surrounding the verandah, complete with a deep red climbing bougainvillea.

'Thank you, it's been a labour of love for a lot of years,' she said, indicating Erin should take a seat at the large timber outdoor setting before them. 'But we've just about finished. So, what did you want to know?' she asked after they were settled with a cold drink.

'Well, I'm not sure exactly. Gran had lots of Christmas cards from Dolly and some letters they'd written over the years. I thought you might like them,' she said, handing over the small pile of cards.

'How lovely.'

'I didn't find much other correspondence from any other old friends, which is why I thought I'd come and talk with you on the off-chance you might know anything about my gran when she was younger.'

'Well, they were close friends as young girls,' Cheryl said with a soft smile. 'Mum often talked about Evelyn and the things they got up to.'

'That's what I'm hoping you might be able to help me with. During the war, I think something happened, and I'm trying to piece it together.'

'Ahh. The Yank,' Cheryl nodded slowly.

'The Yank? You mean Jimmy Crenshaw?'

'Yes, that's the one. Such a sad story.'

'He was killed in a crash,' Erin prompted, feeling her heart begin to pound.

'Yes. Terrible. Mum was the one who called your gran, you know,' she said, tilting her head slightly as she looked across her backyard.

'Called her?'

'To tell her about the crash. She wouldn't have known about it down there, otherwise.'

'Where was Gran?'

'Why, she was in Sydney, dear.'

Thirty-eight

Erin felt the blood drain from her face. *Sydney?* Jimmy was headed to Sydney to get married . . . *to her gran.*

'Are you all right, love? Is it too hot out here for you?'

'No. No, I'm fine,' Erin hurried to assure her. 'I didn't know.'

'Oh, I'm sorry, I thought you must have known all about it . . .'

'I knew bits. I found photos of Jimmy in Gran's belongings, I just wasn't sure how it all fitted together. I thought maybe he was a brief fling . . . or something. I had no idea they were planning to get married.'

'It was all very whirlwind and romantic,' said Cheryl, pouring some cold water into a glass and handing it to Erin. 'Mum used to get this faraway look in her eye when she talked about it. *Just like a movie,* she used to say.'

Erin thought back to the beautiful young woman from the photos.

'Anyway, apparently Evelyn met Jimmy through your grandfather, Roy. The two men met in New Guinea and when Roy discovered Jimmy was going to Townsville he asked him to stop by and visit Evelyn to let her know he was doing okay. But Mum said the moment those two met it was love at first sight. Evelyn was terribly torn about being engaged to Roy, but I guess in the end her love for Jimmy was stronger than either of them could have imagined. You see, Evelyn and Roy had grown up together, they'd been neighbours their entire lives, and from what Mum said, getting engaged had just been the inevitable thing to do. She said they were more like best mates than the love of each other's life, but seeing her with Jimmy was like nothing she'd seen before or since. *It was like two halves of a whole finally meeting*, were Mum's exact words,' Cheryl smiled. 'Anyway, apparently Evelyn's parents found out about her and Jimmy and her father sent her to Sydney to stay with his sister until Roy returned from New Guinea.'

Erin hung on Cheryl's every word. This was incredible. It *did* sound like a Hollywood movie; no wonder Dolly had liked talking about it over the years. Thank God, too, or she'd never have heard all this.

'Anyway, Jimmy supposedly told Evelyn to go to Sydney and he would follow her on the next flight out and they'd get married so that it would be too late for anyone to interfere. I think Mum was a little bit envious and wishing she could find *herself* a Yank to marry,' Cheryl said with a chuckle. 'My mother was a bit of a hussy in her younger years, from all accounts. Then she ended up marrying my father, who was a minister.'

Erin shared a smile before looking back down at the table. 'So Evelyn was in Sydney waiting for Jimmy . . . and he never made it.' The thought saddened her. Poor Gran.

Cheryl sighed. 'It was a war. People were losing loved ones every day. I guess we forget how hard it must have been for them.'

'He only just made that flight,' said Erin, her voice thick with emotion. 'If he hadn't gotten on that plane . . .' What would have happened? Her life would have been altered. She would have been born in America . . . Actually, no, she wouldn't have even been born at all because Evelyn wouldn't have gone on to marry Roy. It only took one simple twist of fate to alter everything.

'Look, I don't quite know how to say this, but there *was* one more thing.'

Erin looked up at the woman across from her.

'When Evelyn left Townsville, she was pregnant.'

'What!'

'Now, before you get too alarmed, you have to remember this is all hearsay, but apparently Evelyn swore Dolly to silence over the plan to get married and about the baby, but then after Jimmy's crash, when Dolly spoke to Evelyn again, Evelyn said there *wasn't* a baby any more. Mum said she tried to ask her what she meant, but Evelyn was still grieving for Jimmy and they lost touch with each other for a few years. When they eventually did get back in touch, Evelyn was married to Roy and Mum said they never mentioned Jimmy or anything about him ever again.'

'Wait,' Erin said, putting up a hand as a jumble of thoughts began bouncing about inside her head. 'Evelyn was *pregnant* when she left Townsville . . . *to Jimmy* . . . but then she lost the baby?' None of this made sense.

Cheryl gave Erin a hesitant look before she pulled a folder that had been on the table across and opened it up. 'Take a look at this. Mum was a bit like your gran, she kept everything. When you called to say you were coming over, I dug through all the bits I had, to find anything you might be interested in. I found this.' She held out a Christmas card and inside was a black and white portrait shot of Erin's mother at maybe two years of age. 'Now look at this,' she said, withdrawing a second photo. This one was similar to the beach party one Gran had. 'That's Dolly,' Cheryl pointed out. 'That's Evelyn . . . and that's Jimmy,' she said, holding up the image beside the photo of her mother and waiting silently.

'Oh, my God,' said Erin, gasping at the photos of the baby and the American pilot. The resemblance was uncanny. Jimmy had dark eyes and thick eyelashes; his olive complexion hinted at some kind of distant Mediterranean heritage, maybe Cajun. He looked like a young Elvis Presley, with those sleepy bedroom eyes. Even as a baby her mother had had similar features—which were nothing like her sandy-haired, blue-eyed grandfather in old photos she'd seen.

'Mum said she took one look at that photo of your mother as a baby and knew, beyond a doubt, that she was Jimmy's child.'

'But . . . how? She married Pop, *Roy*,' she corrected hastily, because it was all too confusing to keep track of everyone, '*six weeks* after this crash date. And my mother was born nine months after that.'

'It wasn't hard to smudge the term of a pregnancy back then, they didn't have the tests and accurate measurements they have nowadays. And your grandparents moved to Tuendoc under the soldier settlement scheme; a brand-new town where no one knew them. And, more importantly, where no one would question dates.'

Erin was dumbfounded. *Jimmy* was her grandfather? This changed everything. What about her mother? How would she react to this? Should she even tell her? A thousand questions raced through her mind, and before she could answer one, it triggered off even more.

'As I said before, I don't have any evidence, and there's no one left to verify all this . . . I'm just going off what I see in these photos and what my mother told me growing up.'

'I don't know what to think. If you'd told me this a few months ago, I would have laughed and said no way . . . but since then I've realised how little I actually know about my grandmother.'

'Don't let this change the way you think about her. This all happened a long time ago in a different era. There was a war happening and life was changing around them. The choices they made then probably wouldn't have been the same ones they'd have made had it been peacetime.'

'You're right.' And she was. In her head she understood this—probably better than anyone. She remembered her own intense romance with Jamie at the same age her gran had been when she met Jimmy. Throw in a war and death happening all around them and it was only logical that life would move far more quickly than usual. But still . . . this was her *grandmother!* And now she'd discovered there was the very real possibility her family tree had just received a massive shake-up.

Maybe this hadn't been a great idea after all. She'd come here to find answers but all she seemed to be uncovering were more questions.

Thirty-nine

Erin drove slowly along the rough dirt track that led from the main road into the Namaste Retreat. Off to one side in a clearing which backed onto bushland, she saw a small group of people sitting in a circle with their eyes closed. A bare-chested man dressed in tie-dyed baggy pants walked around the outside of the circle, waving a branch of smoking gum leaves over the participants while chanting something she couldn't hear. As she approached the end of the driveway, the facility spread out before her. There was a cluster of small teepees used for guest accommodation as well as cabins scattered along the small ridge behind the main building. Within a long wooden structure was reception and more luxurious guest accommodation for less adventurous types.

Inside, an open-plan common room dominated the foyer, holding lounges grouped in twos and threes, as well as some single seats. There were no televisions or computers; staying here meant giving up all forms of communication with the outside world in order to free oneself from stress and clear one's mind.

Further along, on either side of the hallway, were two conference rooms used to hold seminars and workshops, and today both seemed to be in use judging from the muted sounds coming from behind the closed doors.

A young woman wearing a long braid down her back and sporting a large peacock feather in her hair appeared from an office behind the front desk. 'Nah-mah-stay,' she said, placing her hands together and bowing slightly in Erin's direction.

Namaste was not only the name of the resort but it was also the word derived from Sanskrit that loosely translated to mean 'the divine light within me salutes the divine light within you'. *Kind of like an acknowledgement of mutual awesomeness*, Erin thought.

'Hello. Is Serenity here?'

'Serenity is wherever and whenever you choose it to be,' she smiled with her head slightly tilted to one side.

Erin smiled back and silently counted to ten. She really hadn't had anywhere near the amount of coffee required to deal with this yet. 'My *mother*, Serenity. Is she available?'

'Oh, the Acarya.' Her eyes brightened immediately.

Erin had no idea what Acarya meant and, quite frankly, this young woman's dry-as-a-bone, Walgett accent was making her attempt to sound spiritual hard to take seriously.

'She's in the middle of a rebirthing ceremony.'

Of course she is, thought Erin, resisting the urge to sigh. 'Can you please tell her that Erin is waiting for her in her private quarters when she's finished birthing?' Sometimes her mind struggled to believe the things that came out of her mouth when it came to her mother.

'Umm, I'm sorry, but I don't think you—'

'You're new here. I'm Erin, Serenity's daughter. What was your name?' Erin asked.

'Clover,' she said, looking anxious.

'Hi, Clover.' Erin shook her hand firmly. 'Just let her know I'm here when you see her, okay?'

Erin turned away and headed through the back to her mother's private rooms. She dropped her handbag on the small table in the kitchenette and looked around at the decor. The furniture was rustic, handmade from timber. The mats and wall-hangings adorning the floor and walls had been brought back from her mother's many trips to far-off places around the world. Tibetan masks and ornaments sat side by side with African tribal masks and woven pots. It was a cultural mishmash of colour and textures that gave a warmth and cosiness to the cabin-like room. It never ceased to amaze her, the transformation in her mother. This woman who had raised her in a stable, semi-normal environment had undergone a radical personality change once Erin left home. She hadn't just made a tree change, she'd reinvented her whole life. It seemed to happen so quickly, but in truth it had probably been unfolding slowly over the years and Erin had been too caught up in her own teenage dramas and then university to notice the exact moment it began.

There wasn't much of the woman Erin had known left in Serenity. In some ways this was good; Irene had always been so busy. Part of the reason Erin spent so much time with Gran had been because her mother was always so snowed under with work. It wasn't the life her mother had envisioned when she'd started her little shop. She would have been happy running a small business selling health foods. Who knew the health food industry would suddenly boom the way it had? Carol had been the main motivator behind the franchises. She was the businesswoman and had picked up that ball and run with it, dragging Irene along for the ride. To her credit, she had adapted to the business world extremely well. She had been a good mum, too, always trying her best to be at the important events in Erin's life, but she hadn't really been present. Her head had always been stuck back at work, trying to keep up with the empire that had become a life-sapping monster. Erin could see now that her mother had been spreading herself too thin for too many years. It wasn't the life she'd wanted, but the life she'd created now made her genuinely happy.

Erin tried hard not to feel resentful. Her mother had finally found some kind of peace in her life, and she was much calmer and more relaxed, and yet she still somehow didn't have time for her daughter. There were times when Erin wished she could have her mum all to herself for a little while. That was why she'd grown so close to Gran, she supposed. Gran had always been there to provide a sympathetic ear and give warm hugs that could pretty much fix anything. Gran would listen to Erin complaining about her mother's lack of attention and then pat her hand gently. 'Don't give up on her, darling. She's just taking a while to work out who she is.'

Somehow it made Erin feel less alone to know that her gran seemed to miss her daughter as much as she missed her mum. In that way, they were united.

Erin sank down onto the lounge and looked out over the pretty view of the mountains in the distance. Her recent tripping around must have taken more out of her than she realised because one minute she was looking out over the sunlit scenery and the next she was waking up to discover it was dark and she was covered with a patchwork quilt.

Erin sat up and looked around, finding her mother sitting in a chair across from her, peacefully threading beads onto a long string. 'And she awakens, finally.'

'I'm so sorry, Mum. I just sat down for a minute.'

'You looked like you needed the sleep,' she said. 'This is a nice surprise.'

Erin ran her fingers through her tousled hair and tried to wake up. 'I should have called first, but it was kind of a spur-of-the-moment thing.'

'And what was so urgent you needed to embark on such a long road trip?'

'It's not urgent,' she said, moving the blanket aside and folding it up. 'I've just gotten back from a trip up north and I wanted to talk to you about a few things.'

'North?'

'Townsville.'

Her mother's expression froze for the briefest of moments. 'What were you doing all the way up there?'

'I wanted to follow up a few things.'

'You must be hungry. I saved you some dinner if you want it,' she said, putting down her beadwork and standing.

Erin got to her feet as well. 'Mum, I found out something and I think you need to hear it.'

'I hope you like chickpeas,' her mother continued.

'Mum! I don't want anything to eat. I want you to listen to me.'

'Fine. What is it you want to tell me so badly?'

'It's about Gran and Pop.'

Her mother stood in front of her, one hand on the refrigerator door, waiting impassively for her to continue. 'What about them?'

'I found some old photos . . . and I went up to Townsville to meet with the daughter of an old friend of Gran's. She told me a story about when Gran was young, before she married Pop. There was another man she was in love with.'

Her mother's expression didn't change as she continued to stare at her silently. And then Erin realised something. 'You know,' she breathed.

'That Roy Macalister wasn't my biological father? Yes.'

'Why didn't you tell me?'

'Why would I?'

'Why?' Erin repeated, the disbelief heavy in her tone. 'Maybe because this affects me too?'

'How? Your grandfather's been dead for years. They're all gone now, so how could this possibly affect you?'

'Because it means we could have family on the other side of the world.'

'Who don't even know we exist.'

'Don't you want to find out who they are?'

'No.'

Erin continued to stare at her mother as she moved about the small kitchen and reheated their meal.

'I don't understand you at all.'

'I know,' her mother said sadly. 'But that's all right. You don't have to.'

'But I want to, don't you see?' Erin said, stepping in her mother's path so she would look at her. 'I don't want you to shut me out any more.'

'I'm not shutting you out. I'm allowing you to be the person you want to be.'

'I just want my mother.'

'I'm always here. But at this point in my life, I've found a calling, to help others find inner peace.'

'Just like you have?' Erin challenged. 'Really? You're at peace inside?'

'Yes, I am.'

'You couldn't even come back and see Gran before she died.'

'Sometimes forgiving and forgetting are two very different things.'

'Forgetting what? I don't understand. What happened between you two?'

'It's in the past.'

'I'm so tired of all this. If you want me to understand you, then help me by explaining things to me.'

'Are you really sure you want to hear it?' her mother asked, holding her gaze steadily.

'I need to. How can I understand if I don't even know what happened?'

Her mother gave a weary sigh before moving back across to the table to take a seat. 'I knew from an early age that there was something different about my father. He used to look at me sometimes with this expression of pure loathing. Can you imagine how confusing that was for a child? Oh, he was never cruel,' she explained. 'He always provided for me, but he never *loved* me. I would cry to my mother about it for years, trying so hard to be the daughter he would finally love. I exceeded in school. I made sure my room was spotless. I tried to be the perfect child, but nothing I did ever made him show the slightest bit of interest. Then I met . . .' Her mother stopped abruptly, seeming to weigh up something in her mind before continuing slowly, almost as though the words physically hurt her to speak out loud. 'I met Peter. I fell head over heels in love,' a soft fleeting smile floated across her lips before it was replaced by a tight line. 'But he didn't feel the same.'

'Is this the boy you made your debut with?' Erin asked, recalling the photo of her mother and a dark-haired boy.

Her mother glanced at her, hesitated briefly, then gave a small nod. 'I found out I was pregnant, and he promised we'd get married, that he'd find a way for us to be together, but then his parents stepped in and he . . . changed his mind. They all wanted me to get rid of it. I remember looking at Mum, begging her to stand up for me, but she didn't.'

'What are you saying, Mum?'

Her mother blinked quickly. 'They made me have an abortion.'

Erin could only stare at her mother in astonishment.

'Your grandfather and Dr Brown, Peter's father, took me to some backyard surgery and let them rip my baby from me, and your grandmother just stood by and allowed it to happen,' her mother said in a hollow, empty tone.

Erin was still struggling to comprehend the fact her mother had been pregnant. That Erin would have had an older sibling. How could she have never known this? How could they all have kept such a big secret all this time?

'Afterwards, I was heartbroken. Numb. I felt betrayed by everyone: Peter, my mother . . . people who should have protected me.'

Erin felt her eyes begin to sting with unshed tears for the pain her mother must have gone through.

'We never spoke about it. The house became a tomb. I can still remember sitting at the table and the only sound was cutlery, and that damn clock on the mantle. I couldn't wait to leave.'

Erin could only stare at her mother in dismay. 'When did you find out about Jimmy?'

'Around the same time as they found out about the baby,' she said. 'A few months later I found the same box you discovered. I knew as soon as I saw the photograph it was true. He was my father.

'All those years I'd tried to please Roy, tried to fix whatever I'd done to make him dislike me so much, and the whole time she *knew*. She could have made me see that it wasn't anything *I* had done. It was because I wasn't his child and he couldn't get past it. It was *him* who was the problem, not me. But she didn't say a word. She just let him treat me like I was invisible.'

Erin sat silently, waiting for her mother to continue.

'I left home not long afterwards and spent a lot of time rebelling. I bounced from one job to another. One man to another,' she said, shaking her head. 'I could never bring myself to have a proper relationship; they'd killed off that part of me. I couldn't trust anyone. I didn't *want* to trust anyone, because I never wanted to feel so utterly helpless ever again.' Her tone turned brittle. 'So I didn't find a man and settle down like most women my age were doing. For years I believed I didn't have the right to want another child when I'd let them take my first one, but then when Roy died, without him alive to remind me of all that pain and guilt, I slowly allowed myself to dream about it. I wanted that baby so much,' she said, looking up.

Erin saw all the years of pain and heartache in her mother's eyes.

'Oh, Mum,' she whispered sadly.

Her mother wiped her eyes quickly. 'Then I met your father. I was attracted to him and he was married, so I knew he wouldn't want a commitment. Yes, it was wrong, but at the time all I knew was that I desperately wanted a baby. I didn't think about any of the consequences; how it would affect you later. It was selfish of me and I do regret that now,' she said, gently placing her hand on top of Erin's.

Erin had tears in her eyes as she listened to her mother. She'd had no idea about *any* of this. How could Roy have been so hard on a child? And why had her gentle grandmother stood by and allowed him to treat her child that way? *Because Roy felt cheated and Gran felt guilty,* she realised. As a result they'd unwittingly taken out their bitterness and betrayal on their child. 'Oh, Mum. I'm so sorry,' she whispered.

'Like I said, it's in the past—some *other* woman's past. The new me has no past and no regrets.'

And like a cold splash of water hitting her in the face, the moment ended. 'There's only one problem with that,' Erin said, battling to keep the quiver from her voice. '*I'm* part of that past you've let go,' she said and tears of hurt gathered in her eyes. 'You're doing the same thing they did. I'm being sacrificed in order for you to have your clean slate. I'm *you*.'

'That's not true. I gave you everything they never gave me. I'm nothing like them.'

'Really? When was the last time you called just to check in? To say hi and see what was happening in my life?' Erin challenged.

'We talk all the time,' Serenity said, a crease forming between her eyebrows.

'We don't *talk*, Mum—if we did you'd know by now that Phillip has left me.'

'I knew it! I knew something was wrong,' she shot back, before noticing Erin's frown. 'I asked you at the funeral,' she reminded her a little defensively.

'You would have known weeks before that if you'd bothered to visit once and a while.'

'There was nothing stopping you picking up the phone to tell me.'

'The point is, Mum, I shouldn't have to. If you just made an effort to come and spend time with me, maybe I'd feel like I could confide in you, but you don't, because apparently I'm no longer your responsibility.'

'I have *never* said that,' she denied.

'You taught me to be self-sufficient, so I didn't have to depend on anyone else, just like you,' Erin parroted back the words her mother had said to her.

'That's not the same as saying I don't care.'

'Well, it's certainly not the same as being there for me either. My husband left me because I can't have children.'

'Says who? Have you tried holistic therapies?'

'I don't want you to sell me your hippie voodoo crap, I just want a tiny bit of sympathy. I want to wallow in self-pity for just *one minute,* and have my mother hold me and tell me it's all going to be okay. After everything you went through, I would have thought you'd be the first one to understand that.'

This seemed to take her mother aback a little. She opened her mouth but then abruptly closed it once more, at a loss as to what to say.

Erin shook her head sadly. Inside she was hurting. Everything she thought she knew about her life was unravelling. She'd heard the truth from her mother, finally, but the truth had been bitter and hard to swallow.

Erin stood up, picking up her handbag and walked to the door without looking back. She heard her mother's weak protest but didn't stop, she couldn't. She'd lost everyone. It was finally time to give up wanting what she was never going to get from her mother. Maybe she needed to take some of her mother's advice and create a new life for herself. One that no longer involved depending on other people to bring her happiness.

Forty

As soon as she arrived at the airport Erin sent Jamie a message letting him know she was on her way home. They'd talked on the phone every day, but she'd still missed him. The closer she got to Tuendoc the less she could blame the airline food on her churning stomach. It was excitement, pure and simple. She couldn't wait to see Jamie again.

As she pulled into Gran's driveway she smiled as she saw all the lights were on inside the house. He was already walking down the steps as she opened her car door, and she was in his arms before she'd had a chance to close it. He held her against him tightly and kissed her long and deep. Erin ran her hands through his hair, dragging him closer, and they were both breathing heavily when they finally pulled apart.

'I missed you,' he groaned, rubbing a thumb against the side of her face gently. The look in his eye made Erin's heart race even faster.

'I missed you too. I couldn't wait to get home.'

'I like the sound of that,' he said, smiling.

Erin smiled back. It was true, ever since she'd come back to care for Gran this place had felt more like home than anywhere she'd ever lived. She didn't want to ruin the moment by worrying about all the messy details making that happen would entail, so she pushed it away and simply enjoyed being back in Jamie's arms once more.

Inside the house, Erin couldn't help gasping in delight as she surveyed his afternoon's handiwork. Candles lit a beautifully set table for two, complete with a vase of roses in the middle and Gran's best china. 'Wow, you sure know how to impress a girl,' she murmured as he pulled out her seat and settled her at the table.

He came back carrying a tray from the oven and Erin bit back her smile as he placed a piece of steak and some barbecued vegetables on her fine bone china dinner plate. 'I only know how to cook on the barbie,' he said.

'It's perfect. I've been dreaming of Tallowood-fattened beef the whole time I've been gone,' she said.

'I hope that's not all you've been dreaming about,' he grinned, taking his own seat across from her.

'No,' she said, slicing into the tender steak. 'That's pretty much it.'

'Well, in that case,' he said, reaching across to take her plate away.

'Okay, okay, I may have also dreamed of you a few times.'

'That's much better,' he said, smiling as he put her plate back down.

'But I dreamed of steak more,' she added, laughing and closing her eyes as she savoured the taste of the steak.

'You better eat fast, woman,' said Jamie, looking at her in a way that made her heart quicken.

Suddenly she wasn't hungry any more, at least not for the meal on her plate. 'I'm done,' she said, pushing her plate away.

The words had barely left her mouth before Jamie was at her side, swooping her into his arms like some romantic hero from a novel. Then, ignoring her squeal of surprise and warning that he'd do himself an injury, he carried her into her bedroom for a proper welcome home.

Forty-one

It was amazing the resources available to search for almost anything online. Cheryl had been excited to learn of Erin's quest to locate Jimmy's family and had thrown herself into helping straightaway. Whilst Cheryl worked her family research magic in North Queensland, Erin dug around into a few of her leads, but it was proving a little more difficult than she'd expected. Then one afternoon, Cheryl called.

'I found Jimmy!' she cried.

'Where? How? . . . No, don't bother with the explanations, just tell me!' said Erin.

'After a few false leads, I finally found him through the US Census. He lived in Louisiana. A place called Franklin. I was able to find a few of his family members: his parents, Erin Mae and James Crenshaw. He had two other brothers,

Patrick and Thomas. From what I can tell, Thomas is still alive but both his parents and brother Patrick have long gone. I'll send you an email with the info I've got so far.'

'Oh, my God, Cheryl, that's fantastic!'

'Once I sorted through the details and made sure we had the right Jimmy Crenshaw, the rest was fairly easy. Now, I couldn't get anything on the living relatives, because that kind of information isn't available online through Births, Deaths and Marriages, but I have found a niece of Jimmy's who *has* compiled a family history on a family genealogy site I belong to. I reckon if you get in touch with her, she'd be really excited to meet you.'

This was what she'd had in the back of her mind since learning Jimmy was her biological grandfather, but thinking about it and being confronted with the opportunity to actually *do* it were two completely different things. She was about to open a can of worms for these people. How would she feel if some stranger contacted her out of the blue claiming to be a long-lost relative? Now that she'd actually found them, she was a little nervous as to what their reaction might be.

The email from Cheryl arrived within minutes of their phone call ending, and Erin stared at the details on her computer screen for a long time before shutting her laptop and going for a walk.

The clean air cleared her mind, although it didn't give her any answers.

∽

It took a further two days of tossing and turning to finally open her computer and compose her email. Within twenty-four hours, she had established contact with Gwendolyn, the daughter of Jimmy's youngest brother, Thomas.

Any doubts she'd had over being mistaken for some kind of con artist were dispelled after Gwendolyn's second email. She wrote that they had always known Jimmy had fallen in love with an Australian girl and was planning on getting married. After Jimmy's death the family had even considered hiring an investigator to try to find out who this mysterious woman was, but with only a first name and nothing more, they were told it was unlikely to be successful. The news that Jimmy had had a child wasn't as big a shock as she'd expected.

She had a family and they wanted to meet her.

Forty-two

Erin placed the last plastic bag of groceries into the boot of her car. Life had fallen into a comfortable routine. Jamie had more or less moved into Gran's house, going out to work and returning at the end of the day, dusty, tired and happy. She'd been back to the office a few times for important meetings, but the rest of her work was done via video-conferencing.

Tonight she planned on cooking a baked dinner, hoping to get Jamie into a relaxed mood before she broached the subject of travelling to America. She'd been in almost daily contact with her American family over the last few weeks and her aunt had invited her to come over and meet everyone. However, judging from the reaction Jamie had had over Townsville, she wasn't overly confident he was going to be thrilled about her heading to the other side of the world.

She wished she didn't have to upset the sweet calm that had settled between them, but she wasn't prepared to avoid the subject just in case it started an argument. That was not how she wanted to live.

Closing the boot with a satisfying thunk, Erin turned around just as Vanessa walked past, heading for the supermarket.

'Enjoy it while it lasts,' she said, coming to a stop beside Erin's car.

'Excuse me?'

'This thing you've got going with Jamie. It won't last. He'll come back to me, like he did last time.'

'That was a long time ago. I think it's safe to say we've all grown up since then and moved on.'

'I wasn't talking about *then*,' she said with a smirk. 'Ask him where he was while you were up north.'

Erin frowned as she watched her walk away, her earlier good mood gone, replaced by a knot of unease in her stomach.

✍

'Something smells fantastic in here,' Jamie said, coming into the kitchen, catching Erin off guard. She'd been so preoccupied with her thoughts, she hadn't heard him come in.

'Thought I'd do a roast.'

'Sounds good.' He slid his arms around her waist and nuzzled her neck, but stilled and pulled back slightly when she didn't respond. 'What's the matter?'

Erin shook her head, and continued to peel the vegetables in the sink. 'I bumped into Vanessa in town earlier.'

'Did she say something to upset you?'

'It was more what she *didn't* say.'

'Okay. What *didn't* she say, then?' he asked slowly.

'Have you . . . seen her lately?'

Jamie frowned but gave an offhand shrug. 'It's Tuendoc, kinda hard *not* to see someone around here.'

Erin's hand stilled on the potato peeler. It wasn't her imagination, he was being deliberately noncommittal.

'What do you really want to know, Erin?'

Erin dropped the peeler and the potato into the sink and turned around to face him. 'Vanessa gave the impression that the two of you had . . . *been* together recently.'

'Been together?'

'You know what I mean,' Erin snapped.

'I told you she and I had a history. I haven't hidden that.'

'She didn't seem to be referring to that.'

'So you think I've been seeing her while I've been with you? I'm flattered that you think I'm man enough to keep two women happy at once.' His tight expression looked anything but pleased.

'The night we had an argument about my going to Townsville, where did you go when you left here?' Erin asked, striving to keep her tone calm, but her hands were beginning to shake and she braced them on the sink behind her.

She'd been thinking about it all afternoon, and that was the only thing that made sense, the only occasion she could think of that Vanessa could have been referring to. She'd been hoping she was just lying to cause trouble. Now she wasn't so sure.

Jamie was angry, she could see it in the tight set of his lips and the way he'd folded his arms across his broad chest. But it wasn't his demeanour that made her stomach drop, it was the momentary look of apprehension flashing across his face.

'So you don't trust me?'

'I didn't say that.'

'The fact you're asking tells me you don't.'

'You didn't answer the question,' she said quietly.

'I went to Vanessa's.' His answer was blunt and held no apology.

Even though Erin had been expecting it, to hear him confirm it still shocked her. Maybe somewhere deep down she'd hoped he'd deny it and, despite a flicker of apprehension, she'd be able to shrug it off.

But he'd confirmed it. What was she supposed to do with that? 'I see.'

'*Sure* you see,' snorted Jamie.

'What's that supposed to mean?'

'You don't *see* anything. You've just jumped to a whole bunch of conclusions.'

'Then clarify it for me.'

'I shouldn't have to. If you trusted me, you wouldn't be assuming the worst.'

'I'm not assuming anything, I'm just trying to figure out why you'd be so defensive of something if it were completely innocent.'

'Maybe because you're standing there doubting me.'

'What am I supposed to think? She said you'd go running back to her like you always did, and clearly she was right. You were angry with me and you ran to her.'

'Did I? Just like that? You believe that's how it was?'

'You just told me you went to Vanessa's after our fight.' This was getting exasperating.

'I did. I have no reason to lie to you.'

'Obviously,' she said sarcastically.

'So that means I must have slept with her?'

'No, I don't believe you slept with her,' Erin said tightly, moving away from the sink and pacing the floor. 'But running to *her* for comfort or a shoulder to cry on every single time we argue is just as bad.'

'I did that *once*,' he growled, frustration heavy in his tone. 'Look, you want to believe the worst? Go for it. I'm not going to stand here and argue.'

Well, she figured, she might as well get the rest of it out in the open while he was already annoyed. 'I'm going to America.'

'You're what?' he said, turning back to stare at her in disbelief.

'Going to America,' she repeated firmly. 'You know that I've been in touch with one of Mum's aunties, Gwendolyn. She has invited me to go over and stay with them.'

Jamie stared at her. 'You don't even know these people. They could be a bunch of hillbilly psychopaths.'

Erin rolled her eyes. 'I'm not stupid, Jamie. I've booked a motel to stay in and I'm pretty sure I'll be able to tell if my life is in danger once I meet them. If I do, I promise I will not follow them down into a basement, especially if they're carrying an axe, okay?'

'Joke all you like, but weird shit happens over there. You *have* watched the news on occasion, haven't you?'

'Sometimes I seriously worry about you, Jamie. Small-town living has its good points, but small-mindedness is not one of them. You need to get out into the world and see what's beyond Tuendoc.'

'Wow, you know for a minute there I thought I was listening to your husband talking.'

Jamie's snarled comment felt like a slap across the face.

He let out a long frustrated sigh. 'I'm sorry, okay? I'm trying to be the voice of reason. When did you decide all this anyway? And how come this is the first I've even heard of it?'

'This morning.'

'Is that what this whole Vanessa thing was about tonight? Were you trying to pick a fight so you could justify leaving?'

'What? No. Of course not.'

''Cause it seems a little bit too convenient to me.'

'Don't be ridiculous.' Erin felt a strange flutter of panic begin to stir in her stomach. 'I bumped into her in town this afternoon.'

'You don't see this? You don't see that you're running again? It's that night all over again. You're throwing that car in reverse and hightailing it outta town.'

'Oh, please.'

'Think about it. When was the last time you actually stayed and confronted a problem? The only reason you've stayed here this long and buried yourself so deep in all this family history is because you don't want to go back and confront your arsehole husband and his new girlfriend.'

Erin stared at him, fearing her face might show her uncertainty.

'You've done nothing wrong. They're the ones who should be ashamed, but you're the one who's in hiding.'

'I'm not hiding from anyone,' she said tersely. She didn't particularly want to have to face all the gossip and knowing looks either, but it wasn't hiding, it was delaying until the whole thing either blew over or she felt a bit stronger. Just thinking about her husband was enough to irritate her at this moment. 'You have no idea what you're talking about.'

'Course not, I'm just a dumb farmer from Hicksville. What would I possibly know about anything, right?'

'I didn't say that.'

'You didn't have to. Clearly I'm not sophisticated enough for you, I haven't travelled the world, I'm not a university lecturer, I only know how to cheat and slink around behind your back.'

Erin couldn't believe this was all coming out now. It was as though she'd picked the scab off a wound to find all these issues had been festering below.

'You know what? You're right, I'm none of the things your prick of a husband was. I'm better than that. You just don't want to see it.'

'I've *never* compared you to him.'

'You're doing it now, when you've decided the worst, instead of giving me the benefit of the doubt,' he said sadly. 'You can't trust me.'

Erin gave a bitter snort, but closed her eyes briefly against the pain. 'Trust? I *trusted* that marriage was forever, but apparently the whole "unto death do us part" bit becomes null and void if you can't have a baby. Then I discover my family has these secrets in their past, and my gran, the one person I trusted most of all, had a whole secret life she never talked about . . . so forgive me if my trust is a little shaky right now.'

'Do you want to try to make this thing between us work, Erin?' he asked quietly.

His question surprised her. Part of her did want to, very much. But there was still that little part that wasn't sure she could trust in the possibility of a future with this man.

'I guess that answered my question,' he said dully when she hesitated.

'That's not fair.'

'It was a simple question.'

'There's nothing simple about it. I've just come out of a marriage, Jamie. I'm not sure I want to get back into a serious relationship so soon. And quite frankly, I don't think you've thought any of this through enough to be asking.'

'I've thought about nothing else ever since you came back to town.'

'Okay, so have you thought about not having kids?' This was the crux of the issue, and she almost wished she could take the question back now.

'I have, actually,' he told her tightly. 'It's not a deal-breaker for me.'

'Really?' she said with a hefty dose of scepticism. 'So you're quite okay with the fact your family line runs out if you don't have any kids?'

'This isn't medieval England, Erin. Anyway, Dad's got brothers and we have plenty of heirs to the McBride name and vast fortune,' he said sarcastically.

'You can't possibly know how you'll feel in a few years' time, when you wake up and suddenly realise the enormity of never being a father.'

'Maybe you're right. Maybe I will have regrets about the kids we could have had but didn't,' he said, and held her gaze determinedly. 'But you know what? I'm not stupid enough to throw away a future with the woman I love just because we can't have kids.'

'I don't know if I can risk being discarded a second time,' she said quietly. And that's what it all boiled down to. She was afraid.

Erin hated the look of defeat on his face. Jamie was the most confident man she'd ever known and to see him look defeated felt like a physical blow to her stomach.

'This trip to America isn't about running away, and it's nothing to do with you and I. It's just something I need to do.'

'Then you do whatever you have to do.'

He turned away and she was left staring after him. She blinked back tears as she heard his car roar off down the driveway. She needed to start organising her travel arrangements but her heart felt so heavy all she could do was fall into bed. She went to sleep with only the company of warm tears trickling onto her pillow.

Forty-three

Erin zipped her suitcase closed and sat down on the end of the bed. Her upcoming trip had lost a lot of its shine since her argument with Jamie the night before. Instead of excitement, all she felt now was drained.

She looked down at the tin box beside her on the bed and gave a small sigh. For such a small box, it had certainly contained a lot of trouble. She unzipped her bag just enough to slip in the box, then stood, grabbing the handle and pulling the suitcase along behind her as she headed out the door.

Most of the main street was empty as she drove through town. The only sign of life was at the far end at the hotel, where an assortment of vehicles was parked out the front. One in particular caught her eye and sadness was replaced by disbelief. Jamie's car. She didn't want to trust this horrible feeling in her gut, but it was never usually wrong. Erin touched her brakes, slowing down before making a spur-of-the-moment decision and swinging her car into a parking space.

It wasn't a busy night, although there was a decent crowd scattered throughout the old hotel, and Erin spotted him without much difficulty.

Jamie sat, his shoulders slumped, cupping an almost empty glass where it sat on the bar in front of him. But it was the arm draped across his shoulders that had Erin's full attention. She should turn and walk away, but she couldn't. She was furious. All his denying and playing the outraged victim last night had been a lie. Here he was, right back at the scene of the crime with his faithful accomplice. It was history repeating itself.

'Wouldn't work. It was never love. We're just not right for each other,' she heard Jamie saying, his voice sounding slightly slurred but full of conviction. At that moment Vanessa turned and Erin saw something flash in the other woman's eye before she looked away, pressing even closer against Jamie's side and rubbing herself against him.

'You'll never be good enough for her. I don't know why you tried for so long,' said Vanessa.

Erin couldn't believe this was happening . . . *again*. How dare he stand in her kitchen and make her feel bad about calling him on Vanessa's comments. *Damn him!* She'd wanted to trust him but instead of just explaining himself, he had turned it all around to make *her* feel like a paranoid drama queen. How was she supposed to trust him when the very first person he went to after their argument was *Vanessa? Again.*

Erin turned on her heel, her heart paining. She'd heard more than enough. What was the point? The last thing she felt like right now was making a scene. She had enough drama to deal with, she did not need to add a public display in the middle of the damn pub to the pile.

She didn't look back and she didn't slow down until she was in the car and driving out of town, and even then she refused to let her eyes stray to the rear-view mirror. What an idiot she'd been to believe him.

Just don't look back, she told herself firmly. She needed to look forward; she had a family to meet and nothing was going to ruin that moment. Not now.

⁐

Erin sat in the departure lounge of the airport, staring bleakly through the large window. She'd spent the last few days in Sydney organising the trip. It had been good to see Roxy again; she'd missed her friend more than she'd realised. Erin had been back to her apartment briefly over the last few weeks when she'd come down for meetings, but she hadn't done anything about arranging for any of Phillip's things to be removed. She started to write him a text message but deleted it before she hit send. She couldn't deal with that on top of everything else right now. She looked down at the phone in her hand and sighed. There'd been one missed call from Jamie, but she'd been too hurt to return the call.

It was never love.

Whatever he'd been wanting to say obviously hadn't been too important—he hadn't called again. What was there left to say anyway?

The man beside her was taking up his own seat plus a considerable amount of hers, and she couldn't decide whether the family with two small children behind her needed a medal for patience as their children threw tantrum after tantrum, or a slap up the head for raising such obnoxious children in the first place. They'd alternated between crying and whining the entire time they'd been sitting down. It didn't bode well for the upcoming fourteen-hour flight.

Erin glanced up as someone squeezed into the seat on the other side of her. She reshuffled her position, but her irritated frown changed immediately as she noticed the burnt orange poncho draped across the woman, who was turned towards her, watching expectantly.

'Mum?' Erin gasped.

'Surprise,' her mother said calmly.

'What are you *doing* here?'

'I've been thinking about what you said the other day, and it made me face a few home truths. You were right. I have been too wrapped up in my life lately and I've missed out on what was happening with yours.' She searched Erin's eyes and reached out to cover her hand. 'I'm sorry.'

Erin swallowed past a rapidly tightening throat. 'Oh, Mum, I'm so sorry about everything that happened to you.'

'It was a long time ago,' her mother said with a sad smile. 'I've been thinking about it a lot though. I've always prided myself on being strong, not allowing my past to define who I am, but I made a rather unsettling discovery about myself after you left,' she said, dropping her gaze to rest on their clasped hands. 'Turning my back on my past wasn't being strong. It was weak. Confronting the memories made me realise that I was refusing to remember it because I was scared. It hurt too much to think about the child I could have had, and by refusing to think about it, it was like he or she never existed at all. That baby deserves to be remembered, and by forgetting I did exactly what Roy and the Browns wanted me to do. I should have talked about that child instead of allowing them to pretend it never existed.'

Erin felt a tear as it slipped down her face, followed by a steady warm stream she couldn't stop.

She knew her mother carried a heavy burden because of the man who had raised her. Erin could distance herself enough to realise some of the blame for Roy's behaviour could be traced back to the things he'd been through during the war. New Guinea had been a bloody and brutal chapter in World War Two. But her mother had been a child, a baby. An innocent. There was no real excuse for the mental abuse he'd inflicted on his wife and child as payment for Evelyn's infidelity while he was away fighting. Why hadn't he simply ended the engagement and walked away? Why marry Evelyn knowing she was pregnant with another man's baby and then subject them both to all that hostility? What purpose did that serve? Had the war made him so anguished that he wanted everyone else to be as miserable as he was? They'd never know now, and maybe there was no logical reason. War was war, and the consequences lasted for generations after it ended.

Her mother released her hand to dig through her massive tote, bringing out two tissues. Handing one over to Erin, she quickly blew her nose and straightened her shoulders.

When Erin had sent her mother a rather sardonic text about flying out to meet Jimmy's family, she hadn't expected a reply, let alone her mother to actually come with her.

'I'm so glad you changed your mind about coming to meet them, Mum,' Erin said after they'd composed themselves.

'Before you get too excited,' she said lightly, 'I'm only coming along to support *you*. I can hardly expect you to go off and meet these people all alone. They could be serial killers or something.'

'This from the woman who disappears for months on end into the wilds of Borneo,' Erin said drolly.

'I trust animals more than I trust most humans. Besides, I've seen that alligator show. They eat *rats* in the bayous,' she said with a shudder.

Erin shook her head and gave a helpless smile. She had no idea what kind of alternate universe she'd fallen into where her mother was actually being, well, a *mother,* but she wasn't going to complain. She blinked quickly and dabbed her eyes with her tissue.

Hours later, after most of the passengers had settled into the long flight, Erin sat with her head pressed against the cold glass of her window, looking out at the inky blackness below. *So much ocean.* Her thoughts turned to Jimmy and how many times he would have looked out from his plane while on missions. Had he found the immensity of it all as breathtaking as she did? She tried to imagine how she'd feel as a pilot during the war, in a much smaller plane, out hunting for the enemy in the dark, each time you went out knowing it could be your last.

Her fingers went to the heavy ring that hung around her neck. The metal was warm where it had been resting against her skin and she rubbed the large smooth ruby under her thumb as she continued to stare out over the silver river of moonlight spilling across the ocean below.

Forty-four

The three-hour layover in San Francisco seemed to drag on forever, and she sent a text to Gwendolyn to let her know she'd made it onto US soil and that she had a surprise.

Erin still couldn't believe her mum was here with her. She was so happy that she didn't even get annoyed when Serenity gave the purple-haired teenage girl making their coffee at the airport a lecture about why it was so important not only to buy organic coffee beans but also to research how fair trade the coffee beans were. The fact that the girl a) couldn't have cared less, and b) was not likely the buyer for the coffee shop was apparently completely lost on Serenity.

It didn't matter, her mother was here.

The wait to depart the plane once they finally landed in New Orleans was excruciatingly slow. Erin was having trouble keeping what little food she'd managed to eat on the flight in her stomach as a mixture of nerves and excitement fought a battle inside her.

Gwen had assured her she would be waiting at the arrivals gate. Erin had seen enough photos over the last few weeks to feel confident she'd recognise her aunty, and hopefully a few others in the family as well, but still, a photo was one thing, seeing someone in real life was another altogether. What if she walked straight past them? Her aunt had chuckled when Erin had joked about her going home with the wrong family. 'You won't be able to miss us, darlin',' she'd assured her.

Following the other passengers up the long corridor and out into the arrivals hall, Erin took a fortifying breath and gave her mother a confidant smile before searching the crowd of people waiting for loved ones. She skimmed a large gathering and searched for a few people who might resemble her aunty, but she couldn't see any familiar faces. At a growing murmur her gaze moved back to the large group assembled at the gate and she gaped in surprise.

She was so surprised that she actually stopped in her tracks, which caused a small pile-up of travellers behind her. The large group were all waiting for the same person . . . *her.* A large sign had been made with 'Welcome to the family' written in glitter across the front. *There had to be at least twenty people*, she thought, still stunned, but she managed to shake off some of her numbness and forced herself to keep walking towards them. *There were so many of them*, she thought, feeling a little overwhelmed and, at the same time, incredibly touched.

A small stout woman stepped forward from the group and gathered her into a warm hug. 'You're finally here!'

Erin gathered her wits long enough to remember her own little surprise, grabbing her mother's hand and pulling her forward. 'Look who came with me,' she smiled at the woman who looked to be close to her mother's age. 'Mum, this is your cousin Gwen,' she said, watching the surprise on the older woman's face melt into a tearful smile before she moved forward and hugged her mother tightly.

'You have no idea how happy I am to see you,' she said, pulling away briefly to study Serenity's face intently.

Erin watched her mother's expression waver slightly and her eyes gleamed with a sheen of unshed tears. She'd rarely seen her mother lose the composure she was renowned for.

When she let go, Gwen turned them both around to face the others and, with a flurry of names thrown about in introduction, various people smiled or waved. Children were lifted up for their inspection and all Erin could do was smile and nod, without a hope of remembering who belonged to whom or what their names were.

It was every bit as terrifying and beautiful as she'd imagined, and she gave her mother's hand a quick squeeze as they were swept into a sea of something neither of them had ever had before.

Family.

Forty-five

After collecting their bags, the entourage moved out of the airport and dispersed into various vehicles with the assurance they would all be meeting up again for dinner.

It was late May and the weather was warm. It wasn't the blast of hot air she'd encountered in Townsville and had been expecting here, considering this was the equivalent of Australia's far north. Her American cousins found it amusing when Erin explained that Australia's south was the opposite of theirs.

'Give it another few weeks and it'll be the start of our *nasty* hot weather,' Gwen informed them when her mother remarked on the heat.

The airport was a little way out of New Orleans, and as her mother and relatives chatted and asked questions,

Erin took in her surroundings. It was a surprise that there really was no evidence of the damage Katrina had done to this big city in 2005. Erin recalled the news footage of flood-waters and grief-stricken people wandering the streets. There were apparently some parts that had not been rebuilt, but these were the places where people had moved on and never returned.

The closer they got to New Orleans the bigger the houses were. She gaped at some of the big southern plantation-style buildings that lined the streets as they hit New Orleans, passing trams in the middle of the road.

'You just wait,' her aunty said, turning around in the front seat to smile at her. 'In Franklin, where I live, there are some beautiful old plantation homes. In fact, one of them is run by a good friend of mine and she's offered to give you a tour while you're here.'

Erin was blown away by the entire family's generosity. They seemed just as excited as she was.

'Now, depending on how tired you are, we thought we could give you a quick tour of New Orleans. I plan on bringing you back here for a whole day of sightseeing, but since we're here now, it seems a shame not to show you around.'

'I'm fine,' Erin reassured her aunty without hesitation. 'Mum? You feel okay?' They only had eight days here and she didn't want to waste a single minute. In fact she'd gone past tired about five hours back. Now she was running on pure adrenaline. She planned on holding out until it was late enough local time to go to bed; the last thing she needed was jet lag messing with her precious stay.

As they walked along the old streets of downtown New Orleans, Erin snapped photo after photo, just like every other tourist was doing. Some of the buildings seemed familiar and she realised that they had been used in numerous movies she'd watched over the years. The narrow streets were lined with old brick buildings in shades of yellows, pinks, reds, greens and blues, all blending into a gorgeous, vibrant display of spectacular Spanish architecture. Many of their wrought-iron balconies were draped in cascades of potted colour: ivy, begonias and huge green ferns all added to an amazing display. Everywhere she looked there was a vibrancy she could physically feel.

They walked down a shaded back street, past an old church and an alleyway her aunt took great delight in telling her was called the pirate's alley, before crossing the street and stopping for the obligatory beignet at Café du Monde. The sugary delight was a French donut of sorts, covered in an absurd amount of powdery icing sugar, and it tasted absolutely divine.

Erin could have stayed all day, just walking the streets and soaking up the atmosphere of the old port city, but it was heading towards mid-afternoon and her relatives were planning a huge family feast that evening and they had things to organise.

With the promise of being picked up at six, Erin and her mother waved off their family and dragged the suitcases inside the motel where they'd be staying. It would have been nice to have taken up the offer to stay with Gwen and her husband, but when she'd made her travel arrangements Erin had been thinking ahead about how confronting it was going to be to suddenly meet so many new cousins, aunties and uncles and had figured it wouldn't hurt to have a place she could escape to for a breather.

The room was gorgeous and the bed looked so inviting, but she turned away from the four big fluffy pillows and smooth clean sheets and headed instead for the shower. She washed her hair and turned her back under the hot water, letting it cascade over her tired muscles, crammed into an unnatural position for too many hours.

Feeling better after washing away the long hours of travel, Erin picked up her phone to send Jamie a message, but ended up erasing it before she hit send. She was hurt and angry; old memories of that night in the car park fuelled her confusion. It might have been a teenage romance but the betrayal had been real, and it had hurt her terribly at the time. She didn't believe he'd actually cheated on her with Vanessa since she'd returned to Tuendoc, but the fact he could confide in a woman he *had* once cheated on her with still stung. Had he really meant what he said? Had he really believed it wouldn't have worked and that it wasn't love? Or had that been his injured pride talking? She knew she was equally to blame for the fight, but her feelings were just as relevant as his. She *was* scared of losing him down the track; it had happened once, and Phillip had also sworn he'd never wanted children. Why couldn't he understand her concerns?

She put the phone down with a sigh and went in search of an energy drink. She was going to need it.

Forty-six

Dinner was an eye-opener to say the least.

After being collected from their motel by Gwen's husband, Ronan, Serenity and Erin were taken to a sprawling old house on a quiet street right on the bayou. The house, with its neat trim and pretty gardens, had an enclosed front verandah and a huge American flag. They followed Ronan to the backyard where a crowd of people mingled around a long picnic table lined with newspaper. The family looked to have multiplied since the greeting at the airport. The age group spanned from babies in their parents' arms right through to an older gentleman in a wheelchair. Children weaved through the adults as they ran and laughed and played. Huge pots boiled on various burners off to one side, and a delicious aroma filled the air.

'Now, Mum, please don't start about your views on veganism. We're guests and they're . . . well . . . they're American. They do things differently here.'

'Give me some credit,' her mother said, keeping a smile on her face as they moved towards the crowd. 'I do know how to respect another culture.'

'Then how come you always lecture me?'

'Because it's my job to lecture you. I'm your mother,' she said, patting Erin's cheek lightly.

Gwen took her mother by the arm and steered her over towards the old man in the wheelchair. 'I want to introduce you to someone who has been very excited to meet you,' she said as they arrived by the old man's side.

'Dad, this is Serenity, she's your niece,' Gwen said, squeezing her mother's hand reassuringly. 'This is your Uncle Thomas.'

Erin held her breath as the old man leaned forward and peered at her mother silently for a few moments, before reaching out a wrinkled hand. Her mother took a step closer and took his hand in hers gently.

'Jimmy's baby,' he said in a voice thick with emotion. 'I've been waiting to meet you, young lady. I hoped one day we'd find you.'

'You . . . knew about me?'

The old man smiled sadly. 'I got something to show you.' He pulled out a folded letter and handed it to her. 'Your daddy wrote that to me the night before he died. He was head over heels in love with your mama, he told us all about her, told us he was bringing her home after the war, and that he was headin' off to get married as soon as he could get to

Sydney. He told me she was expectin', too. He was mighty proud. Couldn't wait to be a daddy.'

Tears blurred Erin's vision at the old man's words and her mother let out a tiny sob and bowed her head. Erin placed an arm around her mother's shoulders and smiled at the old man.

'We never could track down your mother. We had no idea what happened to either her or you, but we never really gave up hope of one day finding out. It might be a few years too late, but you're finally here,' he said, patting her mother's arm.

Thomas was the only surviving member of Jimmy's immediate family. Gwen had told them that the oldest brother, Patrick, had died only five years earlier, but both men had left behind a legacy of children and grandchildren and even great-grandchildren. And what a legacy it was. Patrick had had seven children, and Thomas five.

'It's good to finally be here,' her mother said, smiling through her tears, but her eyes shone with happiness.

A chair was brought over for them to sit on, but Erin decided to give her mother and her uncle a chance to talk in private about Jimmy.

Women disappeared in and out of the back door bringing out platters of food. Erin lost count of how many trips they made. She tried to go inside and help but was waved off and told she was the guest and to relax and enjoy herself. It was a little hard to relax when she didn't know anyone, but she did enjoy herself, and felt incredibly welcomed by everyone she talked to. She did her best to remember names, but there were so many of them!

Erin was waved over to a small group of women, two of whom were holding babies, and a tall auburn-haired beauty introduced herself as Gwen's daughter, Ronny.

'Are you ready to run yet?' one of the younger women asked with a smile.

'No, not quite,' said Erin, hoping she sounded more confident than she felt.

'We can be a little full on,' Ronny agreed.

'Is it always like this?' Erin asked as she became an obstacle for two young boys of about five and seven who were chasing each other in circles around her.

'Boys, run off and play somewhere else,' the third woman, Tracey, chided. 'Pretty much,' she nodded.

'Do you get together a lot?' Erin asked.

'Most weekends,' Ronny smiled, tilting her head slightly as she looked at Erin curiously. 'Don't y'all have cookouts in Australia?'

'Well, we do. We usually just call them barbecues. But I don't have much experience with get-togethers like this . . . with family.'

'Really? You don't have family?'

'Well, I do. At least I *did* . . . There was my gran, I'm sure you've heard about her. She and Jimmy . . .' Erin paused, unsure how to put it.

'Did the *wild thang*, yeah, we know about that,' Tracey chuckled.

'Yeah. Well. There was only ever really Gran, my mother and me. Now it's only Mum.'

'That's really sad. I don't know what I'd do without this rowdy lot,' Tracey said, looking around with a tolerant smile.

'Are you kidding? Imagine the peace and quiet,' the other woman sighed wistfully. 'No one having an opinion about your life . . .' She looked across at Erin and asked, 'Do you think maybe we could switch for a while?'

Erin shook her head and chuckled. 'I think you'd get bored pretty quick.'

'I'd miss these monsters, I suppose,' she agreed, nuzzling the baby in her arms with a loving smile that caused a stab of longing in Erin.

She looked away, but not before catching Ronny's eye.

'Are you married? Do you have any children?' Tracey asked.

'No. Actually, I'm going through a divorce.'

'Oh. I'm sorry.' Tracey looked mortified.

'Oh, no. It's all right. Really. It's fine,' Erin said, trying to reassure her.

The conversation moved on to something else, and Erin found herself enjoying the company immensely. She loved listening to the soothing New Orleans accent, but everyone seemed to want her to talk so they could listen to hers. She caught glimpses of her mother as she was moved through the crowd of mainly older relatives, and marvelled at how relaxed she looked.

Soon enough, dinner was served and Erin found herself caught up in the rush for the table. She watched in bemusement as the large pots which had been bubbling earlier were tipped rather unceremoniously straight onto the table. She looked sideways to see if anyone else was surprised, but judging by the way they all quickly began reaching for things to put on their plates, she guessed this was quite normal.

'Dig in,' said Ronny, smiling as she handed her a plate then reached past her to snag some large crawfish, which looked a lot like yabbies. There were huge prawns, which they called shrimp, as well as potatoes, cobs of corn, onions and slices of lemon. Her mother politely declined any seafood but piled her plate high with vegetables and salad.

It was delicious. When Erin had first seen the enormous quantities of food on the table, she'd been unable to imagine how they would possibly get through it all, but by the end of the night there was barely anything left. Erin ate so much seafood she could barely move, but it wasn't over yet, there was still dessert.

Again, Erin was shooed away from clearing the table and Ronny was assigned to keep her entertained. The two women found a seat and Ronny handed her a glass of wine. 'So tell me to mind my own business if you want, but how come you haven't had kids yet?'

'I can't.'

'I'm sorry. I should have minded my own business,' said Ronny.

'No, that's all right. It was never a big secret.'

'Is that why your marriage broke up?' When Erin looked up in surprise, Ronny put a hand out quickly. 'I'm sorry. You don't have to answer. It's just me. I'm really nosey. It's always getting me in trouble.'

It was impossible to be annoyed by the questions, her cousin was just too likeable. 'Actually, it was. My husband found someone else to have his children.'

'Ouch.'

'Yeah.'

'What an asshole.'

Erin took a sip of her wine and kept silent. She'd thought much worse things about Phillip, but somehow she no longer cared enough to hold on to her anger. The hurt would take a long time to heal, and the trust he'd thrown to the ground and stomped all over would take even longer.

Maybe Jamie had been right remind her that he wasn't her husband. Maybe part of her reaction to Vanessa's suggestion of Jamie cheating again had been a knee-jerk reaction to her husband's betrayal. Perhaps she had overreacted a little. Yet when was it safe to let your guard down after having had your trust destroyed like that?

'It's sad really,' she said. 'He suddenly realised being the last of his line, he needed to reproduce to keep the lineage going, and suddenly I've found a whole new line of my family I never knew existed.'

'I'm glad you found us.'

'I am too,' she smiled, and she really was. While it was odd to feel like a stranger amongst people who shared her blood, she also felt something else: a sense of belonging . . . of acceptance. A twinge of sadness caught her unexpectedly as she thought of Gran. *This* was what Evelyn should have experienced—would have experienced if only fate hadn't cruelly ripped Jimmy from her life.

It would take a long time before she was as relaxed around these people as they clearly were around each other, but somehow she felt as though she belonged.

Forty-seven

The next day they spent the afternoon sitting around Gwen's kitchen table going through her impressive family album. Gwen was a budding genealogist, and clearly in her element when it came to filling Serenity in on their family tree. Erin watched her mother tentatively take the photos her cousin passed across, explaining who was who, but when she found the ones of Jimmy, she saw something change in her mother's expression.

As she held the photos of Jimmy as a baby, Jimmy posing with his brothers in front of a plane as a teenager, Jimmy in his uniform with his parents before leaving for the war, a smile hovered on her lips. It was a smile that soon wobbled and dissolved into tears, before she pushed her chair away from the table and hurried from the room.

Erin made to follow her mother, but Gwen put a hand out and stopped her gently. 'Leave her be a while, sweetheart. As tough as your mamma tries to be on the outside, she can't hide that big ol' hole she's got inside. Just give her a minute to adjust to all this.'

When coffee and cake was ready a little later, Erin volunteered to go out and tell her mother. She found Serenity sitting on a bench on the bank of the bayou, out the back of Gwen's house.

'Are you okay?' Erin asked tentatively.

'I am,' she said softly, sounding surprised. 'It was always too hard to think about him. I thought if he wasn't real to me, it would make it easier. Not knowing him,' she explained. 'But I was wrong. After you left the retreat, I thought about the way life turned out.

'I think somehow she thought she was protecting me by not stepping in and stopping what happened when she found out I was pregnant. Maybe she didn't want me marrying Peter for the sake of a child, maybe she was thinking that she could save me having to pay for a mistake for the rest of my life like she did.' Serenity dropped her gaze to the photos once more and closed her eyes tightly. 'I've been living a lie for more years than I can count. I told myself I'd forgiven my parents, that I'd released all the anger and hurt and healed. But the truth was I hadn't forgiven, I'd just tried to forget. I tried to help other people, knowing that while I was concentrating on the pain of others, I could bury my own. But you forced me to face my own pain and grief and deal with it once and for all. Thank you, darling.'

Erin swallowed hard over the lump in her throat. 'I'm proud of you, Mum.'

'I'm proud of you,' her mother said, slipping her arm around Erin's waist. 'I promise I won't make the same mistake with us,' she vowed. 'I don't want to live with any more regrets.'

'It won't happen to us, Mum. We won't let it.'

⁓

The next day, over breakfast, Erin cautiously brought something up with her mother.

'I know how you feel about funerals and the whole death thing, but I was wondering if you'd come out to the cemetery with me later to visit Jimmy's grave?'

She watched her mother pause between bites of homemade muesli. They'd gone in search of a health food outlet the very first morning they'd arrived to purchase the necessary ethical and organic ingredients.

'If you like.'

'You don't have to. I just thought you might want to see it since we came all this way and—'

'I want to. I'd like to go with you,' she said, cutting her off firmly.

'Okay then.' Erin was a little surprised. She'd been sure she wouldn't be able to convince her to come along.

It was incredibly moving to stand at the foot of the grave where the man she only knew from photos and a few letters lay buried. This man who had meant so much to her gran. This man who was her grandfather. This man who had been so incredibly young and taken far too soon.

She looked across at her mother and wondered what was going through her mind. This was the man who had created her and he was just as much a stranger to her as he was to Erin.

She reached over and slipped her hand into her mother's, giving her fingers a gentle squeeze.

She wished she could have somehow brought something of Gran's to lay beside him, but in her heart she knew they would already have found each other again. A love that strong couldn't possibly be constrained by the laws of life here on earth. At least it made her feel better to think of them together at last and happy once more.

'Thank you,' her mother said, turning her gaze from the headstone carved with her father's name.

Gwen came up behind and put and arm around each of them and squeezed. They stood there, women tied to each other by blood, each lost in their own thoughts as a breeze tickled their hair and birds sang sweetly from the shady trees above.

Forty-eight

Erin pulled out the small box she'd packed the ring in and handed it across to her mother. Serenity opened it and stared at it for a few moments, then held it out to Thomas. 'It's Jimmy's ring,' Erin said quietly. 'That's what started this whole search. I wanted to bring the ring back to his family where it belongs.'

Thomas carefully picked out the large ring and turned it around to read the inscription. 'It always *was* where it belonged. It belonged to Evelyn and then to you and your mother.'

'But we didn't even know him,' Erin said.

'So many died too young, and without making any lasting memories for the remaining generations. But we *have* something of him with us still: you and your mom. You're both living, breathing monuments to his life, and he would have been very proud to call you his granddaughter. And you his daughter,' he said, turning to place a hand on her mother's arm gently.

As she watched tears run down her mother's face, Erin tried unsuccessfully to blink back her own. It was hard to imagine Jimmy as her grandfather, but when she tried to imagine her mother's pain at never having known this man as her father, the grief was hard to ignore.

It made her angry to think of all the hurt her mother had gone through over the years, trying to please a man who had never shown her any love. She knew how close Jimmy's family was and how much he would have loved having a daughter. Her mother would have been a very different person had she grown up here amongst these people.

'You keep it,' Thomas said.

'I'm not sure I'm worthy of it. I feel ashamed. I should have come looking for you a long time ago, but instead I turned my back on you all. If it wasn't for Erin,' she turned her watery gaze on her daughter.

'You hush now. Everything in its own time. You're here now and that's all that matters,' Gwen said, stepping in. She turned to Erin. 'You mentioned that you'd like to go and see the World War Two museum in New Orleans?'

'Yes, I would. I wanted to donate a photo of Jimmy to them.'

'I think that's a wonderful idea,' Gwen said with a beaming smile.

Erin was awed by The National WWII Museum's enormity. It was like nothing she'd ever seen before. They made their way through a maze of exhibits, searching for the one thing Erin was longing to see up close. She found what she was looking for in a huge space that resembled a hangar. There in the centre of the room behind a rope was the *French Quarter*. The painted starlet in all her buxom glory gleamed beneath the overhead lights.

'Honey, this is Captain Graham; he's a volunteer here at the museum. I called him up the other day and mentioned that you were coming here to visit,' Gwen said, introducing an elderly man.

'It's a pleasure to meet you, ma'am,' he said, shaking her hand gently. 'I believe you have a special connection to this old gal.'

Erin smiled at how strange it all was. She'd first seen this plane in an old photo hidden in a tin box in the bottom of her gran's wardrobe. The journey that had started there had taken her from Townsville all the way to Louisiana. And along the way she'd not only uncovered the name of her biological grandfather, she'd also found her mother once more. *Yes, I do have a special connection to this plane,* she thought with a wistful smile.

Carefully Erin withdrew an envelope from her handbag and took out her grandmother's photo of Jimmy standing beside the plane on the tarmac in Townsville. She handed it across to the captain. 'I thought these two should be reunited again,' she said, looking between the photo in the man's hand and the plane. 'I'd like to donate it to your museum.'

'Would you look at this,' the captain breathed out slowly. When he lifted his gaze from the photo again his eyes were shining with excitement. 'Young lady, this is very generous of you. The museum and the United States Air Force would be honoured to accept this donation.'

A small part of Erin wanted to snatch back the photo. She'd developed a very strong bond to the images in Gran's tin box, but she knew that this part of Jimmy, the military part, belonged to the country and the people he'd died serving.

'There's one more thing I thought might interest you,' Captain Graham said, leading his small group to another part of the museum. 'Right here.'

They stopped in front of an entrance to a photo gallery entitled *Love and War,* and Erin led the way into a dark hallway where images of women and uniformed men lined the walls. Erin slowly walked along, loving the many photos and reading the written accounts of men and women who had found love during war in far-off places. Extracts of old letters and diaries made for fascinating reading.

Was this how it had been for Evelyn and Jimmy, she wondered as she read about dances and shore leave, young American men falling in love with women from all over the world during their stays in foreign lands. There was a section dedicated to the women from all across the world who had married US soldiers and the journeys they had undertaken to be reunited with the men they loved. Fifteen thousand Australian women had married American servicemen during World War Two.

Erin stopped in front of a photo of a ship departing Sydney Harbour. Her gaze roamed across the faces of the hundreds of women hanging over the rails of the ship as it departed. Many carried babies. Some looked excited as they waved goodbye to their homeland to set off on a grand adventure across the ocean; others looked tearful and more than a little daunted, and some were crying openly as they waved goodbye to mothers, fathers and siblings watching from the docks.

What had these women, some still teenagers, given up? And for what? Men they'd only known for a handful of days if they were lucky? The faith these women had put in those men was staggering to think about. Evelyn had been one of these women . . . *would* have been one of these women, Erin corrected sadly. Had Jimmy gotten on any other plane that day, she would have married him and maybe even been in this very photo hanging on the museum wall. She swallowed hard over a lump in her throat and blinked back the pressing tears. There was so much heartache and pain. She ached for Gran and Jimmy and what might have been. Life was so very short and precious. And you never knew what lay around the corner.

Forty-nine

On the eve of Erin's final day in New Orleans, Gwen organised yet another family dinner. There was no cookout this time, but the amount of food was no less daunting. The women had been busy cooking up just about every southern dish they could think of: seafood jumbo, chicken jumbo, boudin and rice, jambalaya, étouffée, fried chicken, and more mashed potatoes and side dishes than she could poke a stick at. She was positive she gained five kilos just by inhaling the glorious smell of all this food.

The day before, her mother had suggested a walk by the bayou that backed onto her aunty's house. It seemed like ages since she'd had her Mum to herself; with so many people around it was often impossible to sit and talk with just one person at a time.

'You seem to be having a great time. Glad you came?' Erin asked.

'So glad. Darling, I wanted to apologise for that last visit we had. No,' she held up her hand when Erin went to protest. 'I need to. You were right, I had been too wrapped up in my own life. I should have realised you were in pain and I didn't. That's inexcusable for a mother, a healer and an activist. What use is helping everyone else if I can't help my own daughter?'

'Mum, it's okay.'

'No, it's not.'

Erin looked at her mother, who stood gazing out over the water before them. 'I haven't exactly been the most understanding daughter in the world either. I guess I was jealous of everyone else who seemed to be dominating your time. But the truth is, I'm incredibly proud of who you are. I don't know of any other person with the amount of passion you have for helping others. The risks you take with your animal projects, the amount of money you donate to make this world a better place . . . It's amazing. You're amazing,' Erin said quietly.

She saw her mother's lip wobble slightly before she turned and drew Erin into a tight hug. 'I'm the one who's proud. You are a beautiful, intelligent young woman and I couldn't ask for a better daughter. Thank you for not giving up on me . . . or on this,' she said, throwing her arm out to encompass her cousin's property. 'I don't think I would ever have been brave enough to do this on my own.'

Erin dug into her pocket and withdrew two tissues, handing one to her mother. 'I don't know why but I seem to be doing this a lot lately, and I've learned to always be prepared,' she laughed, waving the tissue in the air between them.

'Would you be terribly upset if I didn't return to Australia with you tomorrow?'

Erin looked at her mother in surprise. 'You're staying?'

Serenity nodded. 'I thought I might. Eight days just hasn't been long enough to catch up on a lifetime. But if you'd rather I came home with you, I'll come back later.'

'No,' said Erin, smiling at her. 'Stay. I'll be fine. I love you, Mum,' she said and hugged her fiercely. *Goddamn these stupid tears*, she thought helplessly as yet another flood started. They sat and watched life on the bayou drift past for a long while, enjoying the warm sunshine on their faces and the newfound peace between them.

∽

Erin was getting used to the noise and crowd by now. As she sat in a deckchair beside Ronny and Tracey, an empty plate on her lap, she realised how much she was going to miss these people. She quickly wiped at the corner of her eye and took a deep breath.

'I can't believe you're leaving tomorrow. You just got here,' Tracey pouted sadly.

'I know. It's flown past. It's been one hell of a roller-coaster ride,' she added, sniffing slightly.

'Here,' Ronny said, handing her a tissue.

Erin shook her head. 'I don't know what the hell is wrong with me. I never cry and now that's all I seem to do. It's crazy.

I cried this morning because my hair straightener wouldn't fit into your power point! How insane is that?'

'Would a glass of wine help?' Ronny asked, holding up a bottle.

Erin shook her head and frowned as she realised this was the third time in last few days she'd turned down wine. She loved wine. She hadn't felt like it at all. Or coffee for that matter. Her frown deepened. What was happening to her? She couldn't usually function without caffeine. Maybe she was coming down with something.

'Uh-huh,' Ronny said in a long drawl.

'What's that supposed to mean?' Erin asked.

'Nothing,' she said, looking across at Tracey. She saw the two women raise an eyebrow as if in silent agreement.

'What?' Erin demanded.

'Honey, it's completely normal,' Tracey said, patting her arm comfortingly.

'Normal? For what?'

'Being pregnant,' Ronny said simply.

'What?'

'You've been showing all the symptoms,' Tracey added frankly.

Erin stared at the two women blankly. Clearly they'd both lost their minds.

Ronny sighed. 'You're an emotional train wreck. You're tired. You're boobs are huge,' she said, pointedly looking at Erin's T-shirt, which stretched tightly across her chest. 'And you don't feel like alcohol,' she added.

'Well, I do *now*,' Erin muttered.

'You seriously didn't suspect?' asked Tracey.

'*No*. It's not possible. I can't get pregnant,' she said, and realised her tone was a mixture of disbelief and panic.

'Well, there's one way to find out for sure,' Ronny said, getting to her feet.

Oh, my God, Erin thought. They were about to perform some ancient Cajun voodoo magic on her. 'It doesn't involve chicken blood, does it?' she asked, only half joking.

'I was thinking a home pregnancy test would be easier,' her cousin said drolly.

'You've got it all wrong. There's no way I can get pregnant.'

'The doctors didn't take *everything* out, did they?' Ronny reminded her.

'No, but I tried it all. IVF, diet, naturopathy, acupuncture,' she ticked them off. 'I could *never* fall pregnant.'

'Maybe it was stress? Sounds like that was an awful lot of pressure you were putting yourself under,' Tracey suggested.

Could it be as simple as that? That all she'd needed to do was give up and accept she could never fall pregnant? It sounded like a sick kind of joke to her.

'You've had sex recently, I take it?' Tracey went on, folding her arms across her chest stubbornly. 'Then take it from me, it's possible. This is from one who can get pregnant just by just thinking about sex. I'm telling you—you're knocked up, girl.'

Erin was too shocked to bother protesting when Ronny held out a hand to pull her to her feet. She barely noticed when they made the excuse of heading out to help Erin finish packing. She just sat in the passenger seat, staring blindly out the window as they drove through the dark, quiet streets.

Back in her motel room, Erin stared blankly at the little stick in her hand.

Life as she'd known it had suddenly ceased to exist.

∽

Erin spent a long time on the flight home looking through the photos she had taken during her trip. She'd fallen a little bit in love with Louisiana and knew she'd go back again some day. It was in her blood. She smiled when she realised that sounded a lot like something Gwen would say then sobered as she thought about the bombshell she'd been hit with before leaving Louisiana.

She was pregnant. A bubble of excitement made her place a hand against her stomach protectively. *What am I going to do once I return to Tuendoc?* The thought dimmed some of her earlier happiness. She wouldn't be able to put off facing Jamie for much longer. Although maybe he wouldn't want anything to do with her anyway.

He'd said himself that he wasn't ready to settle down. That it hadn't been love. How was she supposed to show up on his doorstep and make the big announcement that she was pregnant with his child? He had a life he'd been leading quite contentedly before she barged her way back into it. Maybe if she'd just been able to put aside her trust issues, she could have given a future with him a chance. Now it was probably too late. She squeezed her eyes shut tightly at the thought. Had she thrown away happiness by wasting the chance on fear? She couldn't help but think of Jimmy and Evelyn and what they would have given for another shot at life together.

The thought made her sad.

The drone of the plane eventually lulled her into a light sleep. There wasn't much point worrying about it now, she couldn't do anything from up here. She'd just have to wait until she got home and see what happened.

Fifty

The traffic seemed louder than she remembered as she walked along the footpath and headed into the restaurant. She'd been back in Sydney three days, but she needed a few more before she could face work again. She was still in shock over her pregnancy, it was almost too surreal to believe; although there were times when she caught herself smiling idiotically as she contemplated the fact that she was *having a baby*. She hadn't even been able to face Roxy. Especially Roxy. She knew her better than anyone, and right now, when she wasn't sure of anything, she knew Roxy would see right through her and know something was going on. She needed a bit of space to deal with things first.

She told herself she wasn't delaying facing Jamie, either. The fact was, she needed to get back to work. Her time at

Tallowood had been an escape from reality, a shelter from the emotional storm she'd been going through, but she always knew that one day it would have to end. She needed to be back in the office. She could take a weekend and drive back to Tallowood once she was settled back into her old life and tell Jamie then. She wasn't being a coward . . . not really.

However, her old life came back sooner than she'd anticipated with a phone call from Phillip asking her to meet so they could discuss their situation.

It was inevitable that decisions would have to be made about property and settlement but, added to her recent discovery, it felt a little overwhelming. Still, she'd prefer to deal with Phillip sooner rather than later and get things out of the way.

She found Phillip seated at a table in the back of the restaurant, the table they had always sat at on their regular visits to the place. She smiled at a familiar waiter as she passed by, and wondered why Phillip had chosen this place to meet. She thought she'd feel sad to return after so many years coming here during their marriage, but instead she felt . . . nothing.

Phillip stood up as she approached and moved to hug her, but quickly changed his mind at her startled expression and gestured for her to take a seat instead. His hair needed cutting, and he looked older. Tired. *Maybe it was a lot harder running after a pregnant mistress*, she thought a little snidely.

'I'm sorry about your grandmother. I know you two were close.'

'Thank you.' Erin took her time settling into her seat before looking across at Phillip. She didn't want to talk about

Gran with him. He'd always found it rather inconvenient to visit, and she'd made most of the trips alone.

'Thank you for meeting me, Erin. I wasn't sure you would.'

She shrugged. 'I was in town. How's Dakota?' she asked, adjusting the cutlery in front of her.

'Fine, as far as I know,' he said hesitantly, and Erin looked up curiously.

'As far as you know?'

'We . . . are no longer together.'

Well, that's certainly unexpected, she thought, struggling to contain her surprise. 'That's . . .' She couldn't bring herself to use a socially acceptable *Sorry to hear that.* '. . . unfortunate.'

'Yes,' he agreed awkwardly.

'What about the . . . baby?'

Phillip shifted in seat. 'There is no baby.'

'She lost it?' asked Erin. Despite what she thought of the woman, no one deserved the heartache of losing a baby. 'I'm sorry.'

'No,' he said, shaking his head. 'She was never pregnant in the first place.'

'What?'

'I feel like such a fool, Erin. I was so caught up in having a baby, so distraught after all our failed attempts, that I rushed into a relationship, seeing and hearing only what I wanted to see and hear. I'm so, so sorry I hurt you.'

Erin was dumbfounded. This woman broke up a marriage by pretending to be pregnant?

'I don't know what to say, Phillip.' Part of her wanted to cheer that karma did indeed work, but she could never honestly feel happy about someone suffering like that. Phillip's desire to have a child had been real, and the truth must have been devastating. He would have made a great father, despite his betrayal of her, she'd always thought so. Erin froze. Once upon a time he would have been the father to a child they'd hoped to make together. He was stable, settled. He was still officially her husband. Thoughts whirled about inside her head, making her feel giddy. Did she really want her child, this miracle child, to grow up as she had, with no father in its life?

It has a father, her voice of reason added sternly. Which was technically true, but Jamie wanting her in his life was under question. Why would she subject her child to having two separate lives, two separate parents, divided between them for holidays and birthdays? She didn't have to. The solution was staring her, quite literally, in the face. Who would know? She had no reason ever to go back to Tallowood, she didn't have to ever see Jamie again. All she had to do was give Phillip another chance. He would never have to know how far along she was.

'Erin?'

At her name being called urgently, she looked up guiltily. 'Sorry?'

'Are you all right? You look a little pale.'

'I'm fine. I'm just . . . surprised . . . by your news.'

'I didn't bring you here to feel sorry for me. I just didn't want you to find out from someone else.'

Erin was too confused by her own thoughts. 'I'm sorry, Phillip, but I don't think I can stay for lunch after all.'

'I understand. Thank you for at least hearing me out.'

Erin managed a brief nod, before she got to her feet and picked up her handbag.

'Would it be all right if I called you tomorrow?'

'Called me?' Erin asked cautiously.

'I . . . Look, I know I don't deserve it, but I'd like a chance to make it up to you. Please. I just need . . . you were the only one I could ever talk to . . .' He sighed, lowering his gaze to the tabletop. 'I miss you.'

She wanted to laugh in his face, or yell at him; a few weeks ago she might have done both, but she wasn't the same person any more. Her life was no longer her own; she had another person to think about.

'I can't do this right now,' she murmured turning away quickly and leaving before Phillip had a chance to stop her. She couldn't think straight. She couldn't breathe. Pushing through the front door of the restaurant, she took a deep breath and tried to calm the crazy thoughts running through her head.

Fifty-one

Digging through her handbag she located her mobile, bringing up her contact list and pressing call.

'Roxy, it's me.'

'Where the *hell* have you been? Do you *know* how many times I've tried calling you?' Roxy demanded.

'I know. I'm sorry,' Erin groaned.

'Where are you?'

'Here. In town. Can you meet me? It's important.'

Her friend was quiet for a moment. 'Are you all right?'

'No. I don't think so,' Erin said on a shaky sigh.

'Tell me where.'

Half an hour later, seated in a cosy little cafe with a hot chocolate in her hands, Erin filled her best friend in on what had been happening over the last few weeks.

'So, the sexy cowboy turned out to be a two-timing jerk, and the two-timing jerk you married was duped by his bimbo?' she summed up with a shake of her head.

'Pretty much.'

'Well, as far as I'm concerned, Phillip got everything he deserved, the slimy lowlife creep.'

That wasn't any surprise. There had never been any love lost between the two of them.

'And as for the cowboy, well, maybe a little fling did you good.' Her eyes narrowed suspiciously when Erin flinched and dropped her gaze to the cup cradled in her hands. 'What aren't you telling me?'

Damn that girl's perception, Erin thought. 'It's complicated,' she hedged.

'When is it ever *not?*'

'It's more complicated than usual,' Erin amended miserably.

'Okay, tell Aunt Roxy all about it,' she said, leaning back in her chair and waiting patiently.

She could tell by the look in her friend's eye there was no getting out of telling her everything, and she had to admit part of her was relieved to be able to air her confused thoughts out loud just so she wouldn't feel as though she really were going crazy. 'I'm pregnant,' she said in a whisper.

'Pregnant!' Roxy gasped loudly, sitting up so fast she knocked the table.

'Would you keep your voice down,' Erin hissed, straightening her cup and glaring at her friend.

'How?'

'Surprisingly, by the usual old-fashioned way,' she said.

'But you *can't!*'

Erin really did feel for her friend's confusion. After all, Roxy had been there with her through quite a few of the failed attempts at conceiving and been there to help pick up the pieces afterwards. Erin herself had been in a shocked form of denial until she'd made an appointment with her doctor and had the pregnancy confirmed.

'Apparently the joke's on me,' she said gloomily. 'When I had a stable home and husband, even scientists couldn't get me pregnant. Now it's happened and I'm going to put this child through the same life I grew up with.'

'There are plenty of single mums out there. There's no shame in that.'

'I'm not ashamed. It's just that I can't believe I had everything worked out so perfectly before . . . and now it's a complete mess.'

Roxy gave a little snort. 'I hate to break it to you, sweet cheeks, but life is always messy.'

Erin tipped her head back and closed her eyes. *How did everything get so complicated?*

'Have you told the cowboy yet?'

Erin let out a small groan before slowly opening her eyes again. 'No.'

'But you *are?*' Roxy prompted slowly, watching her carefully. 'Right?'

'I don't know,' Erin hedged.

'What's to not know? He's the father. You have to tell him.'

'Considering he's managed to avoid settling down and having kids for this long, I'm pretty sure finding out would be something of an inconvenience to him. It would be a lot less stressful if I just stayed out of his life.'

'I can't believe you of all people would consider not telling him. You know how it felt to not know your own father. How can you think doing it to *your* child would be okay? What happens when he or she wants to know who their dad is? You think they'll be happy that you didn't even tell him?'

Erin felt the last of her energy drain out of her body and she dropped her head into her hands. Roxy was right. Of course she had to tell Jamie. She was just tired. Everything seemed too overwhelming to get her head around at the moment. She was thinking all kinds of stupid things.

'Come on,' Roxy said gently a few moments later. 'Let's get you home. You have plenty of time to sort all this out.'

Erin was so grateful to Roxy for taking charge. She didn't know what was happening to her. Once she would have thought she could handle just about anything, but at this very moment she realised she wasn't coping very well at all.

'Go and have a nice hot shower and get into your PJs,' Roxy said once they arrived home.

'But it's only 3 pm,' said Erin.

'Don't argue. You look terrible.'

'Gee thanks,' Erin muttered.

'Nothing a good sleep won't cure, now get.'

'You're so pushy,' Erin grumbled, but at the mention of a sleep, she was already picturing her nice soft bed and snuggling down beneath the covers.

Roxy left soon afterwards, telling her she had to duck out for a minute, and Erin began unpacking. A little while later, after hopping out of the shower and pulling on her pyjamas, Erin heard the door unlock and Roxy call out, 'It's only me. I've just put a few things in the fridge for your dinner.'

Erin came out of her bedroom and found her friend unpacking items into her refrigerator. 'You didn't have to do all this,' she said, feeling touched and more than a little spoilt.

'Of course I did. It won't hurt you to take a little TLC until you get yourself sorted out. Now go and have a rest.'

'Yes, boss.'

Roxy gave her a brief hug and headed towards the front door. 'Speaking of which, I need to get back to the office. I'll call you in the morning and check on you.'

'I may have to give you a raise after this,' Erin called.

Roxy waved over her head without turning back. 'I'll make a note in your diary.'

Erin smiled then headed to her bedroom. Maybe Roxy was right. Maybe things would look better once she had a sleep.

Fifty-two

Erin awoke the next morning feeling better than she had in days. After a shower, she decided she was well enough to go into the office.

It was nice to be back. Her office felt strange to work in after months of being away from it, but if she wanted to move on with her life, she needed to start letting go of the old one. No more hiding away from the world and working from home. It was good to have the distraction of work and other people around to take her mind off her problems. By Friday of the first week back, Erin felt as though she'd never been gone.

The next afternoon her mother was due home and Erin drove to the airport to meet her. The change in her was remarkable. She looked relaxed and happier than Erin had seen her in a long time. On the drive home, she listened as her mother filled her in on the upcoming visits various members of the family were planning to make and marvelled at the difference in her.

'So how have you been?'

Erin glanced at her mother before focusing back on the road. 'Fine. Busy. I started back at the office this week.'

'Have you decided what to do?'

'About what?'

'Darling, don't be obtuse,' said her mother, rolling her eyes when Erin didn't immediately reply. 'The *baby*,' she said.

'You've been talking to Ronny,' said Erin.

'I already had my suspicions.'

She may as well have had a flashing neon sign on her head, it seemed. Clearly she came from a family of women who were far too observant for their own good. 'I don't know,' she said, keeping her eyes on the road. 'I guess I'll figure it out as I go.'

'Have you been back to Tallowood yet?'

'No.'

'Are you going back?'

'I don't think so.'

'Have you at least spoken to Jamie?'

'No.'

'Why not?'

'Because I'm not even sure I want him to know yet.'

After a few minutes of somewhat terse silence, Erin risked a quick glimpse at her mother. Her grim-set features were not comforting.

'Don't go getting all judgemental on me,' she said irritably.

'I'm the last one to judge anybody,' she replied matter-of-factly.

The silence continued to hang uncomfortably between them. 'I *will* tell him,' Erin said firmly. 'When *I* think it's the right time.'

'There's never a right time,' her mother said, looking out her window. 'I think you should tell him sooner rather than later.'

'I'm thinking maybe you had the right idea in doing it by yourself.'

'My reasons were very different. I purposely set out to have a child. I'm not proud of the choices I made, but at the time I wasn't thinking straight. I was reacting out of anger. I had no right to put a child in the position I did. I'm sorry for that, more sorry than you can possibly know.'

Erin heard the huskiness of her mother's voice and knew how hard it was for her to bring up her past.

'Don't make the same mistakes your grandmother and I made. Give this child a chance to know its father.'

Her mother's words stayed with Erin later that night as she lay in bed and stared at the ceiling. Two generations of women in her family had made decisions that had had lasting effects on the next generation, and now it was her turn. The thought was not comforting. In fact it was a whole lot of pressure she wasn't sure she was equipped to deal with.

Fifty-three

Two days later, Erin said goodbye to her mother as she prepared to head back to Tallowood to start packing up Gran's things.

'Are you sure you don't want to come with me?'

'I don't think so, Mum. I don't think I can face that.'

Over the last few days her mother had revealed the plans she had for the charity empire she'd been steadily building over the years. Erin knew she had been doing a lot of work, but she hadn't truly appreciated just what she had accomplished. Erin now understood how selling Tallowood would help make a real difference to some of her projects. It was hard to protest selling off the place of her childhood memories when the money could be invested into things that would make a difference to so many lives.

'Okay. Well, I'll be storing your gran's things, so you can go through them later when you feel up to it.'

'Thanks, Mum. I love you,' she said, holding her mother's hand through the driver's window.

'I love you too,' she replied, squeezing her hand. 'Everything will work out, just trust in the universe.'

Erin watched her mother drive away and shook her head. Trust in the universe? Sure, why not, she may as well. The universe couldn't do any worse a job of stuffing up her life than she had already done herself.

At her first ultrasound appointment the day before, Erin had been so happy her mother was there to share the experience with her. While she lay on the bed waiting for the technician to get started, Erin stared at the screen. She was about to see her baby for the very first time. As she watched an image appear it took a moment for her to work out what she was seeing. 'Is that . . . ?'

'That's your baby,' said the technician, smiling at Erin before returning to her keyboard and busily taking measurements on the screen.

Her mother held Erin's hand tightly in both of hers, but she couldn't drag her eyes away from the image on the screen. *Her baby.*

She didn't realise she was crying until the technician reached over and handed her a tissue. 'Everything is perfect.'

'Can you tell what sex it is yet?' Erin asked, dropping her mother's hand and blowing her nose quickly.

'Not yet, it's a bit too early, but they will be able to tell you at the next ultrasound appointment.'

She'd walked from the radiologist's in a daze. This whole time she'd had so much else on her mind that she'd hardly thought about *who* she had inside her. She wasn't just pregnant—she was having a *baby*. A baby she'd been trying to have for so long she'd given up hope it was going to happen. But it had. She placed a hand across her abdomen and closed her eyes. *Here's the deal. You keep hanging in there, little one, and I promise I'll do my best not to stuff up our future.*

She opened her eyes and smiled at her mother, who was also dabbing a tissue at her eyes.

Fifty-four

The phone rang, interrupting her absent scribbling on the desk blotter. She tilted her head as she considered the two names she'd written, *Benji* and *Maddison*.

'Erin, it's me,' Phillip's voice came over the line.

Her gaze snapped away from the blotter. 'Hello,' she said cautiously.

'I was wondering if you'd mind if I dropped by sometime this week to go through a few things?'

'Things?' Erin repeated guardedly.

'Sort out some of our stuff.'

'Oh. Ah, sure. I guess. When?'

'Is tonight okay with you?'

She didn't know how to answer that. Her emotions were conflicting. She was angry at him, and hurt by the way he'd dismissed her so easily from his life, but part of her still cared enough to feel sorry for him. She was outraged on his behalf, over the fact a woman could . . . She froze mid-thought. He'd already been deceived by one woman who supposedly cared for him and, not so long ago, *she'd* been considering the possibility of doing the same thing. Erin felt the sting of shame. No matter how briefly she'd considered the idea, it had still been wrong.

'Erin?'

'Sorry, yes, I'm still here. Tonight's fine.'

'I'll see you then,' he said, sounding relieved. 'And Erin? Thank you. You're being incredibly generous, considering . . . well, you know, after everything.'

It was unusual to hear Phillip sounding flustered.

Erin was still staring at the phone reflectively when Roxy stuck her head around the corner on her way past her office. 'Everything okay?'

Erin forced a bright smile to her lips. 'Yep.'

'Okay, spill,' Roxy said, dropping into the chair on the other side of her desk.

Oh, for goodness sake, she thought, exasperated by her friend's uncanny ESP. 'I just had a call from Phillip.'

'So what did the slimeball want?'

Erin shook her head and gave a weary smile at her friend's protective streak. 'He just wants to pick up a few of his things.'

'A likely story,' Roxy scoffed. 'You know what he's trying to do, don't you? He's trying to wear you down and beg you to take him back.'

'He's just—'

'Getting what he deserves,' Roxy finished firmly.

'No one deserved that,' Erin said sadly, guilt once more gnawing at her conscience.

The expression her friend shot her across the desk left little doubt that she did not agree with that statement, but there was no point trying to change Roxy's mind—she and Phillip had always rubbed each other the wrong way.

Erin wished her friend had seen the side of Phillip that she had fallen in love with, but he was a difficult man to get to know. His shyness could often be interpreted as arrogance and his passion for his work sometimes made him sound a little pompous. Erin conceded she'd been partly to blame as well: she'd never complained when he'd talk about his work, only to seem less interested in her own day's events. Maybe if she'd spoken up and pointed out that he was being self-centred . . . But then that wasn't entirely true either—he'd been nothing but considerate and supportive during their IVF treatments. Erin sighed, she was so tired of trying to unravel this mess her life had become.

Could she forgive Phillip and try to save her marriage? Yes, he'd hurt her, yes, he'd betrayed her and turned his back on her to find his own happiness, but she hadn't understood how much he'd suffered each time their IVF attempts failed. She also couldn't ignore the fact that Phillip offered her the stability she'd always craved. Her dream had always been to raise her children in a house with both parents present. It was something she hadn't had as a child and had desperately wanted. She'd loved sleepovers at friends' places when she was younger. Being part of a family. Having a dad at the dinner table, seeing him interact with his children. Her friends all seemed to have wonderful fathers who joked and laughed and teased them. She'd hang back, watching, longing to have that in her life. She'd clung to that dream from a young age and still held it firmly in her heart and mind. To give up something that had meant so much to her wasn't to be done lightly.

And then there was Jamie.

Erin closed her eyes as the familiar wave of loneliness washed over her. She missed him. She could see him as a father, and the image was enough to make her heart ache. But telling Jamie about the baby was a huge risk. It would mean big changes to her life if they reconciled and tried to be a couple. Would money always be an issue between them? And what happened when they had another fight? Would he go skulking back to Vanessa? Could she live with the fact the woman would hear all about their relationship? No. She couldn't live like that. She wouldn't live like that. They were both too proud, she supposed, and that would always have the potential to cause fights between them. How could they raise a child when their relationship was so volatile?

Fifty-five

Later that evening, Erin put the mug on the coffee table next to Phillip and sat down on the lounge opposite him.

'Remember this?' he asked, holding up a plate from their trip to Venice.

'The plate that made us miss our flight,' she said.

'It was worth it, though,' he said, chuckling.

Looking at him she was briefly taken back to another place and time when she'd thought their life was perfect. Back when he'd loved her for who she was, not what she could do for him. Then, lowering her gaze, Erin said, 'So you say. I still think that street vendor ripped you off.'

'It's a one of a kind, a complete original,' he said, shaking his head adamantly.

'Then you better not try googling it. You'll be crushed to see they mass produce them in China.'

'Do you mind if I take it?' he asked.

Why he hadn't come and done all this while she'd been at Tallowood she'd never know. 'It's yours,' she said.

'It was *ours* once,' he said sadly. 'I'm finding this whole process incredibly difficult. How do we split a life together into two piles of belongings?'

'It didn't seem to concern you when you made the decision to leave.'

'You have every right to be angry,' he said quietly. 'I don't blame you at all. I'm furious at myself. But you have to understand, Erin, the strain our marriage had been under had taken its toll on me. Dakota came along when I was in an incredibly fragile state of mind.'

'Oh and I was having such an easy time of it? You don't think I was hurting too? You don't think that with each failed attempt to conceive I didn't die a little more? You didn't think I was carrying around the added guilt that I was also failing *you*?'

'I know you did. Why do you think I tried so hard to pretend that it didn't matter? But while I was trying to make *you* feel better, I was also having to hide my own pain,' he said, dropping his head in defeat.

His words dulled her anger slightly. It didn't excuse his betrayal, and it didn't justify him sneaking around behind her back to have an affair with his assistant, but she did have to admit that he was right: she had been so caught up in her own failings and grief that she hadn't stopped to consider that he might be hurting as well. 'I'm sorry for that.'

Phillip stood up. 'Erin—'

A loud knock at the door interrupted and he sighed, sitting down on the lounge and picking up his cup again.

Another round of insistent knocking sounded, louder this time, and Erin frowned as she turned the handle and opened the door, then gasped when she saw who it was on the other side. 'Jamie?'

'When were you going to tell me?'

'What?' Erin stared at him, dumbfounded by his sudden appearance.

'About the *baby*, Erin. When were you going to tell me about the baby?' he said, raising his voice.

'What's going on?' Phillip demanded, coming to a stop behind Erin.

'What the hell is *he* doing here?' Jamie asked, sounding none too pleased.

'This is *my* house. What the hell are *you* doing here would be a better question,' Phillip snapped.

'I'm here to talk to Erin.'

'Well, I'm pretty sure she doesn't want to talk to you while you're in this mood.'

'Mood? How would you know what kind of mood I'm in?'

'Phillip, it's all right,' said Erin, struggling to keep the anxiety from her voice. *How in God's name had he found out about the baby?*

'I'm still her husband,' Phillip snapped.

'Yeah, well, I'm pretty sure that ship sailed a while back now, mate,' Jamie snarled.

'Leave before I call the police,' Phillip threatened, then grabbed Erin's arm to pull her away from the door.

It happened in a split second. One minute Phillip was standing behind her, the next he was sprawled out on the hallway floor at her feet after Jamie's fist connected with his face.

'Call the police.' Phillip's muffled voice came from behind the hand cupped around his nose.

'What on earth are you doing?' Erin gasped, gaping at Jamie as he stood shaking his hand and glaring at the man on the floor.

'Don't you *ever* lay a hand on her again. You hear me?' Jamie snarled.

'I'll touch her whenever I damn well please. She's my wife!'

Erin quickly stepped forward, placing herself between the two men when she saw Jamie move towards Phillip again. 'That's enough,' she said firmly. 'Jamie, just go. I'll speak with you later.'

'I didn't drive all this way to get the shove off. We're talking about this *now*.'

'*I'll* call the police then,' Phillip muttered, taking his mobile from his pocket.

'Put it away, Phillip. No one's calling the police.'

'He just assaulted me.'

'He didn't mean it, he thought you were hurting me.'

'*Again*,' Jamie added.

'Who the hell do you think you are?' Phillip demanded.

'I'm the father of her child,' he said in a tone that made them all fall silent.

'The . . . *what?*' Phillip asked, giving Erin a confused look.

'Jamie, not now,' Erin groaned.

'Oh? Well, when would be a good time for you?' he asked sarcastically. 'When the kid was grown? When exactly *were* you planning to tell me about it?'

'Oh, for goodness sake! I've only just found out myself.'

'You've been back for a week.'

'*What* child?' Phillip insisted. 'Erin, what's he talking about?'

The look of confused betrayal in Phillip's eye was the same look she'd given him the night he'd told her that Dakota was pregnant. She should have felt triumphant, she should have felt justified. All she felt was sorrow.

'I'm pregnant.'

His expression mirrored his hollow tone. 'Pregnant?'

Erin swallowed past the unexpected emotions which were tightening her throat. He had no right to feel cheated, she'd done nothing wrong, and yet a little part of her still felt guilty.

'I'm sorry, Phillip.'

'You're *sorry?*' Jamie breathed incredulously from behind her.

'Jamie, please.' He didn't understand the history of pain they'd shared to this point.

'No, he's right. You have nothing to feel sorry about,' Phillip said, clearing his throat and turning away. 'I'll come back . . . later . . . for my things,' he added haltingly.

'Don't hurry,' Jamie muttered as he moved aside for the older man to leave.

For a long while after the front door closed, they remained standing in the hallway. Erin was reeling, trying to recover from the roller-coaster of emotions she'd just experienced. Surprise, shock, sorrow and everything in between had left her feeling emotionally drained.

Fifty-six

'I need to sit down,' she said, turning away from Jamie, not caring if he followed or not.

He did.

Once she was seated on the lounge, he disappeared briefly into the kitchen, and she heard the tap go on before he reappeared with a glass of water. He handed it to her then took a seat on the edge of the lounge, watching her closely.

'Are you feeling all right?' he asked after she took a sip of the water and placed the glass on the coffee table before her.

'Not really.'

'Look, I'm sorry. I wasn't thinking too clearly. I was already in a bit of a tailspin, but then when I saw your ex . . .'

'How did you find out? How did you even *find* me?'

'I went by your office to see if you were there and met your friend. The tall redhead with a temper to match.'

'Roxy?' She couldn't believe her best friend would sell her out like that.

Her expression must have given her away because Jamie added, 'Yeah, well, I don't think she meant to tell me about the baby. It slipped out while she was tearing strips off me. She's got quite an impressive vocabulary on her when she's angry. I didn't know you could combine so many expletives into one sentence.'

Erin could all too easily picture the incident. Roxy's temper, although not a regular occurrence, was legendary throughout the office. 'Then how did you get my address?'

'She eventually calmed down and I charmed it out of her.' He shrugged. 'But I found out you were back in the city from your mother.'

'Wait. My *mother*?' Erin wasn't sure if it was some weird side effect of pregnancy that was making her so dim-witted that she was struggling to keep up, or if this was just really confusing.

'I was waiting for you to come home from your trip and had just about given up when I saw the lights on at Tallowood and assumed you were home. I went over to see you, only it was your mother. She invited me in for a cuppa and before I knew it I was pouring my guts out to her about what an idiot I'd been.'

'You and my mother had a deep and meaningful?'

'Trust me, no one's more surprised than me,' he said, shaking his head. 'You had me so twisted up inside, I had to tell someone . . . I don't why, but once we started talking about you, it just all came out. She told me if I didn't want to lose you, I needed to get down here and do something about it,' he said, gazing down at his hands.

'She said that?'

'She was different somehow. Less . . . weird. Anyway, I came over to explain that I was not sleeping with Vanessa while we were together,' he said, turning sideways to face her. 'You keep leaving town before we have a chance to clear the air. You just left. I tried calling you, but when you didn't return my call . . .' He let out a frustrated sigh. 'I didn't even know if we were still together or not.'

'You must have figured it out pretty quick. The night I left I saw your ute outside the pub on my way out of town, only to find your on-again off-again girlfriend draped over you like a second bloody skin, and you telling her how you weren't ready to settle down yet and that you didn't really love me. I got the message loud and clear that you and I were over.'

Jamie frowned, then his expression cleared. 'That wasn't about you and me,' he said. 'Vanessa asked why *she* and I had never worked out when we were younger. I didn't even know you were there. Why the hell didn't you say something?'

'Me? Why were you even there in the first place? If you were so cut up about our fight, why would you go running to her for a shoulder to cry on?'

'I didn't go there to cry on her shoulder. I went there to have a drink and to try to work out what the hell had happened.'

'And she just happened to be there?'

'Well, considering she works at the pub, it isn't all that unusual.'

It would have been helpful to know that little piece of information earlier, she thought. 'Maybe if that had been the only time I'd seen something similar play out between you two, it would be different, but it looked a little too much like the last time I found you together. I wasn't thinking straight. I never am around you.'

'Yeah? Well, join the club,' he told her gruffly. 'I didn't go to the pub that night planning on picking up Vanessa, you know. I was leaving and she'd just finished work . . . It just . . . happened.'

Erin let her gaze drop to the lounge between them as she fiddled with the fringe of a throw cushion. 'But you two have a history.' She hated the note of jealousy that had crept into her voice, but she was helpless to stop it.

'Yeah, Vanessa and I *had* a history. I've never claimed to be a bloody monk. How is it any different to you being married?' he demanded.

'The day I saw her down the street, she indicated that you two were still seeing each other. That you always came back to her eventually. When you admitted you'd gone to her place while I was in Townsville, I figured she was right.'

'I didn't lie to you, I *did* go to her place. I spend a lot of time with her kids. Their dad was a good mate of mine. I made a promise to him that I'd keep an eye on them when he couldn't be there to do it. And as for Vanessa, we didn't get together as much as she would have you believe, but we did see each other from time to time. I'm not going to defend myself, I shouldn't have to. It's a small town and we were both single. Occasionally we were there for each other.'

Erin flinched a little, but at the same time she knew he was right, he didn't owe her anything. She'd been married; he'd been living his own life.

Jamie's voice softened a little. 'I've only ever loved one woman, Erin. Back then everyone thought what we had was too fast, too young . . . but that feeling never went away. It was there every time I saw you. Year after year. It just about killed me when I saw you with *him*,' he said, gesturing in the direction of the front door as though Phillip had just this minute left.

Erin saw the uncertainty in his gaze and tried to guard her heart against crumbling. She had too much to think about and her baby's future depended on her keeping a clear head.

'I never stopped loving you, Erin,' he said simply. 'Marry me.'

'What?'

'Marry me.'

'I can't,' she said, her mind in a confused whirl. 'I'm not even divorced yet,' she added, nearly laughing at the absurdity of the conversation. Oh, what a proud moment this was, dumped by her husband, who was now sorry he'd walked out on her, and knocked up by her commitment-phobic old flame, who was now asking her to marry him.

'I don't care. We'll get married as soon as it's official. Until then, just say yes.'

'You don't have to marry me because of the baby. We can work around it.'

'Christ, woman, you can be so infuriating. What part of *I love you* don't you understand?'

'Maybe the part where I remember you saying you weren't ready for a relationship,' she snapped.

'I told you, that wasn't about you and me.'

'You were happy not settling, remember?'

'I said I wasn't going to make do with something that didn't make me happy. I knew what made me happy, Erin. It was you. I wanted what we had when we were nineteen. I've only ever had that feeling with you. How could I settle for anyone else when it didn't feel that good?'

Erin stared at him. How was she supposed to keep a clear head when he said things that made her heart melt?

'I waited for a long time for you to come back, Erin. I finally thought we had a shot at a future. But I'm tired of worrying each time we disagree about something that I'll lose you.'

'You didn't lose me, I was just going overseas.'

'That's the problem, you're *always* going away. I was worried that one day you wouldn't come back.'

'Why would you think that?'

'Because,' he said as though forcing the words from his mouth, 'I thought you'd figure out that I wasn't good enough for you.'

'Are you serious?'

'You were married to a bloody professor. You like living in the city, and you've been all over the world. Yeah, the thought crossed my mind a time or two that one day you'd start wondering what the hell you even saw in some boring farmer who raises beef.'

Erin was taken aback. She hadn't understood how vulnerable he felt in the face of her career and life experiences.

'I don't know how we could make this work,' she said, throwing her hands up helplessly. 'We have different views on everything.'

'We'd have to work them out.'

'I'm not sure I could go back to giving up my independence now.'

'I wouldn't ask you to give up your independence.'

'Having to ask your permission to do things or tiptoeing around sensitive subjects is giving up my independence.'

'We'll both have to make some changes. I have to stop flying off the handle so often. I get that. But you need to stop running away. Every couple has disagreements, there's nothing unusual about us, we just have to figure out how to do things better.'

When did he get so mature? She was the married one, the one who had experience with relationships; she should be the one giving *him* the inspirational couples therapy talk.

'Erin,' he said, stepping closer, his voice dropping low. 'I want this baby. I want you. I want us to be a family.'

Inside her, caution and fear were going head to head, but on the sidelines, tenderness and hope were watching on warily. Her child deserved to grow up with its father. Isn't that what she'd always wanted? Jamie was offering her a shot at a real family; she could be the first woman in three generations to finally do things the right way. All she had to do was find the courage to say yes.

Fifty-seven

Two days. She'd asked Jamie for two days to give him an answer and time was almost up. Her decision had been playing on her mind all day at work. She looked at the text she'd just written, inviting him over for dinner that evening, her thumb nervously hovering over the button before she pressed send.

She'd spent the last two days in a contemplative mood. It made sense that they get married, she knew that. They had chemistry and there was no question that the sex was amazing, but in the back of her mind it still worried her how they would manage to combine their two lifestyles.

As she reached the crossing and took a step, her phone buzzed and she automatically glanced down at the screen.

The screech of tyres, glass shattering and the thump of a body hitting bitumen all blended together in a sickening chorus of screams and pain. Followed by darkness.

Fifty-eight

Erin frowned as an irritating beeping sound roused her from a deep slumber. She tried to lift her hand to shut off the alarm but found she couldn't move her arm. Her eyelids were heavy, too heavy to open, even though something told her she needed to wake up. *I'll be late for work if I stay here much longer*, she thought, but it was too hard to fight it and she gave up, allowing her body to drift back down into the murky darkness.

A low rumble sounded nearby, like a train. Erin tried to turn her head towards the sound but groaned as pain shot through her skull.

After a moment she braced herself, ready this time, and cautiously opened her eyes. The room was dark, but it wasn't night, she could see sunlight in a small gap where the edges of the curtain didn't quite meet. Little black spots danced before her eyes as she tried to focus, but the throbbing inside her head told her she was at least awake and not dreaming.

The strong smell of disinfectant and the humid-like smell of freshly laundered sheets filled her nose. It could only be one place. Hospital.

Why am I in hospital? She tried to think but it hurt her head so she stopped. The rumble started again and she realised it was a cleaner trolley being pushed past her doorway.

Turning her head slowly she fought a wave of nausea and concentrated on breathing carefully so as not to make any sudden movements until her gaze fell on a hunched shadow beside her bed.

As her eyes adjusted to the dimness of the room, she recognised the familiar outline of the rugged face. He looked like he hadn't shaved in days, and his short hair was sticking up as though he'd been running his hands through it restlessly. His head was tipped back slightly, leaning against the wall behind him. His eyes were closed, but he didn't look like he was sleeping, more as though he was resting his eyes for a moment. Almost as though her thoughts had been spoken aloud, his eyes opened and she saw him bolt into an upright position.

'Erin.'

She tried to reassure him that she was all right, but he was reaching for the buzzer above her head, pressing it urgently.

'How do you feel? Can you move your toes? How's your head?'

Erin opened her mouth to answer, but her mind felt foggy, her thoughts slow and clumsy.

346

'Don't talk, it's okay,' he said, jabbing at the buzzer again. 'Christ, Erin, I thought I'd lost you.' The sound of his voice breaking cut through the fog in her head.

A nurse came into the room and looked across at her, a friendly smile on her face. 'Look who's finally decided to wake up and join us,' she said in a calm, no-nonsense tone, taking Erin's wrist in her hand as she pressed cool fingers against her pulse, eyeing the watch pinned to her shirt.

After a few moments she sent a reassuring smile down at Erin and gave a small nod. 'Doctor will be along shortly to check you over. Till then, you just rest up and don't overdo anything.' The last comment came with a pointed look at Jamie and Erin wondered what he'd done to elicit such a warning from the stout nurse.

The room fell quiet again after the nurse had left and Erin looked back over at Jamie, catching him rubbing the back of his neck with one hand. He looked exhausted.

He opened his mouth to speak but a short man in a white coat entered the room, picking up the chart at the end of the bed and flipping rapidly through its contents. After a few moments he peered over the top of his rimless glasses at Erin. 'Any pain?' he asked.

'My head,' Erin said, her voice sounding husky, 'and my throat.'

The doctor replaced her chart and moved to the side of the bed. 'That's to be expected. We had to intubate you, but we removed the tube earlier today. You've also had some brain swelling, but that seems to have reduced nicely.'

He took out a small penlight, waving it across her eyes and completing a quick neurological assessment. 'No deficit or weakness identified,' he murmured more to himself, sounding satisfied, before placing his penlight back into his pocket.

'I'd like to keep you under observation and arrange a CT scan, however all your vitals seem fine, so I'm not anticipating any problems. You may experience some temporary amnesia as a result of your accident, but I expect that to settle down in a day or two.'

Accident? Fear suddenly seized her heart as a memory came crashing back to her. 'The baby,' she croaked.

'We performed an ultrasound. Foetal heart rate is strong and regular and no signs of injury or distress. You're both very lucky,' he added gravely. 'However, I'd like you to remain on bed rest for another few days as a precaution.'

Erin's gaze darted across to Jamie. He stood with his hands braced on the back of the chair, his mouth set in a firm line.

'You'll be having regular neurological observations, and I'll organise a CT scan, X-rays and blood tests for later this afternoon,' the doctor concluded, stepping away from the bedside before giving her a brisk nod and walking from the room.

Erin's hands rested over her stomach protectively as she tried to calm her scattered thoughts. She couldn't remember everything the doctor had just said; it was all a blur after he'd said that her baby was fine. Nothing else really mattered.

'Do I look as bad as I feel?' she asked.

'Just a few scratches and bruises,' Jamie reassured her.

Erin gingerly touched the side of her face and winced. She was almost grateful she couldn't see the damage.

The nurse reappeared, bringing in a jug of water and a plastic cup.

'You better get going. I've just given your friend some forms to fill out, but that won't keep him occupied for long,' she said as she bustled around, straightening the bed covers and propping Erin up against another pillow.

Erin looked over at Jamie and frowned at his grim expression.

'Thanks, Liz,' he said gruffly. 'I'll be back later,' he added to Erin, looking like he wanted to say more.

The nurse hurried him out of the room and a few moments later there was a commotion in the hallway and Phillip came back through the door. 'Oh, thank God. You're awake.'

'What are you doing here?' Erin croaked.

'They called me after the accident. I'm still your husband, after all. The baby's fine,' he told her, taking a seat on the edge of the bed and holding her hand.

'I know. The doctor was just here,' she said quietly.

'Look, Erin, I know you've been through a lot, but I need to say this.'

Erin opened her mouth to stop him; she really wasn't up to this right now. She'd barely had her eyes open for half an hour and her head was pounding in rhythm to her heartbeat, but Phillip placed a finger across her lips, silencing her. She'd always hated when he did that.

'When I received that phone call at work,' he shook his head as though reliving the moment in his mind, 'it brought everything into perspective. I still love you, Erin. We need to put all the pain and the mistakes in the past and start over. This is our second chance at happiness. I don't care where the baby came from. We can work out something with McBride, but that's not important right now,' he dismissed with a wave of his neatly manicured hand. 'What *is* important is *I* can be the kind of father that child deserves. We can be a family. The family we always wanted.' He smiled gently. 'Maybe there was a reason things happened the way they did. Maybe we were *supposed* to go our separate ways so this miracle could happen,' he murmured, gently moving his hand across her stomach.

Erin swallowed painfully as she watched him. Phillip wanted this child more than he wanted her. He hadn't asked her what the doctor had said about her, he'd only spoken about the baby. He was so wrapped up in the notion of becoming a father he didn't even care that it was another man's child.

'No, Phillip,' Erin said softly.

His smile slipped. 'I'm sorry, I should have let you rest up a bit before I got into all this. It's too soon,' he said, patting her hand. 'We'll talk about this again when you feel stronger.'

'No, Phillip,' she said, firmer this time. 'We aren't getting back together. I've changed. You've changed too. I don't want to go back to the way things were.'

'But it'll be different now. We'll have a baby, there'll be no more IVF pressure, we'll—'

'No, Phillip,' she said again, cutting him off. 'I'm sorry, but I'm not coming back. It's over.'

He slowly withdrew his hand and took a step away from the bed. Erin blinked rapidly to stop the tears that were stinging behind her eyelids. She had loved this man once, and she felt for him, wanting a child so desperately, but she didn't love him any more.

'I see. Well, I'll—' He shoved his hands deep in his trouser pockets, edging towards the doorway—'come back a bit later. Or maybe I should just leave you be?' He didn't wait for her to answer, he simply turned his back and left the room.

Erin closed her eyes, feeling exhausted. Maybe she should have stayed unconscious for a while longer. This being awake business was hard work.

Her thoughts drifted to her gran. Evelyn hadn't had the choices that Erin had today. She'd felt that she'd had to sacrifice her happiness to give her child a life she deserved. And for what? In the end they'd all ended up miserable. She wasn't sure what was going to happen, but whatever the future held in store, her child would be put first.

Fifty-nine

As she was having her vitals taken again later that afternoon, she received another visitor and, for the first time all day, she smiled.

'Mum!'

'Oh, darling,' her mother said, rushing to her bedside, her caftan billowing behind her like some exotic sail flapping in the wind.

'It's okay, Mum,' she said, patting her mother's back as she hugged her. 'I'm fine.'

'Are you sure?' she asked, brushing Erin's hair from her face and searching her bruised face carefully.

'I'm positive.' Erin couldn't even pretend to be annoyed by her mother's hovering. It was so wonderfully unexpected that she was too surprised to even think about being exasperated.

Her mother straightened and gave the room a dismissive look. 'I don't know how the public health system can expect patients to make any kind of recovery in an environment like this. A little feng shui would do wonders for the energy in this place,' she said, eyeing the room critically and ignoring the nurse who gave a small snort as she finished recording the data on Erin's chart.

'Never mind, I can work with this.'

'Mum, I'm really not going to be in here long enough for it to make a difference.'

'You'd be surprised. Tomorrow I'll do some work on your chakra,' her mother said, tapping her chin thoughtfully. 'And to get rid of this horrendous chemical smell, maybe a bit of frankincense and myrrh will help.'

'Then all we'll need is three wise men and we'll be set for Christmas,' the nurse said drolly.

Erin bit back a smile at her mother's haughty glare, which was completely wasted on the heavyset nurse who left the room without looking back.

'How did you find out about the accident?'

'Jamie called,' her mother said, dragging her gaze from the empty doorway and back to her daughter. Her expression softened and she sat down on the chair beside the bed.

'Jamie?' Well, that was a surprise.

'We had a good chat the other day. I take it he knows about the baby now?'

'Yes.'

'And Phillip?'

'He knows too,' Erin sighed.

'Everything will work out. You just need to trust in the universe, darling,' she said with a warm smile, cupping Erin's cheek. 'Everything will be if it is *meant to* be.'

'You know, it would be a lot easier if the universe just came out and said exactly what it wanted,' Erin muttered.

'But where would the adventure be in that?' her mother shrugged, before declaring she was nipping out to a nearby vegan cafe to find something wholesome to tempt her appetite.

Erin gave a soft chuckle and tried not to think what weird and wonderful concoctions she was about to be fed.

Sixty

The next morning Erin opened her eyes to the low murmur of voices and found Roxy and Jamie in deep conversation. *At least they don't seem to be killing each other*, she thought with a sigh of relief. Something must have alerted Jamie to her presence, because he turned his head and she saw his expression soften a little. Roxy, noticing Jamie's attention shifting, followed his gaze and her eyes lit up in relief.

'Hey!' she said, a bright smile on her face as she moved closer to the bedside. Erin caught the tremble of her friend's lip as she hugged her tightly before pulling back to sit on the side of the bed. She held one of Erin's hands securely in both of her own.

'I'm okay,' Erin told her with a gentle smile.

'You gave us all a bit of a scare.'

'Sorry.'

'Do you need anything?'

'I'd kill for a decent cup of coffee and a night in my own bed, but other than that, I guess just being alive is enough for now,' Erin said dryly.

'I would break you out of this joint, but the nurse out there on duty scares the crap outta me, so I can't help you there, kiddo. However, I can do something about the coffee situation. I'll be right back. Don't do anything I wouldn't do,' she added at the door, then stopped to roll her eyes at Erin. 'Oh, that's right, you already did!' she said before disappearing out into the hall and leaving Jamie and Erin alone.

'I take it you two have made up since your first encounter,' Erin said, wincing as she sat up further in bed.

'She read me my rights and threatened to castrate me if I stepped out of line. I think that was her way of saying I'm okay.'

Erin reached out for a glass of water but Jamie beat her to it and handed it over courteously. 'What did you have to do to win her over?'

'Get arrested for trying to kill your husband.'

Erin spat water down the front of her pyjamas, brushing Jamie's hands away as he tried to mop up the spill with a tissue.

'I didn't actually *hurt* him,' he protested, before admitting, 'I would have, if he hadn't run in here and locked the bloody door, though.'

Erin stared at him, completely dumbfounded.

Jamie gave an impatient sigh, then took a seat on the edge of her bed. 'I was on my way to your place when I got your text, so I waited for you, but after a while when you didn't show up, I tried calling, and when you didn't answer I got worried and called your office, but they said you'd left already. Then Roxy called me back a few minutes later and told me you'd been hit by a car just outside your office.' He lowered his gaze to the bedspread. 'I came here straightaway but they wouldn't let me see you. The hospital had contacted your husband, and he wasn't allowing any visitors.'

'Didn't anyone tell them we were getting a divorce?'

'He's still listed as your next of kin. Anyway, there was a discussion out in the hall, which turned a bit vocal. When I tried to go in the room, your dickhead ex started yelling for security and then locked himself in here until the cops came.'

'Why did he lock himself in the room?' Erin cocked her eyebrow doubtfully.

'Maybe the fact that if I'd gotten hold of him I would have killed him had a bit to do with it. He's lucky the cops turned up when they did.'

'I don't understand how it got so out of hand.' There had to be more to it than that. 'And they *arrested* you?'

'Nah, they just took me outside to cool down. Roxy filled them in on things and they let me off with a warning. He did take out an AVO though, so, legally, I'm not supposed to go anywhere near him, which suits me fine,' he added darkly.

'That's why the nurse was warning you that he was here yesterday,' she said as it all began to fall into place.

'Anyway, it's not important now. How are you feeling?'

Erin wasn't convinced Jamie was telling her everything, but clearly he wasn't about to get into it any further.

'I'm feeling better than yesterday.'

'What did the doc have to say?'

'All the scans and tests have come back fine, so they're letting me go home later today, as soon as they sort out a few follow-up appointments.'

'That's good news.'

'The best. I can't wait to get out of here.'

'I can stick around and wait to give you a lift home if you like.'

'I was just going to get a taxi.'

'No need. I'll take you.'

'Don't you have things to do back at Tallowood? You've been gone for days.'

'It's under control. I'm not going anywhere, at least until I'm sure you're okay.'

'If that's the only reason you're staying, I'm absolutely fine,' she said, concerned that he may be feeling somehow obliged to remain in the city.

'That may be so, but we still have some unfinished business.'

'Coffee!' Roxy entered the room carrying a tray of coffees. 'And muffins,' she added with a satisfied smirk.

'You are so getting that pay rise,' Erin said, reaching for the bag and giving a moan of delight. Double choc muffins still warm from the oven.

'You know you keep talking about this raise, but I've yet to see it. A lesser friend would have walked out on you by now,' Roxy pointed out.

'I'm sure I gave you a raise just recently.'

'Nope.'

'Well, have my assistant arrange to give you one,' Erin said, sinking her teeth into the chocolatey goodness.

'I'm sure your *assistant* will get right on that.'

In the hallway came an unmistakable voice and all three looked at each other quickly.

'Mum!' Erin groaned. 'No!'

'I thought you two were getting on nowadays?' Jamie said, eyeing her attempt to eat faster with wry amusement.

'We are.' Her answer was muffled between bites of muffin. 'But I can't face another wheat bran and flaxseed muffin and that's what she'll make me eat instead of this.' She held up the half-devoured gooey mess of chocolate.

Jamie shook his head and headed towards the door. 'Fine. I'll go intercept her. You better thank me for this one day,' he threw over his shoulder.

'I will,' she called, taking another bite. 'Thank you.'

'Now *that's* a good man,' Roxy said, sipping at her coffee as her gaze lingered on the empty doorway.

'You called him a jerk,' Erin reminded her.

'That was before.'

'Before what?'

'Before I realised he hates Phillip even more than I do. Anyone who dislikes that man so much can't be all bad. Besides, have you checked out his butt lately?' She fanned her face flamboyantly.

'What happened between those two?'

'He didn't tell you?'

'He said Phillip made a scene and called security, then locked himself in the room,' Erin said, chewing.

'What a tosser,' Roxy laughed with a shake of her head. 'Okay, so Phillip chucks a wobbly as soon as the cowboy arrives and does the whole "she's my wife" bit. And the cowboy, he's like "get the hell outta my way",' Roxy said, tapping into her inner narrator and mimicking Jamie in a deep voice. 'Then Phillip grabs hold of the cowboy and spins him around and tells him that he should just walk away and leave you alone and give the baby a chance to have a life that *he* could never give it. That's when Jamie lost it, and I mean *lost* it,' Roxy said in a low tone. 'Phillip must have realised he'd gone too far because he hid inside the room and locked the door, and that's when security and then the police turned up.'

No wonder Jamie had been so furious. What had Phillip been thinking? Well, clearly he hadn't, she amended.

'Anyway, Jamie and I sat and talked over coffee for a bit, and after Phillip left, Jamie was still determined to see you, so I kept watch and he came in.' Roxy smiled softly; her voice was almost wistful. 'That man really loves you.'

Erin popped the last bite of muffin into her mouth to delay comment. He'd risked getting arrested just to see her, and she couldn't deny that the feelings she'd had before she'd left to go overseas were still as strong as ever.

A movement from the corner of her eye alerted her to Jamie's return, her mother following close behind. She wiped at her mouth to remove any stray crumbs or telltale smear of chocolate.

'Morning, darling,' her mother said, sweeping into the room. 'Look what I've brought you—lovely fresh bran muffins and camomile tea.'

'Your favourite, Erin!' Roxy gushed, wide-eyed.

'Oh. Great. Thanks, Mum,' Erin smiled bravely.

'Don't worry, I didn't forget you two,' she added, unpacking a small cooler bag and passing around the rather bland-looking baked goods.

'What luck!' Erin smiled across at her friend sweetly. 'Rox was just saying how much she missed your muffins, Mum. Maybe she could take the leftovers home?'

'Of course! In fact, I can even drop off a new batch before I leave. I had no idea you enjoyed them so much, Roxy.'

'I wouldn't want to put you out,' Roxy said hurriedly.

'No trouble. I've been having a lovely time going through Erin's pantry and restocking it, so I have plenty.'

Erin's smile wavered a little at that. *Restocking it with what?*

'So, darling, would you like me to pack a bag for you so we can be ready to go as soon as you're released today?'

'Go?' Jamie asked, his gaze switching between mother and daughter.

'Yes, back to Nimbin. A few days at the retreat will do her the world of good.'

'Well, I haven't actually decided,' Erin began, but her mother brushed it off impatiently.

'You can't go back to work yet, you're still battered and bruised, for goodness sake. You need to take it easy for a few more days.'

'She could come back to Tallowood with me,' Jamie offered.

'Tallowood? What would she do there all day? Besides, you'll be working.'

'I can keep an eye on her.'

'Hello? I'm right here,' Erin said irritably.

'I think the healing atmosphere of Namaste would be far more beneficial than being all alone out at Tallowood,' her mother continued.

'She wouldn't be alone.'

Erin's ears pricked up at that. Was Jamie suggesting he would be staying at Gran's *with* her? She should be feeling outraged at his arrogant assumption but there was no denying the spark of interest the idea ignited.

'Erin?' Her mother's concerned question wrenched her from her thoughts.

'Sorry?'

'What do you think about coming back to the retreat for a few days?'

'Actually, Mum,' she said, reaching a decision, 'if you don't mind, I think I would rather go to Tallowood.'

Her mother looked as though she wanted to argue, but then thought better of it, unfolding her arms and crossing to the bedside to hold her daughter's hand. 'Of course I don't mind. Do what makes you happy,' she said, smiling.

She didn't look at Jamie, but from the corner of her eye she saw his shoulders relax a little as he looked through the window at the hospital grounds below.

Roxy offered Serenity a lift back to Erin's apartment to pack, leaving Jamie to bring Erin home when she was released.

'You don't have to babysit me when we get back, you know,' she said, easing back down onto the side of the bed after having showered and dressed inside the small bathroom. 'I'm perfectly capable of taking care of myself. In fact, if you wanted to get back earlier, I can drive myself out.'

'I thought the drive out would give us a chance to talk about a few things.'

'Oh.'

'I'm not going to push you on a decision, if that's what you're worried about,' he said softly.

'I'm not worried.' Things were different between them now. They were acting like strangers: uncertain and nervous. 'Roxy told me what Phillip said.'

Jamie eyed her a little warily but didn't say anything.

'He had no right to say those things. I've never thought you wouldn't make a good father.'

'Then why didn't I know you were pregnant?'

Erin fiddled with the handle of her overnight bag beside her. 'I only found out the day before I flew back from the States. When I got home,' she stopped and shook her head, 'I don't know. I wasn't sure what to do. I didn't even know if we were still together. I needed time to get my thoughts together.'

'So you weren't going to tell me about the baby?'

She swallowed nervously at the tight expression on his face. 'Don't go judging me, you weren't the one who suddenly discovered they were about to have a baby. I was still trying to sort out my own feelings.'

'Look, I know you don't need me to bring up this kid, okay? I get that. I understand you have everything you need to raise a child, *our* child, alone. You've got a house and a fancy car, a good job and plenty of money. And I'm just a farmer. I have a mortgage that resembles the deficit of a small third world country and I still live at home with my parents. On paper I don't add up to much, I know that, but I *know* I can be a good father. Only that's not what I want,' he said, getting to his feet.

Erin's heart lurched momentarily.

'I want to be a husband to you *as well* as a father to our baby. I want the whole package. I want us to be a family.'

Erin wiped the tears spilling over onto her cheeks. 'Are you sure?'

Jamie held his hands out and tugged her to her feet. 'I've never been surer of anything in my whole life. Marry me, Erin.'

'Yes,' she said softly, managing a wobbly smile, closing her eyes as she felt his arms slip around her, bringing her tightly against him. His lips when they touched hers were gentle and loving. God, she'd missed this man. When he touched her, held her so protectively in his arms like this, nothing was too hard to deal with. Nothing else mattered.

'I know this is a private room and all,' came a droll voice from the doorway, 'but it isn't *that* kinda room, folks.'

Erin tried to pull away from Jamie but he kept a firm hold on her, lifting his gaze to the nurse who walked into the room holding the referrals and scrips Erin would need.

'Come on, Liz, we're celebrating here. We're getting married.'

'Well, congratulations, now go do your canoodling somewhere else, I need this room back for sick people.' The nurse held out Erin's overnight bag to him expectantly.

'You're gonna miss us, Liz, admit it,' Jamie grinned as he dropped one arm from Erin's waist and reached for the bag.

'Sure I will, no fights to break up, no more reassuring the other patients that the strange smell in the air isn't marijuana. Yeah, life just won't be the same.'

Jamie looked at Erin and smiled. 'Nope. It'll be even better.'

Epilogue

The house was quiet for a change.

The last eighteen months had gone way too fast, and yet so much had been crammed into that time.

She and Jamie had gotten married, at Jamie's insistence. He'd wanted them to be married before the baby arrived. He could be such a fuddy-duddy sometimes. They'd bought Tallowood from her mother, a big step in their relationship. Erin had made it clear she and Jamie were partners in every aspect of this marriage, including financially. 'If we're going to be equal in this, then I want to be included in the business. Buying Tallowood is an investment in our future,' she'd told him, and it was. Tallowood was their home, it would be their child's home too. 'If I'm part of your life, I need to be part of this too. I want to learn. I want you to teach me more about the business so I can work alongside you.'

'You want to help me drench and mark and ear tag?' he'd asked with a slow smile, sitting back in his chair and crossing his arms as he watched her.

'If that's what you need me to do,' Erin had said weakly. 'Although I was thinking more in terms of the financial side of things.'

She'd laid out a spreadsheet of her proposal and showed him how investing her money into the business was a sensible, and potentially profitable, move for her to make. 'It's not my money or your money. It's ours, to use to build our future.'

'What about your career?'

'I've been thinking about it a lot lately. I'm not ready to give up my job yet. I'll take some maternity leave, but I was thinking I might take some of my mother's advice and cut back a little bit.' She was proud of all that she'd achieved, but with taking on this new business and a baby on the way, she'd known that the pressures of her current job would add stress she no longer wanted in her life. 'I'm going to ask for a demotion,' she'd smiled.

'A demotion?'

'I think I'd be happier working at state manager level, so I'll have more time to spend with you and bub.'

'You do whatever makes you happy,' he'd said, standing up and kissing her tenderly.

'You make me happy,' she'd said softly when they parted.

'Then you should do me,' he'd said, giving her that grin she loved so much.

It felt right. They were finally working together.

Then six months after that, their beautiful dark–haired, blue-eyed girl had made her entrance into the world and immediately proceeded to wrap her daddy around her tiny little finger. Callie Evelyn McBride was the most beautiful baby ever created. Of course Erin thought maybe she was a little biased, but she was pretty sure Jamie had no doubt whatsoever.

Seeing them together had brought Erin to tears on more than one occasion just from the sheer joy of witnessing the love on the man's face as he cradled his newborn baby in his arms.

Now, with nine-month-old Callie, her job and the new business filling every moment of every day, she looked down at the little white stick with the two blue lines and took a deep breath to calm the rising hysteria.

The sound of an approaching vehicle alerted her to Jamie's arrival and she took another series of deep breaths. She'd panicked as soon as she'd seen the results and called him to come home. She watched him hurry across the yard towards her, his shirtsleeves rolled up to his elbows, dusty jeans and hat pulled down low on his head, and despite the nausea she was feeling, felt the familiar flutter of awareness spring to life.

And that is exactly what got you into this situation in the first place, a little voice reminded her prudently.

'What's wrong?'

'I . . .' Erin started to speak but instead began crying.

'Jesus, what's happened? Is it Callie?' he asked, his gaze flying around the room urgently. But Jamie spied his daughter happily jabbering in her playpen.

'No. It's . . . this!' she finally managed, holding up the pregnancy test helplessly.

'Is that a—?'

'Pregnancy test,' she said nervously. 'And it's positive.'

'You're pregnant?' The shocked look on his face would have been comical had she not been on the verge of hyperventilating.

'Apparently.'

'We're having another baby?'

'It seems so.'

'Holy sh—' he started, then stopped, glancing across at his daughter. 'Holy cow.'

'I don't know how it happened,' she told him helplessly.

'Really?' he asked with a grin. 'After all our practising, you still don't know what causes it?'

'It's not funny, Jamie. We have a nine-month-old baby, and now I'm about to have another one. It's—'

'Fantastic,' he finished for her adamantly.

Erin stared up at him hopefully. 'Really? You're happy?'

'I'm over the goddamn moon,' he told her, a grin breaking out over his face as he pulled her to her feet and held her. 'I thought when you came back I was the luckiest guy in the world, then we had Callie and I thought life couldn't get any better . . . until now.'

Relief flooded through her at his words and some of the shock from her early morning discovery began to wear off. Falling pregnant once had been a miracle in itself, but twice? It didn't seem possible. Jamie crossed to his daughter and picked her up, burying his face in her baby softness and enticing happy giggles as he carried her back to Erin and slipped his free arm around her snugly. 'You're going to be a big sister, Munchkin, what do you think about that?'

Erin brushed her hand across their child's soft hair, her gaze drifting to the photo on the wall she'd had enlarged and framed. The photo of a young World War Two pilot and a beautiful young woman wrapped in his arms. She wasn't sure how, but she knew Gran had played an important part in her journey to find happiness.

'Thank you, Gran,' she whispered.

Gran's eyes seemed to twinkle from the image and Erin smiled back.

Acknowledgements and author note

Townsville will forever hold a special place in my heart. Having lived there for a number of years, this story had been simmering in the background ever since the first day I arrived in that beautiful far north Queensland town. Everywhere you go in Townsville there are constant reminders of the huge part the town, and Australia itself, played in World War Two. I remember being amazed by the sheer number of sites marked as World War Two places of interest in almost every suburb or street you pass by on a daily basis. While researching this book, I finally got around to identifying some of these sites and their significance during the war years and found it absolutely fascinating.

I was really surprised to discover that Townsville had actually been bombed during the war. I had no idea! And once I discovered this, I had to, of course, use it in the story.

Parts of Jimmy's story were also based on real events. Twenty-seven people died when a C-47-DL Dakota crashed into Cleveland Bay on 7 August 1943. A Lieutenant Hawver was one of the passengers aboard that morning, having rushed out to the flight line in a jeep and just barely getting aboard before the plane took off. This was quite eerie, as I had already written the scene where Jimmy finally gets on a flight, only for it to crash. To discover this actually happened to someone breaks my heart. What incredibly sad times those were.

I have included some links to sites with lots of information and stories about Townsville during World War Two and urge you to have a read:

http://www.ozatwar.com/ozcrashes/qld146.htm
http://northqueenslandhistory.blogspot.com/2013/07/
    townsville-during-wwii.html
http://www.ozatwar.com

As usual, I wouldn't have been able to make this story happen without the help of many people. Rhonda Dennis, author extraordinaire and a great tour guide; thanks so much for showing us around Louisiana. The inspiration for Jimmy's family blossomed from our visit with you and experiencing true southern hospitality. I'd also like to thank Wendy Simpkins at Townsville Museum and Historical Society and the Townsville library for their help, as well as Kristen Alexander and Dawn Clements-Millen.

A huge thankyou to my publishers at Allen & Unwin: Louise, Christa and all the staff who continue to believe in my books; and to my editor, Julia, who put so much hard work into making my book the best it can be.

ALSO FROM ALLEN & UNWIN

Gemma's Bluff

KARLY LANE

Smart and reliable, Gemma Northcote has always done what's expected of her. So it's not surprising that after uni she defers to her father's wish that she join the family business.

Gemma's best friend, Jasmine, is a different personality altogether. She thrives on spontaneity, is unpredictable and has generally pursued her own path.

When Gemma and Jasmine decide to spend a working holiday on a large rural property, their friends and family are surprised. Neither has any experience of country life (unless you count Jasmine's love of *McLeod's Daughters*) and they're not exactly farming types.

Away from her family, Gemma feels liberated. The longer she's away the more she questions what she really wants to do with her future. Ultimately, she realises she needs to choose between duty and what's right for her in life—and love.

From the bestselling author of *Bridie's Choice* and *Poppy's Dilemma*, this inspirational novel is sure to appeal to anyone who's questioned the direction they should take for true happiness.

ISBN 978 1 76029 041 2

Poppy's Dilemma

KARLY LANE

Poppy Abbott seems to have it all. Bright, successful and attractive, she lives in a beautiful apartment with sweeping views of Sydney. However, since the recent death of her beloved grandmother, she's been struggling to come to terms with her grief.

Feeling nostalgic one evening, Poppy decides to sort through her grandmother's belongings, which she hasn't been able to face before. She's hardly started when she comes across an old leather diary with the name 'Maggie Abbott' written in the front. It's not long before she's drawn into Maggie's life and her fears for her soldier boyfriend during the First World War.

As her interest in Maggie's diary intensifies, Poppy decides to spend some time at her grandmother's house in the country. Away from the city, Poppy begins to wonder if all the things she's always valued so much are what she really wants out of life. And then love intervenes.

From the bestselling author of *Bridie's Choice*, this is the story of a woman leaving a fast-paced existence in the city for a calmer, more meaningful life in the country, where she finds herself re-evaluating just about everything.

ISBN 978 1 76011 133 5